OF GODS AND MUSES

BONDED BY SECRETS

AMBER BUNCH

For the lost and broken.
You are not alone.

Trigger Warnings

- Contains Violence and blood
- A situation or two implies unwanted sex (only implies, no scene actually happens)
- Sexual Content/Sex
- Adult language
- grief, anxiety, loss of loved one, touches on mental health problems

If I have missed anything, please feel free to contact me.

Contents

Prologue

The cold, dark stone of the throne room presses against my bare feet as I stand before my father, Hades. His gaze is like a clout, heavy with expectation and unyielding command. "You are to go to Midgard, Asmodeus," He decrees, his voice echoing off the high, arching walls adorned with the twisted souls of the damned. "She is your soul mate, and she requires protection. Lucius has her parents imprisoned, and she is more vulnerable than ever now."

"Kali," the name tastes like ash on my tongue.

A girl shrouded in problems and bound to me by some ancient prophecy I care nothing for.

"She is about to awaken to her powers, and if we do not act, Lucius will find her." He pauses, watching me, eyes like pits of eternal night.

Fury courses through me, a fire that threatens to consume my reason. "And what of mother? Kora?" My hands clench into fists at my sides. "They are missing likely because of this madness, and you send me on a fool's errand?"

"Your duty—"

"Is to my family first!" I retort, the anger boiling within me.

The thought of my mother, Persephone, and my sister, Kora, lost to us, gnaws at my insides. This prophecy, this preordained destiny linking me to a stranger—it's all a farce.

"Expectations be damned, father," I growl under my breath. "I should be searching for them, not chasing after a girl promised to the Devourer of Souls."

Hades stands from his throne, a towering figure of darkness and power. "We do not choose our fates, Asmodeus. We fulfill them." His words are meant to close the matter, but they only stoke the flames of my rebellion.

"Prophecy or not," I say, defiance lacing every word, "I refuse to believe that my worth lies in being tethered to someone I've never met. Someone marked by Lucius."

"Enough!" The single word crashes through the chamber, a thunderous verdict from the god of the Underworld.

But it does nothing to quell the storm inside me. Yet, despite my resistance, I can feel the inexorable pull of destiny, dragging me toward a path laid out before my birth.

The path to Midgard. To Kali. My supposed soul mate.

The very idea scrapes against my pride, leaving a raw, bleeding wound in its wake.

I feel the weight of my father's gaze, heavy as the iron scepter he wields.

His words are a commandment etched in stone, unyielding and cold. "You will go to Asgard, Asmodeus. As prince of the Underworld, you have responsibilities that surpass your personal desires. Should Lucius reach Kali before you, the delicate balance we've safeguarded will crumble."

I clench my fists, the muscles in my jaw tightening as I hold back a torrent of mutiny. The throne room feels like a crypt, the air thick with the scent of smoldering embers and the silent judgment of the damned. I am trapped, not by walls, but by the inexorable chains of duty that bind me tighter than any physical restraint.

"Your lineage demands obedience," Hades continues, his voice echoing off the cavernous walls, "And your role is crucial. If you fail and Lucius finds her, life as we know it could be extinguished. You know this better than anyone."

The threat hangs between us, a venomous serpent poised to strike. I swallow the bitterness rising in my throat, the taste of scorn and defeat mingling on my tongue.

My anger simmers banked but not quenched, as I bow my head in begrudging acceptance. "Understood, my king," I manage through gritted teeth.

Hades' eyes soften momentarily, a glimpse of the father beneath the god. "I share your worry for Persephone and Kora," He admits, his sigh stirring the eternal twilight of the throne room. "But I have faith that our forces will locate them and return them safely to us. So, right now, I need you to focus on the bigger picture."

"Yes, my king." I repeat the title

with a resigned finality, feeling the weight of my obligations anchor me fully into the role demanded by my heritage.

With a curt nod, Hades dismisses me, his form melding back into the shadows from whence he came, his presence lingering like a specter.

I turn away, each step a battle, my boots whispering across the obsidian floor like the wings of a raven taking flight.

As I march down the corridor, the sconces casting flickering shadows that dance mockingly alongside me. Their whispers seem to echo my own thoughts—doubt, fear, resentment—but I push them aside.

I reach my destination. Before me lies the portal room, its entrance guarded by two statues of Cerberus, their stony gazes fixed on the shimmering pool of water at the chamber's heart.

Without hesitation, I step into the pool, the cool liquid enveloping me in its embrace. For a moment, I am suspended between worlds, the familiar darkness of the Underworld yielding to the unknown light of Midgard. The sensation is a strange comfort, a reminder that even a prince of darkness and death can find solace in the promise of dawn.

And then, with the determination of one who knows his path is both cursed and sacred, I let the portal take me.

CHAPTER ONE

Kali

I hear my mother call to me from a distance.

"Not too far ahead please!"

I let out a light giggle, slowing down my pace. "Okay, Mommy!" I call back as I make my way towards the shoreline.

It's my first time visiting a beach, and although I'm filled with excitement, it does feel odd that we left our home in Colorado at three in the morning to move all the way to Moonstone Beach in California.

The sand is cooler than I expected, soft and forgiving beneath my bare feet. The ocean stretches infinitely before me, a vast expanse of blue that meets the sky at a line so far away I can hardly believe it's real.

According to my mom, we will be staying with some of her friends who have children around my age. Knowing that I will have playmates during the move helps ease my worries a bit.

Being home-schooled I didn't have many friends back home—or any for that matter. The salty sea breeze brushes through my hair as I inch closer to the water, the waves seeming to whisper as they retreat back into the ocean.

I hear my mother's heavy breathing as she catches up to me, and I can't help but laugh as she scoops me up in her arms and spins us around.

The sun glistens off her long dark hair and her fiery green eyes reach mine.

"Kali..." She furrows her brows, a firm expression on her face, "I said not to go too far ahead, my sweet. These waters can be very treacherous."

I want to pout in protest, but she's only trying to keep me safe and I know that.

She calls me an accident waiting to happen. Which isn't too far from the truth, I guess. I mean after all; I did fall in a big hole this morning before we left our cabin, and I scraped up my arms a bit.

Nothing too bad though.

My mom is full of lectures about being careful and making smart choices, especially in new places.

"Nothing is ever as it seems, my sweet. The world is full of mischief, and trickery."

What is that supposed to mean anyways? I wriggle out of her grasp and sit down on the warm sandy beach, letting my feet sink into the edge of the water. The sand is a mix of salt and pepper, creating a unique texture beneath my toes that's squishy, and wet.

The mud in Colorado can't compare to the way this feels.

My mom sits down beside me, drawing her knees up to her chest, and looks out over the ocean, her eyes distant as she seems to lose herself to her thoughts.

I rub my aching feet.

The boardwalk seems to be miles long, but the view has been breathtaking, so I don't necessarily mind.

The aroma of delicious food drifts through the air, mingling with the sweet scent of cypress trees.

Probably the small grill we passed earlier on the boardwalk.

My gaze trails further down the coast taking in the beauty around us.

The green hills are dotted with a vibrant array of wildflowers, each petal ranging in color from bright yellows and pinks to deep purples and blues. The flowers sway gently in the warm breeze, creating a beautiful contrast against the deep green of the hills. Some flowers stand tall and proud, while others peek out from behind lush blades of grass.

It's as if nature herself has taken up painting, crafting a wondrous and enchanting work of art.

I look back toward the Pacific Ocean, watching the foamy waves clash against the sharp rocky cliffs that surround us, while its salty essence mists our faces with tiny kisses.

"Kali, my sweet," My mother says, interrupting my thoughts. "We need to get going."

I nod, pulling my attention back to her.

"It isn't too much farther." She promises, holding out her hand.

I grasp onto her offered hand and she helps me up from the sandy ground. Letting out a deep breath, I brush off the beach that has attached itself to my bottom before we continue walking along the boardwalk that runs alongside the beach.

After a while we approach what I think to be a dead end.

Before us lies a rugged hillside, adorned with a lush mixture of trees, vines, and vegetation. The ocean stretches out to our right, while the left is filled with rolling hills, verdant foliage, and colorful flowers.

My mother's hand stretches forward and separates the thick vines, revealing a concealed entrance. A surge of excitement rushes through me as I realize this is a secret passageway.

Okay.

This. Is. Awesome.

It's like a fairy tale come to life as we stroll through the magical tunnel of trees. The branches reach out like arms, creating a warm embrace. Glistening water dances along the rocks, filling me with wonder and calm.

As the tunnel comes to an end, I am awestruck by what lies before me. The house stands tall, resembling a grand castle with its smooth, sun-bleached walls reaching towards the clear blue sky of summer. The second level boasts large windows that stretch from the floor to the ceiling, offering a panoramic view of the surrounding area.

Through the grand cathedral-style window in the tall and graceful stone tower, I catch a glimpse of the vast library that overlooks the ocean.

Nestled in a picturesque cove, the house is surrounded by lush greenery, almost like a natural fortress.

My mother turns towards me, beaming with excitement. "Are you ready to meet everyone, Kali? I promise they are the most divine of people," She says.

I squeak out a response, my nerves getting the best of me. "I—I guess so."

Without warning, the front door swings open, and a loud, booming voice rings out causing me to almost jump out of my skin, "Helena! Long time, no see, my old friend."

A massive man, with hands as big as Wreck-It Ralph's, storms through the doorway. He has golden blond hair and a full beard to match, and his muscles seem ready to burst out of the Hawaiian-style button-up shirt he's wearing.

I've never seen someone so...*enormous* before.

Although the man appears harmless, I instinctively retreat and hide behind my mother's legs, just to be safe.

"Phil, it's so nice to see you again." "You haven't aged a day, Helena. You're still at lovely as the day we first met!" His gaze lands on me, cowering as I cling to my mother. "Oh my, this can't be little Kali—she's the spitting image of you Hels!" His blue eyes twinkle as he pulls her in for a hug.

I am a spitting image of my mom. Not only do we have identical petite figures, but also vibrant green eyes and long, dark hair. Our noses are remarkably similar as well. It's almost like looking into a crystal ball and seeing my future self.

Phil releases my mother from the embrace and bends down to my level, his massive frame making me feel even smaller. He smiles, revealing a set of perfectly straight teeth, and extends a hand almost as big as my head.

"Hey there, Kali. It's an honor to meet you," He says, his voice now low and soft.

I hesitantly reach out, placing my tiny hand in his. Despite the initial fear, his handshake is gentle, almost cautious, as if he's aware of his own strength and trying not to intimidate me further.

"Thank you, sir," I whisper.

"Oh, please—call me Phil."

I smile, but only a little," Thank you, Phil."

"There we go! You're a brave one, aren't ya?" He glances up at my mother, his expression softening. "Helena, you've raised a fine young lady here."

She beams with pride, her eyes sparkling with unmistakable love and admiration. "Thank you, Phil. It's been a journey, but she's worth every moment."

A strange look passes between them, leaving me with a feeling that I've missed something important.

"Well then, Phil's voice rumbles like the waves crashing against the rocks in a distance. "What are we waiting for? Let's get the two of you girls settled in. Your luggage is already in your rooms, it arrived late last night."

Our luggage arriving before we even left Colorado strikes me as odd. My mother must have already had this move planned.

But why didn't she tell me?

The question swirls in my head for a moment, but then it passes just as quickly as it came.

"Oh good!" I squeal, suddenly grateful that my things are already here. "My everything is tired."

Chuckling, the *blond giant*—as I decided to call him, leads the way into the house.

I glance over my shoulder and take a mental note of their private beach that I hoped to explore later.

As we enter the house, the living room greets us first. It's grand and luxurious. My eyes are immediately drawn to the large, oversized sectional that takes up a significant portion of the space. After a tiring trip and a long walk down the beach, I eagerly kick off my shoes and flop onto the couch in a starfish pose. But before I can get too comfortable, my mother gives me a stern look that says, *"Don't you dare"*.

Whoops.

The couch is like a cloud, soft and fluffy. I could spend an eternity on it. I snuggle into the plush cushions, my eyelids feeling heavier with each passing moment.

"I'm afraid the time has come for that favor now," I hear my mom whisper to the blond giant.

Exhaustion betrays my desire to stay awake and listen further, the words of the speaker trailing off into murmurs as I drift into a blissful slumber, unable to resist the call of sleep.

"We can let no harm come to Kali. She knows nothing about our realms."

As the conversation fades into a distant echo, I sink deeper into the dream world, a place filled with vague shadows and secrets. Still, somewhere at the back of my mind, the whispered words cling stubbornly to my consciousness.

What do they mean—realms? What are they talking about?

I snap awake, feeling rejuvenated from my short rest. Voices resound from somewhere nearby, pulling me out of the cozy depths of the couch.

I sit up, rubbing the sleep from my eyes, trying to focus on where the murmurs are coming from. Glancing around, I notice that the living room is now empty; my mother and the blond giant are gone, and I find that I'm alone.

Curiosity piqued, I stand and stretch, my limbs tingling with stiffness from the unexpected nap, and then make my way to the source of where the voices are coming from.

Silently, I tread across the carpeted floor on my tiptoes and enter a long corridor through the doorway. As I walk towards what I assume to be the kitchen, the muffled voices from across the hall become clearer.

I'm met with exquisite light fixtures hanging above a sprawling island, and bright white cabinets, and marbled sand-colored counter tops that brighten the entire room.

At the rear of the room, there are grand French doors made of glass that provide a view of the tropical paradise outside.

"Well, hello there, sleepy head." My mother greets me, looking up from her place at the table.

I wave, and cautiously edge closer to her.

The smell of freshly baked cookies caresses my nostrils, making my stomach sound like a Wookie in battle.

Bubbling laughter fills the room as a woman, and two young girls breeze in. "Eirene, Rhode, how many times must I tell you to dry off after a swim? You both are dripping everywhere," The lady scolds them. "You wouldn't want anyone cracking a skull, now, would you?"

"No ma'am", The girls reply with a fit of giggles.

"Now go get yourselves dried off and get dressed so you can meet our guests," Mystery woman tells them, mopping up the mess they had just made.

"Kali," Her attention turns toward me, "It's so nice to meet you. My name is Melonie, and those two thorns in my side you saw a moment ago are our daughter's, Rhode and Eirene."

"Nice to meet you, ma'am," I whisper, tinkering with the hem of my shirt.

Melonie has delicate features, with a small nose, full lips, and round cheeks. Her eyes are a warm shade of brown, sparkling with kindness. Her long hair cascades down her back in loose waves, shining in the light with its caramel color. She moves gracefully, like a fairy, floating from place to place. She is dressed in a flowing dress, adorned with flowers and other nature-inspired patterns, adding to her ethereal appearance.

She gracefully wisps across the room, pulling me in a gentle hug, "I'm so glad you both are here. I'm sure you'll grow to love it." She says.

After releasing me from the embrace, Melonie glides over to the kitchen counter, her movements fluid and full of quiet energy.

"I hope you both are ready for a feast!" Phil's voice thunders through the kitchen. "Our chef is out picking up supplies for dinner tonight. You remember Dafina don't you Hel's? She's a hoot."

"Oh yes!" My mom exclaims, "You are going to love her, Kali."

I go to reply but then the young girls from before come dancing into the kitchen.

They both laugh and squeal, as they chase each other around the kitchen island.

"Girls!" Melonie calls out. "Have you introduced yourselves to Kali yet?" She asks.

They skid to a halt, shaking their heads.

"Well, get on with it." Melonie laughs, shooing them towards me.

"Hello!" They sing.

"Ummm...hi." I reply nervously.

"I'm Rhode," The taller girl says, extending her hand.

From the politeness and the hint of maturity in her demeanor, I can only assume that she's the oldest.

"And I'm Eirene!" The smaller girl beams, smiling widely as she bounces on her toes.

The duo instantly ushers me into their world, as if I am a long-lost friend rather than a stranger.

Eirene tugs at my arm, "Do you want to come to the theater room for a movie?" The younger of the pair asks. "Dafina always keeps it stocked with the best snacks, and she left us cookies!"

"Sure! That sounds so fun!" I reply.

Eirene's golden curls bounce around her head as she leads the way upstairs, every bit the spitting image of her father.

Rhode, on the other hand, takes after Melonie in looks but stands tall like their dad, towering over me and Eirene.

They both have the same sun-kissed skin, which makes me feel like a delicate porcelain doll standing between them.

We trudge our way up the stairs, and I let out a gasp when we enter the theater room through a door on the left. Trying to catch my breath from the strenuous climb, I stumble over my own feet as I admire the ginormous projection screen hung on the wall.

The sheer size of it leaves me with my mouth agape.

"Are you okay?" The two girls hurry over, grabbing my arms to steady me.

"I—I think so. My mom says I can be a bit of a klutz." I laugh.

"Don't worry, being clumsy is Eirene's specialty." Rhode says, dodging a jab from the giggling blonde before she takes off running.

"That isn't completely true, you take that back!" Whines the small blonde girl.

"Go ahead and make yourself comfy," Rhode calls out, Eirene hot on her trail. "Grab any snacks you want!"

"O—Okay. Thank you." I stammer.

Following Rhode's warm invitation, I make my way over to the snack table where there's a cornucopia of treats to choose from.

Freshly popped popcorn awaits us in the popcorn machine sitting on top of the table, along with a wide selection of chips packed in neat little rows, and a tempting variety of chocolates and candies. In the corner stands a mini fridge stocked with soda, and juices, its contents gleaming under a soft light.

There's so much to choose from.

I hover a moment, unsure of what to pick first. The buttery smell of popcorn pulls me in like a magnet, so I grab a popcorn bag and fill it up, topping it off with kettle corn seasoning. Next, I grab a chocolate chip cookie from the tray I assume was left for the girls by Dafina, and a chocolate bar and then shuffle over to the plush reclining theater chairs in the center of the room.

Eirene lands a good punch to Rhode's arm before making a beeline to the snack table, cackling as she goes.

Rhode rubs her arm, pretending to be hurt more than she actually is, and chases after Eirene with a playful glint in her eyes. The entire room echoes with their laughter, filling the space with a lively energy that makes me smile.

Eirene, still laughing, reaches the snack table and starts piling up her own assortment of treats.

"You should really try these twisted cheese sticks, they're amazing!" She exclaims, tossing me a bag.

"Mmmhmm," Rhode agrees through a mouthful of candy.

"Thanks!" I chirp, ripping open the bag.

Eirene sits down in the chair on my left, and Rhode takes a seat to my right, clapping her hands together to dim the lights.

The plush chairs hug us as the room darkens, leaving only the faint glow from the screen ahead and the soft lights near the snack table.

Rhode grabs the remote, browsing through the catalog of films available on their streaming services.

"What are you guys in the mood for?" She asks, glancing sideways at me and her sister.

"A princess movie." Eirene suggests, pointing to the one on the screen.

Rhode groans, "Not again. We just watched one last night."

"Fine." Eirene pouts, folding her arms across her chest.

"Kali, and ideas?" They both turn to me.

"Oh, I—ummm...I'm okay with anything." I say, my voice barely above a whisper.

A little while later we're kicked back, throwing back snacks as we laugh and cry at some movie about these lost dogs and their cat friend trying to find their way home.

It's surprisingly intense, despite its simple premise, and all three of us are completely drawn in. Rhode leans forward, her eyes wide as she empathizes with the plucky little terrier leading the pack. Eirene, on the other hand, seems to have a soft spot for the sassy cat who always has a witty comeback.

I personally find it too hard to choose between the animals—I love them all.

As the evening progresses, we gather on the back deck to indulge in Dafina's deliciously prepared meal of steak, fingerling potatoes, and fresh vegetables. The explosion of flavors in my mouth is simply incredible; every bite is a perfect blend of tastes and textures that leave me wanting more.

The deck is illuminated by sparkling lights that cascade down the handrails, creating a picturesque scene for watching the fluffy, cotton candy clouds drift across the sky.

After our meal, Rhode, Eirene, and I take a dip in the ocean while the tide is low, before searching for semi-precious stones along the shore.

The Moonstones and Jade stones are my personal favorites.

We're watching tiny crabs, peek out of their little holes in the tidal pools, when a stench so terrible it has me gagging, hits us.

"Ughhhh! What is that smell?" Eirene whines through her pinched nose.

The putrid odor grows stronger.

I try not to puke as we frantically scramble to get away from it.

Now, I've been around dead animals in Colorado, but even the smell of that can't compare to scent of whatever this is.

It's like someone took rotting flesh, dipped it in poop, and threw it in a dumpster that hasn't been cleaned in six months.

My mom and Melonie run towards us, fear clouding their eyes.

"Get to the house now girls!" My mom screeches.

We don't question her urgency, bolting past the dunes, our bare feet slipping in the soft sand. The fun of the evening evaporates as quickly as our laughter had risen.

Just as we reach the back deck, my mother's terrified screams pierce through the salty air.

I turn around, my stomach dropping as I watch an unusually massive black dog—or *wolf thing* attack her, its teeth ripping at the flesh on her thigh.

The sight of the large, open wound on her leg makes my stomach turn. Blood gushes out, staining the ground a vivid red. She grabs at her leg and collapses to the ground, unable to support herself any longer.

"Mom!" I call out to her. "Mom, are you—"

Suddenly, dark figures dressed in armor with glowing red eyes, emerge from the water, their rotting skin dangling from the parts of their bodies, not hidden behind the tarnished metal. Flashes of white bone peep through as they march towards us

I can't be seeing this right now.

This isn't real...right?

The dead army begins circling my mom and the creature that attacked her. The beast's teeth are still bared, and it has its sights set directly on my mom.

The bony, humanoid creatures charge forward with their swords raised, ready to attack. But then, massive waves, towering like skyscrapers, come crashing down on them, pulling some of the creatures back into the ocean's depths. The water churns and swirls around them, dragging them further and further down.

How is this even possible?

It was almost like the waves are being controlled.

Everything's happening so fast, the world seems to spin around me.

Determined to get to my mom, I jump off the deck, pumping my legs as hard as I can in her direction.

I can't make out what Melonie is screaming at me, and I don't care. I just need to get to my mom and help her—she *needs* my help.

The dark canine leaps towards her, aiming for her throat, but she manages to dodge just in time. Melonie's screams fill the air, causing me to risk a glance back over my shoulder. My eyes meet those of another, with piercing red irises glowing in the darkness that's setting in across the sky.

A strangled cry leaves my parted lips.

In my frantic attempt to flee from the creature, I sprint without direction, until I collide with a sharp and unyielding object. A searing pain shoots through my leg, and I feel a warm wetness spread down it. The jagged edge of the rock I crashed into has left a deep gash, causing me to crumple in agony.

Little black dots dance across my vision—just my luck.

I clutch my throbbing leg, the sounds of battle become muffled, like they're being drowned out by the pounding of my own heartbeat in my ears. My breaths come in ragged gasps, each inhale sharper than the last.

As I struggle to stay conscious, the ground trembles beneath me. The air is thick with the scent of salt and decay, a potent reminder of the nightmare unfolding just feet away. With grim determination, I force myself up, dismissing the pain that screams through every fiber of my being.

Through blurred vision, I see my mom battling fiercely with another of the dark creatures, and I trudge forward only a few steps before large, firm hands grasp me around my waist.

I scream, kicking my assailant as hard as I can muster with my good leg.

"It's okay now. I got you, Kali," The comforting sound of Phil's voice hit my ears.

A wave of relief washes over me. I was convinced that the monster with glowing eyes had caught me.

My mom scrambles to her feet, smiling as she looks over at me, her eyes filled with heart-wrenching sorrow as she shouts over the noise, "I love you Kali, my sweet, sweet girl!"

Her gaze shifts to Phil, "You know what must be done."

He nods.

"Keep her safe."

Tears stream down both mine and my mom's face, my chest pulling tightly in on itself, crushing my heart.

"Kali, I need you to be strong, okay? I—I have to go."

"Mommy, noooo!" Sobs wrack through my tiny body. "Don't leave me, please." My plea is whisper lost in the havoc unfolding around me.

I can't breathe, I can't move.

Nothing about this is making any sense to me. I feel like I'm stuck in a nightmare that I can't wake up from.

I watch in complete horror, tucked in Phil's arms as he carries me back to safety as black veins creep up my mom's body, her bright green eyes, once so full of life, now dull and black.

What the heck is going on?

The strange dog-like creature moves closer to her, and the other glowing-eyed creatures gather around with focused attention. She doesn't back down, ready to accept her impending death. The dog pounces at lightning speed, its sharp teeth piercing her neck.

As my vision begins to fade, I can feel myself losing consciousness, but I fight against it.

Black mist fills the air, mixing the putrid scent of rotting flesh, with the sharp odor of fire and smoke.

I absently reach for my mom, knowing I will never be able to touch her again, never hold her—or hear her say how much she loves me.

I'm going to be left here...alone.

With a deafening blast, searing hot flames burst from my mother's body, consuming her and every living being in the vicinity around her.

The intense heat melts away their flesh, and their screams echo painfully in my mind.

Phil tightly enfolds me in his arms, protective and strong as if he were a shield against the horrifying scene unfolding before us. His body, warm and solid, is a refuge from the chaos and bloodshed surrounding us. He holds me close, trying to shield my eyes from the gruesome sights and sounds that threaten to overwhelm me. But despite his efforts, the images still sear into my brain like branding irons on flesh.

The stench of death and destruction hangs heavy in the air, threatening to suffocate me, and a pile of ash now lay where my mother stood only moments ago.

My breathing becomes shallow, as the reality of the situation sinks in.

I feel like I'm losing control—as if my mind has shattered into a billion little pieces.

Tears stream down my face, uncontrolled and unrelenting, as darkness overtakes my hazy vision, and the world goes black.

CHAPTER TWO

Kali

I awaken yet again, my sheets soaked with sweat, my body on fire. The nightmares seem never-ending anymore.

I feel like I am going insane.

Maybe I am insane.

Seriously, get it together, Kali.

With my chest heaving, I remove the black plush comforter that is currently plastered to my heated skin. The cool night breeze tickles my flushed body as I let the comforter fall to the floor.

My heart is still pounding in my chest as my brain decides to do an instant replay of the same nightmare that's been haunting me every night since I was six years old.

The creatures.

My mother's death.

For as long as I can remember, people have dismissed my memories as mere figments of my imagination. They say that the trauma of witnessing her murder caused me to conjure up a deranged attacker out of thin air, distorting the truth of what truly happened that night.

They say that the monsters I saw the night she died weren't real, and that it's all in my head.

Though, for me, it always feels real.

It always hurts the same no matter how they say it happened, and I still see the same thing every single night.

I feel like there is something wrong with me, and it's a feeling I wish could be easily fixed. However, I doubt anyone will ever be able to fix the mess inside my mind.

A strand of my long, dark hair brushes the small of my back making a shiver run down the length of my spine, and it dawns on me that I'm still sitting in a pool of my own sweat and tears.

With sleep still crusted in my eyes I crawl out of the comfort of my bed and shuffle over to the white sand bleached dresser in the corner of my room. Opening the top drawer, I grab fresh sheets and the adorable crescent moon cami and shorts set I ordered last week.

The icy touch of the hardwood floor sends shivers up my bare feet as I make my way across the room, my footsteps echoing in the empty space. The coolness seeps into my skin, a refreshing sensation against the warmth of my body. I navigate through the dimly lit room, drawn towards the bright light emanating from the bathroom. With each step, my toes curl and uncurl, seeking some form of warmth on the frigid floor.

As I pass the mirror in the bathroom, out of the corner of my eye I catch a glimpse of myself, unprepared to see the ghost of a woman staring back at me.

Intricate lines resembling spiderwebs stretch outwards from my eyes, turning the whites to a deep black. I shake my head and tightly close my eyes, then gradually open one before opening the other.

But of course, I appear completely normal now. Just another trick my mind is playing on me. I quickly discard my damp clothes and make my way to the shower, adjusting the temperature dial to favor the hot water and step inside.

As the showerhead releases scorching hot droplets, I feel some of the tension in my shoulders melt away, providing me with a small sense of relief.

The steam builds, wrapping around me like a comforting shroud, fogging up the mirror and glass that encase my temporary sanctuary. Water sluices down my body, washing away the remnants of last night's torment, yet the relief is fleeting. It's only a matter of time before the cycle repeats, before the shadows lurking in the corners of my mind reemerge to dance their sinister waltz.

I tilt my head back, letting the water cascade over my face and through my tangled hair, trying to wash away not just the physical but also the mental grime that's accumulated. It's like trying to cleanse my soul with torrents of liquid heat, but some stains are too deep, etched forever into the fabric of my being.

After a thorough wash, I turn off the water and reach for my towel.

"Of course, the one thing I didn't grab," I mutter angrily to myself.

Stepping out into the chilly air, my nipples instantly become small beads of steel.

I run towards the towel closet as fast as I can, trying to outrun the cold air, when I slip, falling smack dab onto my bare ass.

"Fucking hell! I just want a towel! Is that too much to ask for!?" I screech, picking myself back up off the floor.

After carefully navigating through the room, I finally reach the closet in one piece and dry off my frozen body.

Then, I remember that I left my clothes in the other room, so I quickly return to retrieve them and get dressed.

And finally, I head back into my room once more to change my sheets.

Walking to each corner of the bed, I take my time smoothing out each wrinkle.

I know it doesn't make any sense because I'm just going to be laying on them anyway, but it's something that's always been satisfying to me.

Climbing in bed, I roll onto my side being mindful of my throbbing tush.

As I nestle into the freshly changed sheets, the fabric cool and crisp against my skin, a small sigh escapes my lips. The simple pleasure of clean linens feels like a balm to my weary spirit.

Slowly, I drift away. Sleep tugs me back into my broken mind full of nightmares.

Back to the worst day of my life.

Chapter Three

Kali

"Kaliiii!" Eirene's sing-song voice rings out, jarring me awake.

What time is it anyway?

I look over at the clock on my nightstand.

'Three forty- two.'

"What in the actual fuck do you want!?" I growl at her. "Do you even know what time it is?"

"I know if you don't get your lazy butt out of bed, you are going to be late for work." She snaps back, giving me one of her Tinker-belle glares; as I like to call them.

She already has the petite build and golden blonde locks, all that's left is for her to add the little *tink-tink* sound as she shakes her fist at me.

Glancing back at the clock, I'm getting ready to rip her a new one for waking me from my slumber, when I suddenly realize my clock reads *'three forty–two p.m.'*

Ahhh…that explains a lot.

"Holy crap I'm going to be late for work!" I yelp.

For the second time this week, I'm running behind schedule for my shift as a bouncer at Phil's nightclub that starts at five minutes to midnight.

Not exactly the job most girls my age have, but it's a job that pays the bills and, honestly, I love the thrill of it.

After my mom was killed, I started taking martial arts classes at seven years old and eventually added weapons training into the mix. The trauma of her murder left me feeling vulnerable and powerless, and I never wanted to experience that again.

So, I guess that's also another reason I love my job, because I get to kick out the creeps that prey on drunk girls, and if they get nasty, I get to kick their ass.

Eirene rolls her eyes, "Uh, yea genius. That's kind of what I just said."

Slinging my curtains open, she laughs as she lets the sun burn holes through my retinas.

"I made you some coffee, and I think there are still some pumpkin muffins left from earlier, that Dafina made."

Dafina makes all my pumpkin favorites during the fall.

She's the absolute best.

Grateful for the mention of coffee and muffins, my irritation with Eirene begins to subside, though I can't resist a parting shot. Thanks, Eirene. You're lucky you're useful," I mutter, rubbing the sleep from my eyes and scrambling out of bed.

"Love you too!" She sings as she exits the room, her laughter echoing down the hallway.

I stumble out of bed, nearly tripping over the rug as the onslaught of sunlight continues to assault my eyes.

I hurriedly brush my teeth and hair, quickly pull on my favorite worn-out jeans and a black hoodie—a requirement for the job and then throw on a pair of high tops before making my way down the stairs.

The aroma of freshly brewed coffee mixed with the scent of pumpkin spices fills the air as I reach the kitchen. Dafina, with her warm smile and flour-dusted apron, greets me at the bottom of the stairs.

"You look like you're in a rush, dear."

"Only a little." I admit.

Grabbing a muffin, I take a large bite and plop onto a stool at the kitchen island.

Dafina walks over and gives me a tight hug before handing me a cup full of the warm caffeinated goodness.

"Looks like someone had a late night visitor," Dafina teases, playfully moving her hips.

In her early fifties, she has more curves than some of us younger girls, and her hair is streaked with grey. But one thing's for sure—she's not afraid to be herself. She always joins in on our jokes and pranks, and knows all about our antics.

"Not this time, Dafina." I grin, taking another bite out of my muffin.

Rhode and Eirene start laughing like maniacs, at the dining table across the room.

"Do you really think Daddy would allow any of us to have a guy here? He doesn't care that we are adults." Rhode scoffs.

"That's why Kali and I sneak out." Eirene chimes in, her mouth dropping crumbs of muffin as she speaks.

"Facts! Sometimes a girl just needs some dick." I laugh.

Rhode's face looks like a tomato about to burst on a hot day, as she screeches, "YOU TWO DO WHAT NOW!?"

I explode in a fit of laughter at her outburst.

She's a rule follower. Never gets into trouble—on her own that is, but Eirene and I somehow always managed to drag her into our antics.

It's a familiar pattern that repeats itself every time; we come up with a seemingly brilliant idea that turns out to be a disaster, and Rhode always comes to our rescue before things get too out of hand.

"Oh, c'mon live a little girl." I stand up, and stretch, the pull against the knots woven in my back feels heavenly.

Although I slept for several hours, it wasn't a restful sleep and now my body is extremely sore.

Rhode rolls her eyes tipping her chair back as she does, "If I didn't always have to worry about the two of you getting into trouble, then maybe I could."

Eirene waves her off, turning to me, her bright blue eyes, filled with excitement. "Hey, speaking of trouble, have you decided which bar we are going to for the big twenty-oner?"

My birthday is coming up soon and Eirene has been begging me to have my party at the new club nearby called, Lust.

Outside of my job as security at the family club I've never actually stepped foot in another similar establishment before, let alone, drink at one.

I am however, looking forward to the change of scenery and the titillation of something new.

"Are you going to die if it's anywhere other than Lust?" I tease.

The corner of her mouth twitches as she tries to hold back her excitement "It is quite the possibility." She says, in a matter-of-fact tone.

I walk over to the sink, turning the water on to rinse out my coffee cup—one less thing for Dafina to worry about.

Sitting the cup in the dish rack, I smirk turning back to my slightly older sister, "I guess you will just have to wait to find out. You can suffer with not knowing in the meantime."

She tosses a muffin straight at my face, its soft squishiness connecting with my cheek.

Tossing her blonde curls over her shoulders she gives me a famous Tinker-belle glare, "Biiiiitch." She says, unnecessarily emphasizing the word.

"I can't stand you two sometimes." Rhode shakes her head. "Uh, shouldn't you be leaving for work?" She points to the clock that now reads *four thirty-nine p.m.*

Great.

Just what I needed. Jeremy is sure to fire me this time.

I shove another muffin in the pocket of my hoodie, not even bothering to wrap it up, earning myself a side eye from both my sisters.

"Late night snack." I shrug.

Seriously, need I say more?

I give them a quick wave and then make my way out the front door.

Our land is blessed with a lengthy, secluded driveway enveloped by lush greenery and beautiful flora. Our security protocols are the best in the business, and the entire hundred acres of our estate is protected by imposing gates.

No one can see in or out.

It's a necessary precaution after my mother's untimely death.

After that night, Phil and Melonie welcomed me into their home and I became a part of their family. Rhode and Eirene were embracing of having another sister, and over time we all became inseparable.

I climb behind the wheel of the custom Jeep that Phil and Melonie surprised me with for my eighteenth birthday.

It's black with neon green trim, and it has leather interior to match. They also put neon green lights underneath the running boards and had an out of this world sound system installed.

I remember being so excited that Phil had to catch me and Melonie both when my failed attempt at a jump-hug knocked her over.

I turn the key in the ignition, and it roars to life. I decide to hope for the best and send Jeremy a quick text before pulling off.

On my way. I figured we could play a game of "time roulette". I may be late… or I may not be late. Depends on how against me the world is tonight. If I am late though, we can play a game of "why we shouldn't fire Kali." Sounds fun right?

I almost miss my turn too busy imagining how Jeremy's face probably matches his ginger-colored hair right about now.

Jer is a decent guy. He's tall, lean, and quite the charmer with the ladies. As head of security at Club Vortex, where we both work, he takes his role seriously.

Okay, he takes it seriously for the most part. Again, he is a ladies man.

A group of girls that are regulars here, dubbed him The Knight—like the shining armor kind since he's always coming to their rescue.

I know, lame right?

I pull into work with no minutes left to spare and wouldn't you know it, Jeremy is standing outside checking IDs, and he's glaring directly at me.

Funny thing…his face really *does* match his hair.

"Seriously Kali, this is the third time this week." He huffs as I jump out of the Jeep, tossing my keys into the air and catching them with a grin.

"I know, I know. And yet, you've still waited for me in this very spot every single time."

"Like I have a choice," He rolls his eyes, "You should be the one checking ID's."

"I guess I'm just lucky like that," I joke, making my way through the crowd of people at the door.

He shakes his head but can't suppress a smirk. "One of these days, your luck is going to run out."

I reach up ruffling his hair. "Oh, you know you love me Jer," I say before pulling my long dark hair up into a ponytail, and shimmy past the group of girls in skin-tight mini dresses and stilettos that are trying to sweet talk him.

I laugh as they all send me death stares when Jeremy chuckles and unclasps the velvet rope, ushering me inside.

"For the time being," He cautions. "But if you continue to arrive late like this, I may have to reconsider."

Though there is a lightness to his voice, I can tell he's about at his fill with me being late.

Okay, then.

Warning noted.

CHAPTER FOUR

Kali

The music seems extra loud, and it it's crazy busy, even for a Friday night.

A group of guys to my right are being loud and obnoxious but, nothing too out of hand so, I just let them continue to do their thing.

I make my way to the u-shaped bar in the middle of the lounge to the bartender, who also happens to be my bestie, Olivia.

"Hey Liv, how are things going tonight? Do I need to kick anyone's butt?" I shout over the thumping music coming from the speakers above us.

She pops up from behind the counter holding a bottle of tequila, "Hey pretty lady, late again I see."

She's wearing black leggings and a low-cut, long sleeve crop top that barely covers anything. Her blonde hair is pulled up in a messy bun and the black diamond kitten charm dangling from the belly ring she's wearing, draws attention to her toned abs.

She's a fucking goddess among men.

"I technically wasn't even late tonight. I pulled in at exactly five o'clock. So really, I should be having Jeremy fix my time."

Olivia laughs, "Of course you would say that."

She sets down a couple of shot glasses on the bar and pulls a couple beers from the cooler, popping off the tops with the bottle opener hanging from her wrist before pointing down to a pretty brunette sitting alone at the far end of the bar.

"Looks like there's gonna be trouble." She says, clicking her tongue. "I hope you're ready for the fun to start."

One of the *"obnoxious"* guys from earlier has made his way over to the brunette and he's getting handsy with her.

"Ewww! Get your filthy hands off me!" She spits, shoving his hand away from the small of her back.

He grabs her by the wrist and pulls her off the stool she's perched on, slamming her small frame into his chest.

"Hey, c'mon. Don't be like that, sweetheart. I'm just having a little fun."

He runs his finger down the curve of her cheek. "How about I take you home with me tonight? I'd really enjoy seeing that dress of yours on my bedroom floor."

With a swift movement, she raises her petite hand and brings it down hard on his cheek with a resounding *'thwack'*. His smug smile instantly turns to surprise as the sting of her slap lingers on his skin.

"You stupid little slut, you're going to pay for that." He growls, his rough hand gripping a fistful of her hair and yanking her down to the ground, "Get on your knees where you belong."

The entire bar falls silent for a heartbeat, the music and laughter dying down as heads turn towards the commotion.

Fury courses through my veins like molten lava, heating up my entire body in an instant.

How dare he!

Without a second thought, I lunge from my seat at the bar, my heart pounding in my ears as adrenaline surges through me.

I weave through the throng of dancers, my gaze locked on the man who has ignited my rage. When I finally reach him, I don't hesitate to take action: I grab his wrist and twist it with all my strength until he cries out and falls to his knees, releasing his grip on the young girl's hair.

"Apologize to her," I command, my voice low and menacing, barely recognizing the harsh tone as my own.

He tries to resist, his face contorted in pain and anger, but the pressure I apply to his wrist only increases. "I said, apologize!" My voice rises over the murmur of the crowd

"Who the hell do you think you are?" He spits out.

Sweat beads his brow as he tries to stand up, but I twist harder, forcing him back down. "Give me one good reason I shouldn't break both of your filthy hands."

The man glares up at me with hatred burning in his eyes, yet there's a flicker of fear as well—fear that perhaps he's finally met someone who won't tolerate his bullshit.

"I'm sorry," He spits, as though the words taste disgusting on his tongue.

The brunette lets out a small squeak of gratitude as she snatches her purse and scurries towards the exit, undoubtedly relieved that I had stepped in.

The crowd around us begins to murmur, some voices filled with approval, others wary and anxious about escalating the confrontation further.

I keep my grip tight, ensuring he fully understands the gravity of his actions. Despite his reluctant apology, his eyes still flash with defiance.

My stare bores into him, unyielding and cold, "Get out and don't ever show your face in my club again. Let this be a lesson, because next time I won't go as easy on you."

With that I allow him back to his feet, and escort him out the front door.

Good fucking riddance.

I turn back to face the interior of the club, my heart still racing, but now with a tinge of relief. The music, momentarily drowned by the commotion, regains its volume and pulses through the space when I nod to the DJ, a silent cue to keep the night moving.

As the beat picks up, people slowly return to their dances and conversations, the tension fading away like a puff of vape smoke.

The rest of the evening goes by fairly quickly without any more drama. Last call finally arrives and the last of the club goers stagger out into the dark of night.

You don't have to go home, but you can't stay here.

"Do you need any help closing up tonight?" I ask Liv.

She looks over her shoulder as she continues to wipe down the surface of the sleek, mahogany bar.

"Nah, I'm good girl. After that circus of crazy tonight, you deserve to go home and rest. I'll see you tomorrow night. Try not to be late again." She says.

I flash her a grateful smile, pulling on my jacket. "Thanks, Liv. I owe you one."

"Sure you do," She chuckles, shaking her head as she tosses the rag into a bucket beneath the bar. "And try to make it on time tomorrow, will ya? You're going to give Jeremy a heart attack." She snickers.

I shrug, "No promises." I say sticking my tongue out at her before I throw the wet cloth clutched in my hand at her, and make a break for the back door.

Her retaliation rag smacks loudly off the metal frame as the door slams shut behind me.

Doing a little victory dance, I flip her off through the small glass pane in the door.

She laughs but flips me the big FU back.

Ugh, got to love that girl.

My keys are excessively stubborn and don't want to come off my belt loop as I walk to my car. A prickly sensation in the back of my neck makes me feel as if I'm being watched.

My muscles tense up and I scan the empty parking lot, trying to pinpoint the source of my unease. There's nothing visible to me in the darkness, but something doesn't feel right.

I shake off the sensation and finally conquer the key chain that has been holding me hostage from being able to get in my Jeep and drive home.

But before I even get to unlock the door, the shifting of gravel re-sounds from behind me in almost an instant, followed by the feeling of something sharp against my ribcage as a chubby hand grasps around my mouth.

A familiar voice rasps in my ear, "Time to put that dirty mouth of yours to use. I'm going to make you suffer for making a fool out of me, girl. By the time I am finished with you, you're going to wish you were fucking dead."

My stomach drops.

I stand there, frozen, my heart thudding so hard, it threatens to burst from my chest. My whole life I swore to myself that I would never wind up in a position like this—I took all those stupid self-defense classes to prevent this very thing from happening.

So why is it I'm standing here unable to react or move?

Well, this just absolutely perfect.

Is this how I'm going to die, by the hands of this scumbag?

Panic claws at my insides, but I don't let my fear show.

His knife sinks a little deeper, the cold steel causing a small amount of blood to drip down my side.

On the bright-side, I'm still wearing black, so it shouldn't stain.

He slides the blade up to my breast, "Maybe this will be the first chunk I cut from that tight, little body." He grunts, pressing himself against me.

Could this guy be any more twisted?

His alcohol-infused breath creeps its way down the back of my neck, and I choke back vomit when I feel his slimy tongue skate across the crease of my neck.

Gross.

I should be scared; I should want to run , but fury overtakes my fear. With every degrading word he spits, a fire builds inside me—a seething, roaring flame.

He thinks he's won me over with fear, cornered me into submission?

No, I can't—I won't—let it end like this.

With a sharp intake of breath, I stomp hard on his foot with all my weight and thrust my head backward with as much force as I can. The sickening crunch in my ear, lets me know I hit the sweet spot, and I've broken his nose.

Turning to face him, I take a moment to enjoy the image of the crimson fluid seeping from his nose, which now sits at an odd angle.

He howls in pain as my knee connects with the soft fleshy meat-tube that dangles between his thighs.

In my panic, I had completely forgotten about the knife in his hand. It isn't until I feel a searing pain that I remember and look down to see it embedded in my body.

My eyes grow wide.

His blow hits one of my lungs, causing excruciating pain and making it nearly impossible to breathe.

My entire body is trembling uncontrollably, and my teeth chatter violently in my skull.

I think I'm going into shock.

The bald, grubby man falls backward as he tries to get away from me.

What is he doing? Isn't he going to finish the job?

His face scrunches and his beady eyes dilate with fear.

I can barely feel the pain anymore, and oddly enough; breathing isn't an excruciating chore anymore, and I'm way calmer than I should be in a situation such as this.

I'm dying.

I think I read somewhere that right before you die, the pain lessens to make death a little bit easier, but that's the internet for you.

The man scrambles to his feet, clutching his bleeding nose, and stumbles towards the dim exit of the alley. His primal instincts to flee override any desire he had to inflict further harm.

"What kind of freak are you lady?" He shrieks as he runs, not daring to look back even once, his arms flailing about him like one of those wacky inflatable guys you see at car lots.

Well, that was weird.

I'm the one with a knife sticking out of my gut after all.

Oh. Yeah. That.

Panic floods through my body once more as I frantically reach for my wound. Out of the corner of my eye, I spot a pocketknife lying on the ground.

It must have fallen out in all the commotion.

I lift my shirt expecting to see a puncture wound, only to reveal the puckering of smooth, fresh pink skin where only moments ago, the blade had been.

I stare in disbelief, my hands trembling as they hover over the un-marred surface of my abdomen.

How is this possible?

I press deeper, half-expecting to encounter some hidden layer of pain, but there's nothing. Just the faint touch of my own pulse, beating steadily against my palm

There's no broken skin, no collapsed lung—I don't even know if any of it was even real.

This isn't happening.

Nope.

I'm not going crazy again.

I refuse to believe that after all this time of doing so well and being out of therapy, that now I'm having another breakdown.

I take a shaky breath trying to calm myself and climb into my Jeep, catching a glance of my reflection in the rear-view mirror. My eyes are solid black and obsidian veins creep along my face and neck, while the intoxicating scent of smoke and fire tickle my nose.

And there it is.

I'm completely fucking losing it again.

Wonderful.

Note to self: Call the shrink in the morning.

CHAPTER FIVE

Kali

I lay on the oversized sectional in our living room awaiting my therapist, Selene.

She has been making house calls since I was a little girl, so formalities are long gone at this point.

When I first started therapy, Melonie believed it would be easier for me to have my sessions in a familiar place, rather than an old stuffy office.

Of course, she had been right.

I have always been able to be open with Selene, and she's always had a way of calming me down and bringing me back to reality.

A loud knock at the front door informs me that she's arrived and it's time to have my brain picked.

I take a deep breath and saunter over to the door, twisting the knob and pulling it open

Not that I'm sure I'm ready for this, but here we go anyway.

No pain. No gain, right?

Selene waltzes through the door, her brows furrowed with worry, causing the wrinkles in her forehead to deepen even more than usual.

Her gray hair adorns a braid tossed across her shoulder, rings line her aged fingers on both hands, and around her neck hangs the black serpent necklace she never takes off.

"Kali dear, it's nice to see you again." She hugs me, "Though, I wish it were on better terms. How are you feeling today?" She asks, releasing me, her long flowy dress breezing across the carpet as she seeks out the recliner across the room.

"Uhhh, I'm feeling...*something*, that's for sure. I'm not exactly sure what it is, but it's something." I reply as I climb on the couch and tuck my feet beneath me.

It isn't a lie.

I really don't have a clue about what I feel.

Confused?

Yeah.

Scared I'm going off the deep end?

Sure.

But there's something else too, I just can't quite seem to be able to put it into words.

Selene starts fumbling with her small briefcase and pulls out a pen and clipboard. Knowing her, she's about to write down every word I say.

"Why don't we start with you telling me about what happened last night? Could there have been anything that triggered you?"

"If being attacked and having a knife shoved in my stomach could be considered a trigger—then yea, you could say that," I think to myself.

Just imagining it again makes me feel queasy.

Should I relive the moment?

The thought of feeling weak and helpless is unappealing, and being vulnerable isn't something that comes easy for me.

It's a tough choice.

But Selene's gentle eyes, though aged and wise, hold a kind of magic—the comforting kind that makes you want to spill your secrets, believing somehow they could be transformed into something less horrifying in her presence.

"Alright take it slow," She says, setting her notepad aside for a moment, "Take a breath, close your eyes, and calm your mind."

"I'm trying." I say, squeezing my eyes together.

"Would you like me to burn some incense? That always seems to help calm you." Selene asks.

But before I can even open my mouth to reply, she's already lighting a sage and lavender incense cone.

She knows me so well.

If nothing else, that should say a lot about how many sessions we've had together.

I take a moment to breathe in the calming scent, letting it saturate my lungs and soothe my rampage thoughts.

"I—I'm not certain how to explain this one." I start, "It felt so real, and I was fully awake this time. I had just gotten off work and I was walking out to my car. A man I had an altercation with earlier that evening was in the parking lot waiting for me." I pause, the memories vivid and painful.

Selene waits patiently, her eyes never leaving mine, encouraging me to continue at my own pace.

"He attacked me, and it just took a turn for the worse from there." The words begin to fall effortlessly from my lips as I tell her everything that had happened the night before, peeping up at occasionally to catch her reaction.

She watches with pursed lips, nodding every now and then while I spew my crazy to her.

She's used to it at this point.

At a young age, she diagnosed with Fantasy Prone Personality disorder. So, when something triggers me, I have a hard time deciphering fantasy, and reality.

Then she taught me how to know when I was daydreaming or having one of my nightmares, by finding an anchor of sorts, like a sound or something nearby that I could physically touch.

But this time, when that man attacked me, it had been different.

Everything around me felt real.

Nothing was pulling me out of it.

And my eyes—my eyes were just like my mothers were the night she died. Pitch black just like they are in my nightmares.

Is that a coincidence? Could it mean something?

Nah.

Maybe I'm just getting sick, and now all the stress of work and life in general is starting to get to me.

"Kali?" Selene's voice has a gentle, inquiring tone, pulling me back from the spiraling thoughts.

"Hmmm.?" I ask, my eyes fluttering open.

Oh, shit.

Was I just been rambling all that nonsense aloud?

The questionable look Selene is wearing on her face, leads me to believe that yes—I indeed just mouth vomited everywhere.

Why is this incense so damn relaxing?

It's not fair.

Selene reaches out, her hand settling on mine, grounding me with her touch, "It's okay, Kali. This is a safe space." She reassures, "Let's start with the nightmares. Are there any changes? Does it seem like they are getting better, or do you think they are getting worse?"

I pick up my coffee from the glass table between us, taking a sip, "Worse. More vivid than usual." I reply.

I pull up the images in my mind, trying to remember if there have been any changes.

The waves!

The waves in my last dream were different this time.

"Actually, there was one minor alteration. In my dream from the other night, it was Phil who caused the typhoon on the night my mom passed away. Not a storm."

"That is—*different*. Tell me about it." Selene is hawk-eyed now, scribbling excessively on the pad attached to her clipboard.

Does she look almost...excited?

"Well..." I begin. "As you are aware, I usually just glance upwards to see the massive waves engulfing all of the creatures. But this time, I saw Phil standing there, somehow controlling the ocean. It was like energy or magic was pulsing from his hands, entwining with the waves like strands of moonlight. I believe he was attempting to save my mother."

My hands are shaking now, so I shove them underneath my legs, hoping to get a grip on myself.

The last thing I need to do right now is lose it right in front of Selene. This is already hard enough as it is.

Suddenly, the sound of glass shattering in the kitchen makes Selene and me both almost jump out of our skin.

But when Dafina starts cursing everything under the sun and shouts a quick apology, we both ease.

Selene meets my gaze once more and speaks softly, "You have gone through a lot of changes in your short life. Changes that would affect anyone's mental state." She pauses as if to collect her thoughts, then continues, "I believe the combination of your changing nightmares, followed by the traumatic experience with the man who attacked the young woman at your workplace and then turned around and attacked you, triggered a state of emotional shock in your mind. This could explain why you began experiencing hypnagogic hallucinations." Her tone shifts to one of certainty as she finishes her explanation, as if she has just solved a mystery like Scooby-Doo and his gang.

I reach my arms above my head in a deep stretch, then prop myself up on the arm of the couch squinting my eyes as I ask Selene, "Do you mind repeating that—in English this time, please?"

She crinkles her nose and flaps her hand in a dismissive gesture. "In essence, the trauma of being attacked caused you to imagine a bleaker situation than what was truly occurring. Earlier, when you suggested this, I believe you were correct; you have been dealing with immense pressure recently. You are still a young adult attempting to discover your path in life—your meaning—if you will."

"Soooo," I draw out. "What now? Do I need medicine—a treatment plan— anything?"

Anxiously, I wait for her to utter the words I've been dreading: that I will finally be sent off to a mental health facility.

But if that's the case, I refuse to go down without a fight.

I have responsibilities and plans—including my upcoming birthday, and I am determined to continue taking my MMA classes.

In fact, I may even increase the frequency of my classes now.

Those things are important too, right?

On second thought, perhaps being sent away for a period of time is the best option.

I don't want to burden Phil and Melonie with all this nonsense.

Like, I know I can come to them for anything, but they've already done so much for me, and they don't need to all this extra stress. I shouldn't bring any more of my darkness into their lives.

They deserve better.

Selene stands up and smooths out the creases in her dress, putting away her pen and clipboard.

"Kali...Kali." She tsks. "You know I prefer herbals. So, no, I will be making up a calming tea for you to drink every night for the next week. You should be drinking the last of it the eve of your birthday, so don't worry about it interfering with any alcohol you may consume." She winks. "I will also be advising time off work for the next couple of weeks. It's important that you rest, and that you avoid getting involved in anymore...situations for a while."

Kayyy. Not what I was expecting.

A calming tea doesn't sound too bad, and taking time off work? That seems like a blessing in disguise right now.

A glimmer of mischief dances in her eyes as she embraces me, "You should spend a day out with Rhode and Eirene, just us girls. You're carrying too much weight and tension on your shoulders. It's important to take some time for yourself and unwind. Plus, I hear you still need to find a dress for your party."

"Okay, I can do that," I agree.

Rhode and Eirene always know how to make things feel light and breezy, a skill I seemed to have lost along the way.

Selene steps back, her hand lingering on my shoulder in a gentle, reassuring squeeze, "I'm going to get going. You have my number if you need to talk. And remember, I'm here not just as your counselor, but as your friend too." She says, with a smile that carries the warmth of a summer afternoon.

She nervously fiddles with the serpent pendant around her neck, as if she has more to say. But then she turns and heads towards the front door.

Just when I go to walk her out, she turns back. grabbing my hand, her light gray eyes searching for something in the depths of my own, "Be careful Kali, nothing is as it seems. The world is full of mischief and trickery." She whispers, her voice barely audible over the growing wind outside.

With a quick, final squeeze of my hand, she slips through the door and disappears into the evening, abandoning her words as they're left swirling around me like leaves in a storm.

I stand there in the doorway, in complete dismay.

My mother used to say that phrase all the time, but it was a secret I never shared with anyone.

Not even Selene. So, where has she heard that phrase?

I guess it's possible that I let it slip when I was a little girl, and I just don't remember it.

Yet, the coincidence almost feels too precise—too pointed.

My mom was the last person who muttered those words to me, the morning we left Colorado to move here.

I had been exploring in the woods and I stepped on what I thought was a pile of leaves, falling into a deep trench.

Luckily, it occurred right outside our cabin and my mom heard my screams for help. When she hauled me out of it, she had wiped the tears from my face and smothered me in kisses.

Then, of course, giving me her lecture about the world and its trickery.

I would give anything to have one of those lectures again.

Choking back the sob forming in the back of my throat, I slowly shut the door, and turn and press my back against it, and allow myself slide to the floor, still trying to wrap my head around the words Selene just slapped me with.

Maybe she knew my mom.

That *must* be it.

Selene is a friend of Phil and Melonie's, so that would make sense.

Maybe it's even just from an old movie they've all seen together before or something.

I'm sure I'm just freaking out over nothing.

Sheesh.

Selene is right; I really do need to relax and do something fun.

Choosing to brush it off, I lift up my left butt cheek and pull my cellphone from the pocket of my jeans, my fingers tapping harshly against the screen as I type out at text to my sisters.

> *Get your asses in the kitchen. It's time for snacks and party planning bitches.*

The vibration of my phone hitting the wooden floor reverberates louder than expected as I wait for their response.

A loud thud followed by insistent giggling from upstairs indicates they've in fact received my message, and their stampede of footsteps signals their approach even before they appear.

Eirene bounds down the steps first, her curly hair bouncing wildly around her face.

"Party planning? Did someone say party?" She exclaims, her eyes sparkling with excitement.

"Yep. Got it in writing and everything," I say, picking up my phone and double tapping the screen to show her the message once again.

She slaps my arm.

"Stop being a cunt. It's not a good look." She says, flipping her hair over her shoulder.

Ever the loving sister.

"RHODE!" Eirene screams from the top of her lungs. "HURRY YOUR ASS UP!"

"I'M COMING!" Rhode shouts back, her voice echoing down the stairwell.

Moments later, she appears at the top of the staircase, a look of mock annoyance plastered across her face as she descends.

"It's about time." Eirene huffs.

"Oh, shut up." Rhode snaps back, rolling her eyes dramatically as she reaches the bottom of the stairs.

I've already made my way into the kitchen and started pulling out bags of chips from the cabinets along with an assortment of dips from the refrigerator.

"Are we thinking a theme, or are we just winging it?" Rhode asks, rummaging through another cabinet for extra bowls.

"Definitely a theme." Eirene responds. "Maybe like—"

"A 90's throwback party?" Rhode interjects.

Eirene's face turns in disgust, "Ewww. No. Not in a million years"

Rhode shrugs, clearly unbothered by Eirene's reaction. "Well, I think it would be cool. Imagine everyone in baggy jeans and crop tops, maybe even some frosted tips and butterfly clips?"

Eirene crinkles her nose.

"What about a masquerade?" I suggest, laying out the snacks on the counter. "Everyone loves a bit of mystery."

Eirene perks up at that. "Masquerade, yes! We can do a whole *'Eyes Wide Shut'* vibe but, like, less creepy."

Rhode nods, warming to the idea, "I can get behind that. Masks, fancy dresses, secret identities—it could be fun."

Eirene claps her hands together, her earlier disdain forgotten, replaced by the bubbling enthusiasm of a new project. "Okay, let's make a list of what we need."

Plopping in a chair, I pop open a bag of chips and start crunching as Rhode pulls a notepad from the drawer and tosses it onto the table.

She searches the drawer eagerly for a pen, before returning, ready to jot down our brainstorming ideas.

"First, we need invitations," Eirene declares, pacing back and forth with a thoughtful look on her face. "Something classy, mysterious. Black cardstock, perhaps." She taps her chin.

"Gold lettering?" Rhode suggests, scribbling down the idea.

Eirene nods approvingly. "Yes, and we should seal them with wax—make it feel authentic."

I munch on another chip. "We'll need to compile a guest list too. How many people are we thinking?"

Not that I have many friends of my own to invite, but our family is well known so there's bound to be a crowd there whether I like it or not.

Rhode ponders this for a moment, her pen hovering above the paper. "Let's keep it intimate. Too many people and it loses the mystique. Maybe fifty? Sixty tops."

Eirene grins, clearly pleased with the numbers. "Perfect. Exclusive but not elitist."

I nod, agreeing silently as I pop the tab open on my soda can, thankful for the smaller number.

I grab another handful of chips as I take a sip and lean back in my chair, watching my siblings get swept away in party planning.

I might as well get comfortable, because with the way they are diving into every detail, this is going to be a long night.

CHAPTER SIX

Kali

After spending the past two days elaborately planning everything for my birthday, Eirene, Rhode and I decided to drive up to the city to shop for dresses.

The V.I.P section at Club Lust was completely reserved for us. Melonie insisted on personalizing the space, so she and Phil took care of it.

Originally, we planned for a small gathering more intimate event, but somehow it turned into a massive party with Dafina catering the event after they paid a hefty fee to use the club's kitchen.

Phil is a very humble man, yet he favors having the finer things in life.

It's well deserved, though.

He is a beloved and renowned businessman who comes from a wealthy lineage. He used his family's inheritance to open Club Vortex, long before my sisters were born, and I became part of the family.

Then, about six years ago when the wildfires ravaged the area, most local businesses were destroyed.

To help rebuild, Phil used some of his inheritance to reconstruct every single one, resulting in him receiving thirty percent ownership of each business.

Needless to say, he is very well off in the financial department.

I gaze at my own reflection, taking in every detail, in the full-length mirror of the dressing room.

As I open the door, I twirl to show off the barely-there blue dress I'm wearing. "I can't decide if I like it or not," I say with uncertainty.

A low whistle reverberates from my best friend, Olivia, "Damn sexy lady. You're giving me a lady boner." She grins, waggling her eyebrows.

Rhode flushes a deep shade of scarlet at the boldness of my friend's statement. She turns quickly, pulling a random dress from the rack she's flipping through and runs into the nearest dressing room.

No one else seems to have the ability to get under her skin quite like Liv does. I've watched her become frazzled around Liv in a way I've never seen before; it's almost amusing.

I run my hands down the sides of my dress, feeling the smooth fabric cling to my curves. The low v-neckline highlights my chest before stopping just below my breasts, and the form-fitting design accentuates my backside.

It's beautiful; however, blue is not my color.

Eirene squeals, pumping her fists in the air, "Holy shit girl, you have to try this one on!"

She prances over to me, holding up the most stunning dress I've ever laid eyes on.

We've been at this for what feels like hours now.

We all can be a tad picky, so we know to make it an entire girls' day out, anytime we go shopping together.

As soon as Eirene hands me the dress, I let out a breath of amazement. The color is stunning, a deep crimson that catches the light in just the right way. I can't help but run my fingers over the soft fabric, reveling in its smoothness.

"Oh, wow. This is absolutely perfect." I breath.

Eirene beams, her eyes lighting up with triumph. "I knew it! That color is going to look killer on you."

Rhode clears her throat nervously before emerging from the dressing room in a stunning emerald green halter dress. The color compliments her caramel skin and hair, cascading perfectly over her toned body. With the addition of a golden arm cuff, she looks like an Amazonian warrior. A peek of her side tattoo, featuring flowers and vines that she got at nineteen, can be seen through the cut-out on the right side of the dress.

She struggles to form coherent words, her arms hugging her body tightly as if she wants to blend into herself. "Wh—what do you think?" She manages to mumble out in a whisper.

Liv's eyes light up, widening, her mouth dropping open just the slightest bit as she chokes on the glass of pink champagne she's been sipping on, some of the liquid splashing and seeping down her chin.

She sucks in a breath, stumbling to find her words. "You're—I mean—*it's* great. It fits you perfectly."

Liv makes her way to a beautifully arranged table adorned with various accessories. She selects a pair of elegant gold earrings in the shape of leaves, with sparkling diamonds adorning the center.

"Here, these will complement all the hotness you're radiating," She says, handing them to Rhode.

I observe the brief hesitation as their hands make contact, causing a flush of pink to reappear on Rhode's cheeks.

Ok?

Am I missing something here?

Rhode's hesitation lingers as she takes the earrings from Liv, a faint smile playing on her lips. "Thanks, Liv. I—I appreciate it."

Eirene gazes back and forth between the two of them and then back at me, giving me a what in the world is going on type of look.

"I'm going to ask the owner for another bottle of champagne, and more ice." She announces. "Kali, do you want to come with?"

I play along. "Yea, I wanted to find a necklace to try on with the dress you found for me, anyhow."

It's not completely untrue.

I really can't wait to try it on, but we need to talk about what I think I saw going on with our sister and my friend.

We navigate through racks filled with glamorous dresses and tables lined with high-end shoes, accessories, and handbags as we approach the front of the boutique. The most luxurious jewelry and items are displayed in a glass case at the forefront of the store, only accessible by the owner, Angel.

As soon as we're out of earshot of Rhode and Liv, Eirene grabs my arm pulling me to a stop.

"So, are you thinking what I'm thinking?" She asks.

I nod, "There's definitely something more than friendship brewing between those two," I whisper, glancing back to ensure we're still out of earshot.

"It all makes so much sense now, doesn't it?" She adds. "Just think about it; when has Rhode ever introduced a guy to us, or snuck out to see one—or even mentioned having sex for that matter?"

She's right. I don't recall Rhode ever having a boyfriend or really ever being interested in men.

I take a moment to idly process our revelations, picking at the dirt under my fingernails that has begun to accumulate.

Good thing we're going to the salon today.

It does make sense, I suppose.

I've always just thought she was a stifler and wanted to keep things peaceful with Phil.

"You have a point. We need to be careful, though," I say, finally meeting Eirene's eyes. "*If* we're right about this, she should know that we support her."

"Absolutely!" Eirene agrees, then her face splits into a wide smile. "Did you see the way they were looking at each other? They were practically boning with their eyeballs."

I am aware that Liv identifies as bisexual, but she has not been in a relationship since we met at the private academy where I began studying at the age of thirteen. This was after Selene convinced Phil to enroll me there instead of continuing to homeschool me, for the sake of my mental well-being.

Now that I think about it—she's always acted a little different around Rhode. It's clear now that she's always been more interested in her than anyone else.

How did I not see it before?

I'm a terrible best friend.

I pick up a slow pace again, waving to Eirene to follow. "I think we should keep our discoveries to ourselves for now. Just until we know for sure. I wouldn't want to upset either of them or make things weird, you know?"

Eirene furrows her brows, clearly distraught over having to keep this between just us. I know good and well that she wants to march back to them and ask a million questions.

Hell, she's probably already planning their wedding in the back of her mind.

She's such a hopeless romantic.

"Ughhh!" She groans. "I hate it when you're right."

Tapping her finger on her bottom lip, she smiles, "They would just be such a cute couple. I don't see the harm in doing a little digging, do you?"

Doing a little hop-skip to lessen the distance between us, she looks up to me with pleading eyes. "Well...do you?"

Shaking my head in defeat, I shrug. "I suppose it wouldn't hurt to ask a few questions, here and there."

Eirene claps her hands gleefully, her excitement barely contained.

"Just a few harmless questions," She echoes, winking conspiratorially as we continue our walk through the leafy campus paths.

I can't help but smile at her exuberance.

Angel, our extravagant host, generously hands us another bottle of champagne, a special treat she reserves for her most high-paying clients. As the daughters of the most esteemed businessman in the region, we are fortunate enough to be considered among this elite group.

Along with the bubbly, Angel presents me with a stunning diamond choker necklace featuring a clustered star-burst design set on black lotus silk. I struggle to zip up my red dress while admiring the luxurious accessory.

The sweet-heart neckline plunges slightly, offering a nice glimpse of my cleavage. It fits snugly around my small waist and flares at the curve of my hips. The black strappy stilettos adorning my feet perfectly compliment the outfit and elongate my legs, giving me that super-model effect.

The dress has long sleeves, but the delicate silk fabric won't be enough to keep me warm in the chilly night air, so I also grabbed a cropped leather jacket to complete the look.

"Are you almost done in there, lady? You're as slow as a sloth." I hear Liv call from outside the dressing room.

After trying on multiple outfits, she finally settled on a stunning metallic shawl that sparkled against the black fabric of her fitted dress with spaghetti straps.

Meanwhile, I of course am the last of us to finish shopping, and the last to try everything on.

I stumble towards the door, my face colliding with it before I can even open it. The jeans I had taken off earlier trip me up as I hurry to unlock the door.

With an irritated scowl, I yank the door open, "I'm done, I'm done. I have no regrets though. With how I look right now, it was totally worth it." I say, wiggling my hips, making them all fall to pieces in a fit of giggles.

I think at this point, we've all probably had one too many glasses of champagne.

Liv rolls her eyes playfully as she steadies herself against the wall, still chuckling. "You look absolutely killer, babe," She says, her voice tinged with amusement and genuine admiration. "That necklace alone is going to make every head turn."

"Agreed." My sisters chime in unison.

"Thank you." I grin. "Okay, I'm going to change really quick and then I'm going to go pay for all of this. After, we should eat. You guys down for the grill down by the boardwalk?"

It's easily become one of my favorite places to eat ever since I moved here.

As the others nod in agreement, I rush back in the dressing room to quickly change back into my jeans and t-shirt, regretting the loss of the glamorous persona I had briefly adopted.

We make our way towards the front counter, carrying all of our items. Angel starts adding up the total, and I can already feel my stomach twisting at the thought.

The necklace alone costs over five-thousand dollars.

Despite the thirty-five percent discount we receive, it's still an exorbitant amount of money for just one outfit.

As I reach for my wallet in my back pocket, Angel dismissively waves me off. "The bill has already been settled, Ms. Adira. You're good to go!"

I glance behind me at Eirene and Rhode. "Do you know anything about this?"

Rhode just gives a shrug.

Maybe Melonie called ahead to approve our purchases before we arrived.

"No, I haven't a clue." Eirene says. "I can call mom to find out though."

"Ms. Adira, if I may, the gentleman that took care of your bill just stepped out about ten minutes ago. He said he didn't want to interrupt you, but that he knew your mother, and this way his way of paying his respects to you.

Strange.

How did he know my mother?

"Did the receipt have a name at least?" I ask.

"No ma'am. I'm afraid not. He paid with cash—left a handsome tip too, but I don't recall him ever giving his name." Pity oozes from her words.

"Ok. Well, thank you, Angel for a wonderful experience. We had a blast here, as always." I give her a grateful smile, feeling a mix of curiosity and unease churn within me.

Grabbing our bags, we head outside. My emotions are a swirly haze, making my chest tighten with grief.

Who could this stranger be?

We unload our days treasures into the back of my Jeep.

Rhode hops into the back seat with Liv, which is a rare sight as she usually sits up front. Seeing their playful conversation eases some of the tension that had been creeping up my spine just moments ago.

We fasten our seatbelts and Eirene inputs the address of the grille into the GPS. The car lurches forward with a loud crunch of gravel, as we head towards Moonstone Beach Grille.

The sun is still high in the sky, so it's not too busy yet. Hopefully we'll be able to find a table easily. In my mind, I plead for an open booth to be waiting for us when we arrive.

As we drive, my thoughts whirl back to the mysterious benefactor who'd settled our bill. My mother had many friends, most of whom I knew, but this act seemed unusually personal for a mere acquaintance. Was it possible that someone from her past was trying to connect with me indirectly?

After a few rounds of laughter and singing along to songs, we finally pull into the parking lot of the restaurant.

"I am starv—" I begin to say, but my eyes lock in on a man standing over on the far side of the parking lot.

Standing beside a lifted blue four door truck, his towering figure still seems dwarfed by its size. His piercing dark brown eyes wander from my face, down my frame, and back up again.

I am convinced that he is the most attractive man I've ever laid my eyes on.

As he flicks his tongue across his lower lip, a wave of heat rushes through me. My body's response to him surprises even myself. I've definitely had one-night stands and been immediately attracted to someone before, but this is on another level.

It's almost absurd how drawn I am to him.

His muscles ripple under his shirt and I have this intense urge to rip from his body. He brushes a hand through his dense, dark hair and my legs turn to jelly. A warm wetness gathers between my thighs.

Is it within the realm of normalcy for someone to elicit such a strong response?

Hardly the norm, I would say.

I feel my cheeks darken at the thought of having the stubble that lines his jaw, tickling my inner thighs, as his tongue slides between the folds of my pussy.

Shit.

I'm losing it again, aren't I?

A forceful blow to my already spinning head slams me back down to reality, and I quickly spin around to find the origin. "What are you looking at?" Eirene asks, her voice confused and curious. I turn back to gesture towards the man who had caught my eye moments ago, but he's gone. Just like that, he's disappeared into thin air.

Or maybe he was never there in the first place.

My mind races as I try to think of a logical explanation.

This has to be the effects of mixing Selene's herbal teas and a few glasses of the bubbly.

"I think I just got a bit woozy from not eating anything yet today." I lie. "I need a burger—stat."

Rhode wraps her arm around me for support, "Why didn't you say something sis? I could have drove. Let's get you inside before you pass out on us." Her face creases with worry.

I try to forget about what just transpired, letting her guide me inside, shame simmering deep within my gut.

But on the bright side, there's an open booth.

Small victories, right?

CHAPTER SEVEN

Kali

My fingers trace the rim of my coffee cup, the ceramic cool against my skin, as I sit across from Melonie in the softly lit kitchen. The air is fragrant with the remains of dinner, a blend of herbs and spices that always makes the house feel more like a home. I hesitate, then, with a furrowed brow of curiosity that seems to deepen the dimples on my cheeks, I venture into the silence between us.

"So—" I begin tentatively, "Do you by chance have any idea who could've paid our bill at the boutique?" My gaze is searching, hopeful for some insight into the unexpected act of generosity that had occurred days earlier—a mystery man's kindness that lingers in my mind like an unsolved riddle.

Melonie pauses, her fork full of pie and midway to her mouth, before setting it down with a clink against the porcelain plate. Leaning back in her chair, she taps a finger against her lips, eyes narrowing slightly as she summons the faces of acquaintances in her mind. "Well, there's Mr. Henderson from the flower shop, but he's far too frugal," she muses. "And then there's Marcus, your mom's fling, but no...I doubt it."

It shouldn't strike me weird, but my mom having a fling with someone that wasn't my dad seems almost impossible. She didn't even date after he died. I never got the chance to meet him, but my mom told me many amazing stories about him.

She said he died a hero.

I watch as Melonie cycles through possibilities, each one seeming less likely than the last. There's an earnestness in her efforts to unravel the enigma, an exemplification to how deeply she cares for my peace of mind.

Finally, Melonie exhales, a gentle sigh escaping her as she shakes her head, her light golden-brown hair catching the light. "Honestly, sweetheart, I haven't the slightest idea." Her voice carries a note of apology, a wish that she could provide the answer I sought. "But you know, it's kind of fun having a little mystery in our lives, isn't it?" her eyes twinkle with a mischievous glint as she picks up her fork again, this time successfully bringing a piece of pie to her lips.

A flicker of suspicion sparks within me.

Could Melonie be concealing the identity of our mysterious benefactor?

Nah.

As quickly as it came, the thought is extinguished by the rational part of my mind. Chiding myself for the baseless doubt, I brush aside the notion with a mental sweep.

"Anyway," Melonie says, breaking into my reverie with a soft, maternal tone, "Did you girls have fun shopping? And are you excited for your party tomorrow?"

The change in topic flows as effortlessly as the silk scarves we had admired at the boutique.

"Of course," I reply, warmth blooming in my chest. My smile is genuine as I add, "Thank you for putting it all together, Mel. It means the world to me."

Melonie beams at the gratitude, but there is a subtle change in her demeanor as she stands from her chair and makes her way around the kitchen table. She wraps me in an embrace that speaks volumes of the years we have shared—the bond that has grown between us, strong and cherishing.

"Kali," She murmurs, her voice muffled against my shoulder, "I can't believe how fast time has flown. You, Rhode, and Eirene—You're all fully grown women now." There's pride in her words, but also a hint of disbelief, as though she's trying to hold onto moments already slipping through her fingers.

I chuckle softly, the sound vibrating against Melonie's embrace. "I know, right? It's wild."

When Melonie pulls back, her eyes glisten with unshed tears, exposing the vulnerability often hidden behind her composed exterior. "I'm just not ready for all of you to leave at once," She confesses, her voice cracking slightly as she dabs at the corner of her eye with the pad of her thumb.

"Hey, we're still here. No one's leaving just yet," I say softly, my own emotions swelling at the thought of eventual goodbyes.

"Thank you, my dear," Melonie forces a small laugh, trying to hide the emotions welling up inside her.

She inhales deeply, trying to steady herself. The air shudders as it exits her lungs. "It's just...you've all grown up so quickly, and I—" She stops, lost in the bittersweet knowledge of time's unceasing progress.

I squeeze her hand, offering what little comfort my touch can provide. "You helped us grow. You've been there, every step of the way. Remember all those late-night talks, the school projects we dragged you into, and even the disastrous first attempts at cooking? We couldn't have done any of it without you. We'll always need you, Mel. No matter where we go or what we do."

She nods, her eyes now brimming with a mix of sorrow and satisfaction. "Yes, those were the days, weren't they? Somehow, I thought they'd never end." She forces a smile, sitting back down in her chair, tracing the lines of the wooden table with her finger.

"You know I'm planning to study Mythology, right? It's like our family tradition or something," I add with a half-smile, hoping to lighten the mood. "Those stories about Zeus, Athena, and all those gods Phil is so fascinated by—they're kind of ingrained in me now." My eyes wander to the bookshelf crammed with well-thumbed volumes of ancient myths and legends. I'll be here for at least another three years, minimum."

Melonie wipes another tear away, her laughter a fragile sound amidst the lingering silence. "I guess I'm just getting ahead of myself with this empty nest syndrome," She says, attempting to brush off her earlier display of emotion. "It's silly. You girls are just starting out, and here I am, acting like you've already flown the coop."

"Mel, you don't even look old enough to have an empty nest," I reassure her, the corners of my lips curving upward genuinely. "What are you, like twenty-eight now?" I reach across the table, squeezing her hand.

"Flattery will get you everywhere," Melonie quips, her smile returning as she gives my hand a reciprocal squeeze.

However, the tears glistening in her eyes contradict the cheeriness of her tone. They hold stories of years gone by—of love, sacrifice, and a fierce protectiveness that has nothing to do with age.

Melonie's voice softens, the timbre rich with a mixture of gratitude and solemnity. "Kali," She begins, her gaze steady and brimming with earnestness, "I know I can never take your mom's place. But I want you to know how honored I am, how deeply privileged I feel to have had the chance to raise you into the incredible woman you are today."

My throat tightens at her words. "You'll always be my mom, too," I say, my voice a whisper that seems to echo through the years of laughter and tears we had woven together. "You stepped into a life full of gaps and made it whole. Mom is mom, but so are you, in every way that counts."

"I know things haven't been easy for you," She mutters, a knowing look passing between us, acknowledging the silent battles I have fought and the strength I've mustered to face each day. "But I've got this feeling, deep down, that everything is about to change for us—change for the better."

"Yeah?" I ask, eager for her to elaborate.

"Yes." She nods. "Maybe it's intuition, or maybe I'm just an eternal optimist."

She laughs at herself, but I grasp onto the notion.

I hold her gaze, searching the depths of those familiar eyes, finding the unwavering belief that has always guided me through the darkest of times.

And somehow, in the quiet confidence of her words, I find myself daring to believe it, too.

Chapter Eight

Kali

I wake up and stretch, feeling rested for the first time since I was a little girl.

Last night I actually slept in a peaceful and dreamless sleep. There was no awaking with my body trembling in terror. No being drenched in a cold sweat, nor was there a single tear that fell from my eyes. Just an embracing and blissful darkness of sleep pulling me deeper into the abyss of something completely unknown to me.

A new energy swirls deep in my veins—likely, the perk of finally getting a full night of sleep. The morning sun trickles in through my

Victorian curtains, casting a symphony of colors that dance across the large oval mirror hanging right above my dresser.

"Today should be filled with loads of sunshine and fucking rainbows." I think to myself, chuckling at the thought before forcing my tepid body out of bed when really, I just want to fall back into the wonderful void of sleep.

I throw on some loose-fitting gray sweats, a tank top, and a pink hoodie, then toss my hair into a messy up-do and get ready to head downstairs.

As soon as I open my bedroom door, I run dead into my sisters who are standing there in front of my door, smiling like lunatics.

"HAPPY BIRTHDAY!" They both screech so loudly, I feel like my poor offended eardrums are going to burst.

They beam at me with stretched smiles, urging me to come along with them. We all laugh like children as we move forward. The air is filled with a wild and carefree exuberance, along with the tempting aroma of Dafina's mouth-watering cake in the kitchen.

Something fishy is going on here.

"What has the two of you acting so...giddy?" I ask, suspicion creeping along my skin.

"Whatever do you mean dear sister." Eirene clutches her chest as if I offended her. "We are just two loving sisters, trying to make sure their baby sister has the best birthday ever. Now, what's so wrong with that?" She teases.

Rhode's face is a ticking time bomb, ready to explode at any moment. Keeping secrets has never been a strong suit for either of them.

As we make our way down the ornate staircase, their giggles and whispers become a musical backdrop to my growing curiosity.

"Oh, shit." Rhode squeaks, "Go ahead without me. I forgot to grab something. I'll meet you guys on the back deck for breakfast" She drops my hand and quickly running back upstairs, leaving me alone with Eirene.

Now is my chance.

"So, "I begin. "Is there a surprise or something that I don't know about?" I pry innocently.

Eirene bounces on the balls of her feet, the corner of her mouth twitching at my question. "I'm not at liberty to say, and I have sworn an oath of secrecy. You'll find out soon enough."

Then she makes a beeline for the kitchen. "Want coffee?" She shouts behind her as she runs.

"I always want coffee. Nice way to change the subject though." I say, running after her.

As we reach the kitchen, the smell of freshly brewed coffee fills the air, mingling with the sweet scent of baked goods. Eirene is already pouring two steaming cups, her hands steady despite the obvious excitement she's trying to hide. I take the mug she offers and sip gingerly, letting the rich flavors wash over my palette.

She's made it clear she isn't saying a peep. Whatever it is they're hiding from me, must be big. I'll just try to sneak attack her again later.

I sneak a quick glance at the cake in the oven. It's not the usual white cake that Dafina bakes for me every year.

Cracking the oven door open a little more, the smell of spices hit my nose: cardamom, cinnamon, ginger, and notes of orange and vanilla caress the air.

Eirene exclaims from behind me, "Oh my goodness, what is that amazing smell?"

I quickly shut the oven and use my sleeve to wipe away the drool escaping down my chin, "Seems like Dafina decided to try something new this year. Today is just full of surprises if you know what I mean." I jest, giving her a wink.

"Ha! As if. Nice try though." She snorts. "Let's go dork-fish, the food is going to get cold."

The cool morning air blasts my face as I open the back door, energizing me, and a salty presence dances in the delicate breeze, from the gentle waves licking at the sandy beach shore.

Birds sing off in a distance to the left of me, and the golden hue of the sun dusts the clouds above, its warm rays making the plant life surrounding us glisten from the morning dew.

A row of buffet warmers lines the front part of the deck, the patio dining table is set with a white lace trimmed tablecloth, the plates and silverware have already been placed at each chair, and a large array of fruits and pastries are displayed in center of the table.

It's all so...perfect. Yet, my heart feels heavy, and my eyes burn with traitorous tears.

"Aye there, don't ya go crying on us now." Phil's strong arms pull me in for a hug, encasing me in his calm, his burly voice vibrating my cheek that's crushed against his chest.

I hadn't even realized everyone else had already came outside.

I take a deep breath and try to force a smile. "It would have been so nice if my mom could have joined us. She would have enjoyed everything Dafina has prepared this morning." I motion towards the spread of food on the table.

"Hels would have loved just being here with you, Kali. She would be so proud of the woman you've become. We all are." He gives me a quick squeeze and places a kiss on the top of my head.

His words hit me like a ton of bricks, and I can no longer help myself, the ache in my chest becomes too painful to endure.

My throat is raw with sobs, my body shaking uncontrollably as a haunting wail escapes my lips. It's been a long time since I've cried this hard, not since the night my mother was taken from me.

Melonie and my sisters join me in the embrace, reminding me that they are here to support me. Our bond may not be biological, but it is strong and unbreakable. I am incredibly grateful to have found this family, especially in a time like this.

"I slave for you lot in the kitchen all morning, and you still haven't touched a damn thing?" Dafina shouts, busting through the back door, unashamedly interrupting the moment, scolding us like we were small children refusing to eat our vegetables.

She marches over to me, pushing the others out of her way, without a care in the world, pulling me into her.

"Happy Birthday, dear. I hope you don't mind me changing up your cake this year. I thought you'd like to try the one I used to make Helena, when she was younger." She smiles.

I blink away tears, touched by Dafina's thoughtfulness. "Thank you, Dafina. That means a lot to me," I manage to say, my voice still shaky.

"Yeah, yeah. Now let's eat before the birds get it all." She pushes me towards the breakfast bar she had worked so diligently on. "Would you like me to make you a plate dear?"

The way I love this woman. She's always devoted to our needs, never her own.

I place a quiet hand on her shoulder. "No, that's ok Dafina. Go, sit down and I'll make *you* a plate."

"Don't you even—" She goes to argue.

"I'm not taking no for an answer!"

Dafina huffs, a smile playing at the edges of her lips as she surrenders. "Alright then," She says, settling down at the end of the table, grabbing herself a cinnamon sugar-coated, beignet.

She angrily shoves a bite of the confectionary treat in her mouth, giving me the stink eye. But to my astonishment, she gives me no further argument.

I can't help but marvel at the delicious spread on the table.

There's fluffy scrambled eggs, golden brown French toast, warm and flaky biscuits with creamy gravy, crispy bacon, and juicy ham. And that's just a small portion of the delectable dishes that Dafina has prepared for us. It's incredible how much care and dedication she puts into every meal she makes for us.

As we all take our seats, I make a loud coughing noise to get everyone's attention and then gesture towards Eirene with the piece of bacon I'm holding. "So, according to Eirene, there's something special planned for me," I state, hoping that someone will accidentally reveal some information.

However, instead of anyone speaking up, they all shoot angry glares towards her.

Her mouth drops, and I just know I that I've started a war.

Her eyes slowly meet my own, "I did no such thing, Kali Adira!" She exclaims, shaking her tiny fist at me. "What I said, was that I wouldn't tell, because you would be finding out anyways."

"Okay, Tink." I reply, throwing my hands up in mock defense. "You know I can't help myself. I hate surprises." I pout.

"And I hate it when you call me Tink." She seethes. "But here the fuck we are. You know, you should all fear me really." She smirks, blowing a burst of air on the back of her freshly manicured nails, and then wiping them on the shoulder of her shirt.

She's such a diva and I love it. It makes messing with her all the more fun.

I'm close with both my sisters, but Eirene and I share a special bond. She had been the first to not treat me like a ticking time bomb after I first arrived, and the one who used to climb in bed with me at night when my nightmares got really bad.

She gave me her favorite stuffed animal telling me he would help keep the demons away. And though to be honest, it never actually helped, but I still sleep with him every night; a white horse with wings and it means the absolute world to me.

"Noted." I laugh. "Sorry, sis. You know I had to try."

Eirene rolls her eyes but the ire in them fades. "Fine, you're off the hook for now, but don't think I won't get back at you," She warns playfully.

Phil reclines in his seat, patting his belly and chuckles at the familiar scene playing out between my sister and me.

"You two are a riot, honestly. How do you manage to keep up this banter all the time?" He asks, his eyes twinkling with amusement.

I shrug, grinning at him. "It's our superpower. Keeps life interesting."

"That's one way to put it." Rhode chides from the other side of the table.

Eirene and I giggle.

"You've truly outdone yourself, Dafina." Phil beams. "My stomach is so full; I couldn't eat another bite even if I wanted to. With all the delicious food you cook for us, I'm surprised I haven't grown a massive belly," He laughs.

"Oh, it was nothing dear." She replies, wiping off her face with a napkin.

"Do you want some help, cleaning this mess up?" I ask Dafina, knowing she just going to refuse my offer.

"That's ok sweetie," Melonie says as she glides over taking the empty plate from in front of me. "Why don't you girls go upstairs and start getting ready for the party this evening? Phil and I can take care of putting the food away and cleaning the dishes."

"You don't have to tell me twice." Dafina says, as she rises from her seat. "I have a cake to finish before I head into town to speak with the head chef at Lust. He's supposed to be assisting me with the Hors d'oeuvres for this evening."

"Thank you so much for catering the event, Dafina." Melonie says, before turning back to scold me for putting food away. "Kali!" She snaps, "You put that down this instant and go get ready for your party."

Before I can even object, my sisters are pulling me back inside the house, and up the massive staircase to our rooms.

Tonight is going to be a blast.

CHAPTER NINE

Kali

The next few hours seem to fly by quickly.

Everyone else has already left to put the final touches on tonight's event at the club, but Eirene has taken it upon herself to do our hair and makeup.

She moves with quick, practiced hands, her fingers deftly applying eyeshadow and smoothing out our hair. She took a couple of semesters at a beauty college a few years ago, but for some reason, she never finished, and whenever I bring it up to ask why, she brushes it off with flimsy excuses or diverts the conversation entirely.

But her talents speak for themselves—she transforms Rhode and I into dazzling stars with just a few brushes and products.

As we sit in front of the mirror, admiring our reflection, I can't help but be grateful for Eirene's skill and her quiet patience. She steps back, surveying her work with a critical eye before nodding, satisfied.

"Alright, you two are all set," Eirene announces, her voice tinged with a hint of pride.

Eirene's face lights up with excitement as she applies her lip gloss in front of the lit vanity mirror.

"I heard the owner's son is going to be there tonight. Rumor is, he's the hottest guy in town. I bet Elliot's probably foaming at the mouth with jealously knowing he's no longer the hot shot anymore." She laughs, placing the lip gloss back into her makeup case.

Elliot is her douche of an ex that stole her heart at fifteen, only to turn around and break it into a million pieces. He kept her on a leash, while he was out screwing every other girl in town.

Disgusting.

If it hadn't been for Melonie, Phil would have beat him to a bloody pulp the day Eirene found him in her room with another girl.

Rhode's face turns to stone, and she glares sternly at Eirene, "Don't. Even. Think. About. It." She sounds out slowly. "Rumor also has it, that he is devious and nothing but trouble. You deserve better than to go through that again."

Always the protector.

"Don't be such a fun sucker. I'm not looking for marriage. Just a little...fun. A girl still has needs you know." Eirene chides.

Rhodes gaze snaps to Eirene's, "I do not suck anything!" She exclaims. "I worry, ok. I'm a worrier. How could I not be with the two of you imbeciles. I want to have a life too, you know. I also have needs. But do you ever care? No!" Rhode's voice starts to rise, her eyes mist over with tears.

I want to laugh at her sucking comment, but I can tell she is starting to get upset.

My phone dings.

A text from Liv.

> Jeremy is letting me off early tonight. I'll be able to come to your party after all. He still feels bad about you getting attacked last week. I think this is his way of making himself feel better. Oh! I almost forgot, he said to tell you Happy Birthday.

Saved by the ding.

I need to change the subject before this becomes an all-out cat fight.

"Hey Rhode." I say, grinning and waving my phone at her. "Liv is coming tonight."

Her cheeks blush at the mention of Liv's name before she crosses her arms over her chest, turning her nose up in the air, "Ok? Exactly why would that matter to me?" She asks.

I throw my hands up in defense, raising my brows. "I just thought you guys...I don't know—clicked, or whatever on our shopping trip."

She attempts to act nonchalant, placing a hand on the wall for support. But she completely misses her mark and ends up grabbing onto the door frame instead, causing her to lose her balance and smack her face against the wall.

Like a chain reaction, Eirene falls out of her chair laughing, which knocks Rhode into me causing my ankles to buckle in the heels I'm wearing, and we fall into an entanglement of bruised body parts, consumed by the kind of laughter that brings tears to your eyes.

Through our tangled heap on the floor, Rhode finally manages to untangle herself, rubbing her forehead where it smacked the wall.

"You're both absolute disasters," She mutters, but the corner of her mouth betrays her with a reluctant smile.

I manage to stand up first, wobbling slightly as I extend my hands to my sisters and help them to their feet. Rhode, still rubbing her forehead, shakes her head but can no longer hide the amusement playing at the edges of her lips. Eirene, ever the peacemaker, wraps an arm around each of our shoulders, pulling us into a clumsy group hug.

"I love you guys." Eirene declares, squeezing us tighter than necessary.

Rhode lets out a small sigh, but leans into the hug, nonetheless.

It's moments like these that remind me why, despite all our squabbles and mishaps, I wouldn't trade my sisters for the world.

The limo Phil sent to pick us up, beeps loudly from outside my bedroom window.

"Oh no! My hair is a disaster!" Eirene exclaims. "I'll be the talk of the club if I show up like this."

Rhode puts her hand across her chest, accepting the challenge, "I promise, sis. If any of those heifers laughs at you tonight, I'll punch them square in the tit! No questions asked." She promises.

This earns a fresh round of giggles from all of more, even as we scramble to make ourselves presentable again.

Eirene rushes back to the vanity, "Seriously though, are you sure my hair looks okay?"

"Better than okay, it's fabulous!" I assure her, picking up a brush and beginning to smooth out the few tangles that the fall had caused.

"Alright, ready?" Rhode asks.

"Ready." Eirene and I chorus together.

Then, interlocking arms, we make our way downstairs and out to the limo, like the bad bitches, we know we are.

About ten minutes and two shots of Patron later, we were pulling into Club Lust.

The crowd here tonight is nuts.

People wrap all the way around the building in hopes of being let in—many of them undoubtedly still underage.

The upper level serves as a balcony that provides a view of the dance floor and leads out to the deck above the main entrance. A group of girls can be seen sitting on this deck, chatting and enjoying cocktails. There is also a lower level that is restricted to members who have paid for access.

According to a few girls from Vortex, they had joined some club members and ventured to the lower level. However, due to being under the influence, their memories of the experience were fuzzy at best. All they could recall was that it was the go-to spot for a good time.

A young male wearing a blue suit with dark slicked back hair opens the door to the limo, causing us to jump, "My apologies ladies, I didn't mean to startle you." He says with a charming smile, extending his hand to Eirene who is sitting closest to the door.

Eirene takes his hand gracefully and steps out of the limo, her dazzling dress glinting under the streetlights, "No worries," She replies, offering him a smile that's both sweet and slightly mischievous.

Rhode and I follow suit, stepping into the cool night air that buzzes with anticipation and the distant thump of bass from inside Club Lust.

After assisting each of us, the gentleman slaps his hand on the hood of the limo, signaling to the driver that he can go.

Eirene's eyes light up with a familiar glimmer, the one she always gets when she finds someone attractive and has her sights set on seducing them.

She bites her lip and flips her hair over her shoulder, revealing a daring amount of cleavage. Her violet dress glitters under the overhead lights as she gives him a smile.

He scans her with his eyes like a predator stalking its prey, "I don't believe we have met before." He begins, grasping her hand in his own. "I would never forget a captivating beauty, such as your own." He lowers his head, pressing his lips gently against the back of her hand.

Damn.

This guy is as hot, as he is smooth.

"Well, I suppose tonight's a night for new acquaintances then," She replies coyly, pulling her hand back slowly, the contact lingering just a moment longer than necessary. "And you are?" She asks.

The man straightens up, his smile widening. "Apologies for my lack of manners. My name is Dante. My father told me of your event this evening and ask that I see you in safely."

"Your father?" I ask.

"Oh, yes...ummm he owns this place."

Eirene's interest deepens, her eyes flickering with curiosity and a hint of amusement. "Well, Dante, it seems we owe you—and your father—our thanks for the warm welcome."

Dante nods, his gaze locked on Eirene with an intensity that suggests he is equally intrigued by her as he offers her his arm, "Shall we, love?"

"Eirene." She corrects, eagerly accepting his arm, and glancing back at us like she's just won the lottery.

Rhode and I share a look behind them as they stride toward the entrance of the club.

Don't get me wrong: dude is sexy as sin, but something about him screams dangerous.

As we step into the dimly lit club, pulsating bass reverberates through the walls. Shirtless men with chiseled abs and women in skimpy outfits sway rhythmically under the neon lights. Their bodies, slick with sweat, shimmer as they press against each other, lost in a haze of primal energy. The atmosphere is heavy with the mix of perfume and sweat, blending as they sway to the entrancing rhythm, their eyes half-shut in a haze of raw desire.

A girl wearing just a thin dress lay sprawled across a guy sitting on a couch in the front corner of the room. She strokes his dick that hangs from the zipper of his jeans, while he thrusts his fingers in and out of her. She moans, writhing against his hand, both of them oblivious to their surroundings.

Well, this place is—unique.

Rhode raises a hand to her face, shielding her eyes from the couple locked in the deep throes of passion and a giggle escapes me.

Dante ushers us through the clubgoers, pushing past a group of dancers who are so absorbed in the rhythm they barely notice our presence. He leads us to a quieter section of the club, a secluded area adorned with plush red velvet booths and dark mahogany tables that offer a stark contrast to the chaos we just walked through.

Liv is already seated in the lounge with the rest of the group when she notices us and waves us over. "Hey girl! We were just starting to think that you guys got lost," She jokes, passing me a shot glass filled with liquor.

I take the shot glass, the liquid cold against my fingers, reflecting the dim lights overhead like tiny, trapped stars, "Wouldn't be the worst place to get lost," I quip back, throwing back the shot.

The liquor burns its way down my throat, setting a fire in my chest that feels oddly comforting amidst the chaos of the club. My eyes water slightly from the strength of the drink, and I cough a little, trying to regain my composure as I take a seat.

Rhode settles next to me, her eyes scanning the dim surroundings with a mixture of curiosity and caution. "This place has a certain...charm, doesn't it?" She remarks.

"Indeed, it does." Eirene agrees staring up at Dante.

Melonie stands up and rushes over to me, "Happy Birthday sweetheart." She exclaims over the loud music.

I hug her even tighter, "Thank you so much, Melonie! Everything is great." I gush. "I can't believe you did all this. Words can't even begin to describe how much I appreciate you guys."

Melonie beams, her eyes twinkling with excitement. "Well, you only turn twenty-one once! We had to make it memorable," She shouts back over the music, her voice barely audible.

With a slight slur in his words, Phil claps his hand on my shoulder. "Today's your big day! Let's get this celebration started!"

He's always been one to embrace a good party.

"Who the hell is this?" Phil asks as he turns around to see Eirene clinging to Dante like a lifeline in a stormy sea.

"Daddy, this is Dante. He's the owner's son."

Dante steps forward offering his hand to Phil, "Nice to meet you, sir."

The smile on Phil's face disappears in an instant and he sizes him up with a scrutinizing gaze before shaking his hand, albeit somewhat reluctantly.

Dante, unfazed by Phil's skeptical expression, maintains his friendly demeanor.

"I hope you're enjoying the evening," He says with a nod towards the bustling dance floor. "If there's anything you need, just let me know."

Phil nods stiffly, his eyes still locked on Dante as if trying to read his intentions. After a moment, he steps back, giving a little grunt that could either be interpreted as acceptance or warning.

"Daddy, Dante is going to show me around and then we're going to go dance." Eirene informs Phil, her voice slightly hesitant.

"Alright, but I'll be watching." Phil warns with a stern look, motioning towards his eyes with two fingers before pointing them at Dante, making the intention clear.

Eirene rolls her eyes but smiles reassuringly at her father. "I'll be fine, Daddy. It's just dancing."

Phil pours another shot of whiskey into the glass before him and lets out a sigh. "Alright, go ahead," He says. But, if I catch you getting handsy with my little girl, don't be surprised when I chop off both your arms leaving you with only tiny little nubs that you won't even be able to pleasure yourself with. Got it?"

Dante stares on, careless to the threats being thrown at him, "Hmmm. I guess I'd better be on my best behavior then." He smirks, offering Eirene his arm again.

Eirene chuckles nervously before glancing in my direction and clearing her throat, "Oh, uh, is it okay if I go, sis? I swear I will come back and celebrate with you. I just need an hour—tops."

I nod, giving her a thumbs up, "Go. Have fun."

Eirene beams at my approval, a weight seemingly lifted from her shoulders as she takes Dante's arm, and he whisks her away.

Liv pours me another shot and then pours herself and Rhode one too, "Hey, you still got us." She grins.

"Facts." Rhode agrees, picking up her shot glass.

I raise my own to make a toast, "To sisters, friends, family, and the ties that bind us—even if one of us is absent and off dancing with trouble."

They both laugh and we clink our glasses together, the sharp sound merging with the lively hum of conversation and music that fills the air around us.

I guess so much for the four of us being single together, tonight.

Chapter Ten

Kali

We sit and sling back shots for the next hour.

Eirene is still long gone. It won't surprise me if I don't see her for the rest of the evening.

She's gotten exactly what she wanted tonight—a chance to disappear into the crowd, to become just another hidden face in a sea of strangers. To shed her identity, almost as easily as one would shed a coat, and revel in the anonymity that the bustling city nightlife offers.

Liv is feeling herself big time, swaying her hips to the music as she tosses back another shot of tequila.

She plops herself down next to Rhode, singing along to the music but slightly off key. Her face mask constantly slides down her nose, causing her to frequently readjust it over her eyes. I catch them stealing glances at each other, their admiration for one another not so secret.

Liv grabs Rhode's arm and pulls her towards the dance floor. "Come on, let's dance!"

Rhode sheepishly confesses, tucking loose strands of hair behind her ear. "To be honest, I'm not really sure how to dance."

Liv laughs, a bright, infectious sound that seems to make the entire room turn a shade lighter, "That's the best part! No one here knows what they're doing. It's all about having fun."

Rhode hesitates for a moment longer her eyes scanning the throng of bodies moving chaotically to the sound of the beat before she gives me pleading eyes to help her out of her hopeless situation.

But I simply raise my glass in a silent toast to her new adventure, my eyes twinkling with deviltry. Rhode sighs, resigned, and finally allows herself to be led by Liv into the pulsating throng of dancers.

As they walk away, I turn back to Phil. He's now gently massaging Melonie's shoulders and whispering something in her ear. She laughs and nuzzles into his chest, running her fingers through his beard.

Yea...things are getting a bit too weird in here for my liking.

"You guys enjoy the lounge. I'm going to go check the rest of the place out. Maybe dance with a stranger or something. I don't know." I tell them, standing from my seat.

They nod, no longer paying any attention to me.

With a casual shrug, I weave my way through the dense crowd, each step taking me further away from my friends and deeper into the beating heart of the nightclub. The music grows louder, the bass vibrating through the soles of my shoes and pulsating against my skin like a second heartbeat.

My drink swishes around in its glass, spilling a few drops onto my dress as I accidentally bump into a solidly built man. I quickly step back and try to regain my balance, but end up stumbling into a nearby table instead.

Man. I'm fucking drunk.

I notice the man I ran into, is seething. His elegant suit is now drenched in the drinks that were once in his hands, and if looks could kill, the one he is giving me right now, would surely slay me on the spot.

"Watch where the hell you're going next time." He shouts.

I give a hasty apology to the stranger and quickly take off, just to bump into yet another stranger.

Out of nowhere, a surge of passion and longing shoots through me, targeting my very essence. My stomach tightens as the scent of Sandalwood, Clove, Vanilla, and...man, overwhelms my senses. I inhale deeply, feeling my nipples harden and my body tremble with desire. I clench my thighs together tightly, afraid that I will lose control at any second.

What the hell is wrong with me?

I straighten my dress and stutter out another apology as I finally glance up at the person I collided with this time around.

To my surprise, it's him—the guy from the grill.

I can hardly believe what my eyes are showing me. Or, at least, what I think they are showing me. For all I know, this man in front of me could just be a product of my overactive imagination.

But I couldn't possibly be *that* drunk, could I?

Or maybe the effects of Selene's tea haven't worn off yet. Yes, that must be it.

I swear, she's a dirty freaking liar, and her herbal concoctions pack quite a punch.

Okay...well, I can't drive; I'm way too sloshed for that, and the driver isn't due back for another two hours. Everyone else is trying to get laid so it's just me and this intoxicating mirage, if that's what he is. I take a tentative step forward, my heels clicking against the hardwood like a ticking clock counting down the seconds of my sanity.

I need to sit down.

"Are you alright?" The voice, whether it's a man, imaginary or something else entirely, inquires.

Despite the oddity of the situation, I can't help but feel an overwhelming sense of pleasure washing over me when he speaks.

This is one vivid hallucination—one that I will be using later when I'm by myself, no doubt.

"Are you ok?" The voice repeats, this time with a hint of impatience creeping into its tone.

I tilt my head to the side and jab my finger at his chest, "None of this is real. You're not even real. So why are you getting mad at me? That's what I really want to know...buddy." The words tumble out of my mouth, slightly slurred but I don't care.

I know I sound ridiculous, but it doesn't bother me in the slightest.

He looks at me, his eyebrows knitting together in confusion—or is it concern? It's hard to tell with imaginary people.

"I assure you, I'm very real, Kali. Maybe you just need to get some fresh air," He suggests, his voice a mixture of amusement and vague annoyance.

I find myself gazing intently at the noticeable bulge in his trousers. Whoops.

But he doesn't seem to mind my indiscretion, and it's clear that he is just as attracted to me as I am to him.

"Yes, even that part of me is real," He chuckles, sending a delicious shiver down my spine.

The reaction my body has with this man drives me insane. I can't help but to think about what it would feel like to be at his mercy—allowing him to destroy me in all the right ways.

"Hold on. How do you know my name?" I question, realizing suddenly that in all the haze of this confusing encounter, I never once introduced myself.

He's a fabrication inside your head. That's how...duh.

His smile widens, revealing perfectly aligned teeth that somehow add to his allure rather than detract from the mystery.

"I know a lot of things about you," He replies.

His tone is playful but there's a seriousness in his eyes that makes my heart beat just a little bit faster.

"Like what?" I challenge, folding my arms across my chest in a defensive posture, even though every fiber of my being is drawn to him.

He steps closer, the distance between us now only inches apart.

"Like how you prefer coffee to tea. Black, no sugar, unless you're feeling particularly desolate." He begins, his proximity unsettling, yet intoxicating. "Then you add just a pinch of sugar, as if that small act of kindness towards yourself could sweeten the darker days. I know how you tap your foot when you're anxious, and how you look up at the sky when you think deeply, and how when you're nervous, you tug on your left earring, just like you're doing now." His voice lowers to a near whisper, his breath mingling with mine.

I freeze, all thoughts of attraction momentarily suspended by the realization that he knows far too much. My hand instinctively drops from the earring, and I take a step back, trying to regain some semblance of control over the situation.

"How—how do you know all this?" I stammer, wanting to step back, to put space between us, but my legs refuse to obey.

I should run, scream, demand answers. But there's something over-whelmingly compelling about his gaze that pins me in place, a moth hypnotized by the light.

"I was—"

"There you are sis!" Eirene's voice echoes through the bar as she sprints towards me, interrupting the man in the middle of his sentence.

She's ditched her date, who is currently making out with an intoxicated girl at the bar.

Still a bit flustered, I redirect my attention from the imaginary figure to my sister, "What happened with the two of you?" I inquire, nodding over to the man in question.

"He was a flop," She shrugs. "Just another Elliot. He's her problem now." Her nose turns up at the sight, a mixture of disgust and disinterest painted plainly across her face as she turns back to me. "But enough about that disaster. Who might this hottie be?" Her eyes dart curiously back to the man who was just intimately listing my habits mere seconds ago.

She sees him too? Holy mother of Gods—he *is* real!

I blink, not sure how to explain the situation without sounding like I'm the one spiraling into madness.

"This is..."

I have no idea who this is.

He steps forward, offering his hand and a charming smile that doesn't quite reach his eyes, "My apologies, we hadn't quite yet made it to introductions. My name is Asmodeus." He says smoothly.

Eirene's eyebrows arch, her earlier flirtatious demeanor evaporating as she looks between us, instantly sensing the tension. "Asmodeus," She repeats, a trace of skepticism in her voice. "Interesting name."

I give a slight nod, trying to keep my emotions in check.

She studies him with her eyes for a moment, then asks, "Do we know each other?"

"Not directly," He replies, his eyes flicking briefly to mine before settling back on Eirene.

"But I believe we have some mutual acquaintances."

He finds a nearby table and sits down, gesturing for us to do the same.

My sister and I have always had the proclivity of diving headfirst into troubled waters; however, this time is different. I see her own caution mirroring the apprehension I feel deep down. But curiosity, as often as it does, wins out.

Following Asmodeus's lead, Eirene slides into the seat on the left of him. I hesitantly join them, taking the seat opposite, my brain throbbing with uncertainty and suspicion.

Clasping his hands together in front of him like a teacher about to lecture a class when he speaks, "I understand my presence may be—surprising," He begins. "But there are matters of great importance that we must discuss, and time is of the essence. You see, there are certain...elements at play, which require our mutual attention."

Eirene's gaze sharpens, her posture subtly shifting, "And what exactly might that be?" My sister asks.

I watch the stranger, not missing how he measures each word, weighing them like a gambler contemplating his next move.

Asmodeus leans slightly forward; the low light of the bar casting shadows across his angular face making his features appear almost chiseled from stone, "I was sent to find Kali here." He says, giving me a lopsided smirk as my name rolls off his tongue.

Eirene moves with the force of a lightning strike, launching herself at the man sitting across from her. She seizes his collar and presses a sharp ivory dagger against his throat, demanding answers.

"Who sent you? And what do you want with my sister?" She questions in rapid fire. "I suggest you start talking right now, before I cut you up into tiny pieces, and feed your rancid carcass to the sharks."

Woah.

Where did she pull that dagger from?

The man's face lights up with amusement, and a smile spreads across his features, sending tingles through my body.

"I come on behalf of someone who is important to both of us. She needs our assistance. She has been captured and I do not know how long she will survive before—" His voice trails off, his expression turning cold and grim, like a winter night full of storms.

"Who?" I demand to know. "Is Liv in trouble?" I ask frantically.

I'm completely confused and lost. None of this is making any sense to me.

"I literally just saw her with Rhode not even twenty minutes ago—."

"No, Kali," he interrupts me. "Let's just say this man, Lucius, has captured your parents and I'm certain he has my mother as well."

I can't help but laugh. This guy must be insane.

"My parents are dead, you asshole." I retort, disgusted by his twisted attempt at humor.

He lets out a heavy sigh and furrows his brow, bringing his left hand up to pinch the bridge of his nose in frustration.

"I was told you probably didn't know much, but WOW." He scoffs, glaring at my sister as if she knows what he was talking about.

"Okay. Well, no point in sugar coating it..."

He takes a deep breath, and his eyes lock onto mine with a seriousness that chills me to the bone. "Your parents are very much alive, Kali. They've been in hiding all these years, protecting you from Lucius's reach. But now, they've been caught, and I've been sent here to the mortal realm as your protector. I am to train you when your powers kick in at midnight tonight."

My mind reels.

The entire world comes crashing down around me, numbness sinking into every fiber of my being.

This guy is a fucking psychopath.

To be able to use something as heart wrenching and as personal as my dead parents without even a hint of remorse—I don't even know him!

What could possibly motivate him to do this?

If there is one thing that's certainly clear: this guy is riding first class on the crazy train to Looney-town.

"You're insane." I spit, slamming my hands in front of me as I shoot up out of my chair.

He remains unfazed by my outburst.

"If only insanity were my problem." He chides. "Fuck! I swear this would have gone so much smoother if you weren't so damn sheltered." He says, running a hand through his hair in a gesture of strained patience.

Eirene lets go of Asmodeus, her hands falling to her sides as she stares at him in shock. Her complexion fades from a warm golden hue to a pale white, and she murmurs something under her breath.

She quickly rebounds and begins barking orders at me, "Kali, take him with you and go find mom and dad. We need to get out of here. Now." She exclaims.

Stunned, I just sit there, my mouth gaped open.

Crossing my arms over my chest I hiss, "What is with you right now? You're seriously expecting me to go with him? Did you not just hear the words spewing from his cakehole!? I'll take a hard pass."

"Kali, please. You must." She pleads. "If only to ease my mind, let him go with you to find Daddy. When we all get back home, I swear to you we'll explain everything, but right now you need to go."

"Eirene, what—what are you saying?" My voice trembles.

"He's telling the truth, Kali."

My heart skips a beat.

She's just acknowledging this madness?

It can't be.

"Come on Eirene. This isn't funny. Just tell me what the hell is going on."

"I promise I'll explain when we get home where it's safe."

I stare at her, betrayal stinging sharply. "You knew?" My voice cracks under the weight of my disbelief.

"Yes, I knew," Eirene admits, her voice barely above a whisper. Her eyes, usually so full of life, now appeared hollow and weary. "But it wasn't my secret to share. Please trust me on this, Kali."

Trust her?

How can I possibly trust her after this?

Everything I thought I knew about my sister, about our life, seems to crumble in an instant.

I feel a coldness creeping into my veins as I look between her and Asmodeus.

Taking a deep breath, I realize the urgency in her voice isn't just fear—it's desperation. My resolve falters. Asmodeus, who had been silent throughout our heated exchange, steps forward, his expression grave.

"Kali, I know this is difficult to digest," He says, his voice smooth yet somehow rugged.

"Don't." I swallow hard, the dryness of my throat making it difficult to speak.

"Kali, I'm—I'm sorry." Eirene's eyes are swelling with tears as she throws her arms around my shoulders and squeezes me. "Please, don't hate me."

I stand rigid in her embrace, my mind racing through a thousand thoughts at once.

Finally, I pull back from her embrace, searching her eyes for answer I know I won't find in them.

"Fine." I say. "But why do I have to go with him?"

Eirene wipes a tear from her cheek with the back of her hand, "Asmodeus will keep you safe while I'm gone. I'm going to go find Rhode and Liv; let them know that we have to go. I'll meet you back at home, okay?"

"I am perfectly capable of taking care of myself. I don't need some weird stalker guy to watch over me," I retort, my voice laced with bitterness and frustration.

Asmodeus's eyes flash a dangerous shade of dark amber, the muscles in his jaw clenching.

Eirene lets out a defeated sigh and places her hands on my shoulders, "I know you are, Kali. But this isn't about capability. It's about safety—yours and ours. There's more at play here than you can understand right now, but the quicker we get out of here, the quicker we can get home to where we can explain it all to you."

Damn it. She's right.

"Alright. Fine. I'll go." I cave.

Asmodeus nods once, sharply, as if sealing the deal with my reluctant agreement. He steps forward, extending his hand but then seems to think better of it and lets it drop to his side. "Shall we?" he asks, his voice unnervingly calm.

"I'll catch you in a bit." Eirene promises before her small frame is swallowed by the sea of masked partygoers.

I give a piercing stare to Asmodeus, gesturing for him to come with me. We make our way to the V.I.P section where I had left Melonie and

Phil earlier. Their expressions instantly turn to ones of panic as soon as they see Asmodeus accompanying me.

I give them a quick rundown of the events that just unfolded with Eirene, hoping someone will brush it off as her being intoxicated, though that is not the case.

My curiosity peaks and I finally speak up, wanting to know what is really going on.

"Can anyone please fill me in on what's going on?" I ask, as we hastily gather our belongings.

Phil's lips purse tightly, his eyes flickering to the others before settling back on me. His response is short and cryptic. "Not here."

A tightness forms in my chest as I realize there is more to this than any of them are letting on. But for now, I am left with no answers and a sense of malaise lingering in the air.

Without giving me any further explanation, they hurriedly guide me out of the building and into the back of a limo.

We try to act as if everything is normal, ignoring the fact that we are riding home with a complete stranger that I've never laid eyes on before this evening.

To say something feels off would be an understatement.

I don't know how to explain it, but something deep in my gut is gnawing at me, like a starving animal devouring its first meal in days.

Liv and my sisters are still nowhere in sight; and where the fuck is Dafina?

I never even got any of the food she was supposed to cater.

Fucking shit.

I am *not* sober enough for any of this.

I lay my head against the back passenger window, trying to silence my stubborn thoughts. But anxiousness creeps in like a hazy fog anyways, and I silently choke on the fear that's bubbling in my throat.

What is with everyone?

If this is supposed to be the surprise they've been keeping from me all day—it sucks, and this will inescapably be going down in history as the most fucked up night of my life.

Happy Birthday to me.

CHAPTER ELEVEN

Kali

I tap my fingers on the dining table in a steady rhythm.

My thoughts are clouded with confusion, and I'm secretly hoping I'm passed out drunk somewhere and that I'll be waking up soon with a massive headache, realizing this is all just a dream. But the tap of my fingers and the hard, cold reality of the wooden table tell me otherwise.

There are countless questions swirling in my mind, some of which I am hesitant to even seek answers for.

I lean my head from side to side, relishing the satisfying cracking sensation that travels down my spine.

"So", I begin. "What in the actual fuck is going on? Can anyone elaborate, or are we going to continue pretending that nothing happened?"

I can feel the anger starting to bubble in my stomach.

Phil is the first to respond.

He reaches up with his hand and scratches his beard, looking over at Melonie and then back at me. His shoulders tremble, and his bright blue eyes are tarnished with the shame of deception.

"It's a lot to take in, Kali," his voice cracks as he struggles to find the right words. "Just know that your parents love you more than anything in this world, and we had all hoped that this day would have turned out differently." He tightens his grip on Melonie's hand, drawing strength from her presence. Taking a deep breath, he continues, "I'll start with the night your mother was attacked. She was sent back to Helheim—when she was bitten that night—the realm where you were conceived. The curse of the hellhound's bite prevented her from being able to return back to the mortal realm. As much as she wanted to, she couldn't be with you. She spent years trying to break the curse, but we still have yet to find a solution."

I click my tongue off the roof of my mouth, "Do you realize how crazy this sounds?" I ask. "Seriously, Helheim and curses? Like, I get we have a wild religion compared to most, but this—this is ridiculous. Why are you putting me through this? I mourned her—*we* mourned her!"

Phil clears his throat and speaks, "Kali, please let us explain. I promise it will all make sense soon enough." He pauses to take a deep breath before continuing, "When you moved here, you were here because Helena had come to us for help. After she had an altercation with some lesser demons that found you, she knew she had to leave Colorado and find you a new home, because she also knew what danger awaited her—and you—if she were to remain there. Ensuring your safety was her top priority, and we all thought bringing you here, having you under our protection, would accomplish just that. But we were sadly mistaken. We were unprepared and caught off-guard when we were attacked that night, and I—I tried to save her but—." Phil's hands tremble as he covers his eyes, tears streaming down his face as he's overcome with sorrow and guilt. "It haunts me with every day that passes, with every lie that has tumbled from my lips. I'm so sorry Kali, we shouldn't have hidden this from you. We should have been honest from the start." His voice is barely audible as he leans towards me, taking my hands in his own and pressing his forehead to them.

It's as if he is pleading for forgiveness, as if he holds himself responsible for my mother's absence.

As I reminisce about that dreadful night, my memories become sharper, and I begin to realize that I was never crazy; everything that happened *was* real.

It wasn't all just in my head.

The waves raged and spun above me, like a relentless tornado determined to obliterate everything in its path. The burning saltwater stung my eyes as it crashed over the shoreline, dragging most of the red-eyed beasts back into the depths of the ocean.

Their bodies were covered in protective armor, their decaying flesh exposing bones beneath. In their hands, they wielded flaming swords that blazed so fiercely, even the water couldn't douse them. I had stumbled while fleeing from one of the creatures with red eyes and gashed my leg open. My mother sent Phil away from her side to save me instead.

If only I had heeded their warnings instead of rushing back to my mother...maybe she would still be alive...maybe she could still be here with me.

My head is spinning like I'm on a never-ending tilt-a-whirl. My stomach churns and I feel the urge to vomit as tears pour down my face, burning like wildfire, and tremors rattle through my body as my heart shatters into countless fragments.

It was all real.

I yank my hands away from Phil's grip. My palms slam down on the table as I push myself up, causing the chair to crash onto the tile floor, "This is all because of me," I manage to say through sobs. "She would still be here if it wasn't for me."

Melonie rushes over and wraps her arms around me, pulling me close to her chest. She gently brushes a tear-soaked strand of hair from my face, her expression turning serious and somber. "It's not your fault, Kali," She whispers soothingly. "Even if you hadn't been there, fate would have taken its course. It was decided long before you were born."

Her words hang in the air, trembling like the delicate strings of a spider's web under the weight of morning dew. They're meant to comfort, perhaps even to heal, but they slice through me like shards of glass.

"I wish I could believe that." I choke out, my voice a broken whisper as I pull away from her embrace.

Asmodeus clenches his jaw, leaning forward in his seat, the muscles of his biceps flexing under the thin material of his white button up, recognition dawning on his face. "It's written in the prophecy." He mutters, his smoldering chocolate eyes glaring directly at me.

"What prophecy?" I snap. "What's he even talking about?"

Asmodeus lets out a deep sigh, his gaze never leaving mine. He runs his fingers through his tousled hair before speaking, "It's the entire reason I'm even here."

Phil shoots Asmodeus a look that says he better shut up and keep that information to himself.

But Asmodeus ignores Phil's warning glare and turns his attention back to me, "The prophecy mentions a girl marked by unparalleled grief and burdened by a legacy of pain," He starts, "A girl whose power and spirit can be the only one who conquers the darkness that threatens to engulf this world."

"Okay?" I question, my sobs beginning to subside as I release myself from Melonie's comforting hug to glower at Asmodeus.

He rolls his eyes, sighing a breath of frustration, "Kali, you need to understand—you're not just any girl...you are *that* girl. The one the prophecy speaks of. Whether you like it or not, your existence is intertwined with the fate of the world."

The room suddenly feels devoid of air.

I'm frozen, trying to process his shocking confession and the heavy burden it carries.

I didn't ask for any of this.

I didn't ask for responsibility for the world's survival, for a destiny penned in secrets and ancient script.

"No," I shake my head, unable to accept what he's saying. "That—that can't be true. I'm just a regular girl."

Folding my arms across my chest, I squeeze my eyes shut, trying to turn off the last few tears that well beneath the surface of my swollen lids.

Asmodeus leans forward, his expression softening slightly. "You may feel ordinary, Kali, but you're far from it. There are things about your past, your lineage—"

"Stop," I interrupt, my voice firm despite the trembling that has taken over my body.

Asmodeus begins to speak but then abruptly clamps his mouth shut when Phil clears his throat as a subtle reminder of his presence. "Asmodeus, maybe this isn't—"

"And you!" I snap at Phil. "What could have possibly been so damn bad that it made you all lie to me about my mom's death and betray me for so long? You made me believe that I was crazy!" I continue. "My entire life you all let me think that I was the sick one—that I was seeing things, feeling things—all those years...all those sessions with Selene I had to endure, and for what...FOR ABSOLUTELY NOTHING!" My frustration is at its boiling point, and I scream the last words.

Melonie's hand flies to her chest, clearly taken aback and wounded by my sudden burst of anger, "It's not that simple Kali." She says with a shaky breath.

An intense, unyielding rage overtakes me, like a bottomless pit devouring the stars in the sky and extinguishing their once vibrant existence, "Oh really? Telling me the truth isn't simple?" I bite out.

"Listen, Kali," Melonie pleads, "Your mother only wanted to protect you. There is so much more to this than we could ever tell you in one night."

"You don't say?" I scoff, my anger turning cold and sharp, a blade that could cut through the thickest armor.

There's a long silence, one that stretches and bends like the horizon just before dawn cracks open the night.

"None of the decisions that were made, were done in light." Phil finally says. "We made those choices under extreme circumstances. You have to understand, there was no right answer." He looks down, his face etched with deep lines of penitence that seem to age him a decade in those mere seconds. "We were trying to shield you from a truth that might have destroyed you much sooner."

I shake my head, disbelief and despair mixing into a toxic concoct in my veins. "Destroyed me sooner? You mean more than you've already done by letting me live a lie? I keep hearing about how it was all to protect me so, why even tell me now at all?"

Asmodeus who has stayed silent since he was basically told to butt out, finally speaks again, "Kali, the dangers you were shielded from are now at your doorstep. It's no longer a matter of hiding you away; it's a matter of making sure your prepared for what's coming." His voice holds a somberness that makes the air seem vapid.

"And what exactly is coming? What are you all so damn afraid of? This—this Lucius guy? He's just one man."

"One man that can unleash chaos unlike anything you've ever seen." Asmodeus warns.

I roll my eyes, "This is just...insane."

"Agreed. I have felt the exact same way since my arrival here. Things would have been easier on the both of us had you known sooner and been more prepared. But we are where we are now, and time isn't exactly on our side. Once your power emerges, we won't have long before one of Lucuis's minions—or worse—your grandfather can track you down."

"Why would my grandfather finding me be a bad thing?"

"Because he's the reason Lucius is after you in the first place."

Mind blown.

The only word that can describe what is happening to my brain right now.

A week ago, I was a somewhat normal girl. Traumatized sure, but I was normal-sh.

Preparing for my birthday party had been my only worry in the world—now I find myself trying to grasp the enormity of a hidden world suddenly thrust upon me. I should be picking out my next tattoo, not strategies for survival.

"Great. Grandpa is evil. What's next? Does he shoot lasers out of his eyes?"

It's a rhetorical question.

Something Asmodeus clearly isn't used to.

"That would be absurd." Asmodeus shrugs off the sarcasm with a slight tic in his jaw, indicating his growing impatience. "He a trickster god. One with abilities that manipulate reality itself. Your grandfather wields illusions so potent; they can turn an army against its own soldiers or make a person doubt their own senses. He thrives on deception, deals, schemes, and control. And he has Lucius wrapped around his finger."

My brow furrow and I lick my lips, "Why me though? Why are they so obsessed with finding me?" I ask, my frustration mounting as the situation grows more and more confusing.

"Loki's status as an immortal god was never enough; he constantly yearned for more, his hunger for power insatiable like the need for air." Phil pinches his lips together and curls his nose as if Loki's name is a bitter taste on his tongue before he continues. "A long time ago, when your mom was a young girl, Loki kidnapped an old seer in hopes of discovering the key to gain the type of power he so desperately seeks. But when the oracle foretold his eventual downfall at the hands of his own offspring, he responded with violence and ripped out her eyes before imprisoning her in his dungeons. He had always feared the potential power of your mothers and her siblings. In a fit of rage and fear, he killed their mother and then banished each of them to separate realms. By the time Helena was able to sneak back through an Asgardian portal to save the seer, it was already too late."

Impatience begins to bubble up inside me. "That's a shame," I reply, trying to keep my tone even. "And kind of gross, but I'm still struggling to see how this connects to me."

Melonie fidgets in her seat, tugging on a strand of her hair. "Well, this is where things start to get complicated."

Right, because this whole ordeal isn't complicated.

Phil leans in, his eyes narrowing as if he's sharing a great secret, "In her final moments, the seer breathed a prophecy to Helena, speaking of future wars and the fall of Tartarus' god, and how in his place, an evil king would rise. Then, the Goddess of Death herself, your mother, would fall in love and become pregnant by a powerful god Loki would deceive.

The prophecy claims that Helena's child would grow up to become as powerful as an Eternal, and that she would be betrothed to the new king by her own blood, and if he succeeds in marrying you, his curse will be broken, and the titans would reign once more. At first, young and naive, Helena dismissed the woman's words. But years later, when she became pregnant with you, everything the seer had foretold started to come true. Your parents did everything in their power to protect you from the clutches of Loki after he betrothed you to Lucius. They were determined to keep you safe and prevent the prophecy from being fulfilled." He pauses, shifting in his seat. "We thought we had time to change things. But fate, it seems, is not so easily swayed."

My eyes jerk toward the clock on the stove—it's almost midnight.

My supposed abilities are on the verge of showing themselves at any moment.

Will I actually have powers? And if so, what will they be like?

I clamp down on my arm with all my might, hoping to snap out of this nightmare. Yet, all I am left with is a throbbing red mark, a harsh reminder that what I am experiencing is indeed real.

It's too overwhelming to process all at once.

Part of me wants to run away—to escape this destiny that seems more like a curse than a blessing. But another part—the part that has always craved answers about my mother's death—urges me to stay.

Melonie notices the conflict in my eyes and reaches across the table, placing a gentle hand on mine. Her touch is surprisingly warm, grounding. "I know this is a lot to take in, and it's okay to be scared. But I promise you, we are here to protect you, and you're not alone in this."

Phil stands up, his enormous frame towering over the dining table, "How about Melonie and I go make some coffee and get something to put in our stomachs after drinking all that alcohol. I have a feeling it's going to be a long night and I'm sure you have many more questions."

I give a slight nod, even though moving my head causes the persistent ache at the back of my neck to spread to my temples.

As they shuffle towards the kitchen, their voices a comforting murmur in the background, I sit frozen in my chair, the ticking of the clock now thunderous in my ears.

Asmodeus stands up, rolling his broad shoulders and smoothing out the wrinkles in his shirt. He places a rough, calloused hand on my shoulder, but surprisingly, his touch is gentle. "I know this isn't easy for you, but there's a lot at stake here. I'm not exactly thrilled about being stuck here babysitting a petulant little princess with trust issues, but I don't have a choice. So, the sooner you can toughen up and harness those powers the prophecy talks about, the sooner I can get back to things that actually matter to me." His words slither through me like a venomous snake, paralyzing me with fear and doubt until it feels like my heart has stopped beating.

In a burst of anger, I push him away as hard as I can and stand up, ready to strike him with an open palm towards his jawline. To my shock, he catches both of my wrists in a firm grip before I can make contact.

His muscular legs carry us quickly across the room and into the hallway, where he presses me against the wall. The cold surface of the wall provides a welcome contrast to the heat of my flushed skin still exposed by the tiny dress I'm wearing.

His gaze darkens and his nostrils flare, as if he can sense the warmth and dampness seeping through the soft fabric between my thighs. He grabs both of my wrists in one hand, holding them above my head and trapping me in place. With his other hand, he traces a finger along my cheek, down my neck, and finally stopping at the curve of my breasts. His chest rises and falls rapidly, accompanied by a low, feral growl from deep within his throat.

This sends shivers of anticipation through my body, like a lone wolf howling at the sight of a full moon. It's an intoxicating thrill I find myself craving more of.

He lowers his head, his face hovering in the crook of my neck, breathing me in. "Mmm...you have some fire in you after all, don't you, little flame?" His full lips graze over the soft fleshy part of my ear, my eyes flutter shut, and a breathy moan to make

He bows his head, bringing his face close to my neck and taking in my scent, "You do have some fire in you after all, don't you, my little flame?" He murmurs.

His lips brush against the sensitive skin behind my ear, causing my eyes to flutter closed and a soft moan to escape my lips.

He lets go of my arms and stands up straight, readjusting himself. A smug grin creeps onto his face as he says, "Good, maybe I won't regret coming here after all. Channel that anger you hide inside, but just know...if you ever raise your hand to me again, I'll have no choice but to bend you over my knee and give that perky little ass of yours a spanking you'll never forget."

The threat, spoken with a teasing edge, sends another jolt of adrenaline through me. I glare at him, my breath still uneven, torn between indignation and a peculiar kind of excitement.

"Is that meant to scare me?" I challenge, regaining some of my composure though my body still betrays my arousal.

Ugh, this guy seriously needs a reality check!

He laughs, a rich, deep sound that seems to vibrate through the air, "Scare you? No, not at all. It's merely a promise, sweetheart." His eyes gleam with mischief and something darker, more primal that I can't quite name.

I push against his chest and my hand instinctively goes to the base of my neck, pulling out the hairpin that kept my locks in place. My long dark waves cascade down my back as I stare at the sharp point of the pin, considering my next move.

His breath hitches, and his gaze flickers back and forth from my hand to my eyes.

Then, without hesitation, I thrust it into the thick muscle of his bicep, a small droplet of blood staining his pristine white shirt.

I quickly extract the pin, bringing it to my lips and savoring the metallic taste of his blood on my tongue. "Try me, asshat. I guarantee you'll be wearing this through your dick next."

His eyes widen in shock, the pain and surprise etched clearly across his face. For a moment, he is silent, merely staring at the small spot of blood that now blooms like a sinister flower on his shirt.

Suddenly, his shock morphs into amusement, and his laughter fills the room once more, "Oh, you really are a wild one, aren't you?" he says, the pain seemingly forgotten as his expression shifts back to one of intrigued fascination. He slowly circles around me, like a predator eyeing its prey, his eyes never leaving mine. "I think I'm going to enjoy this game between us."

The tension between us crackles like a live wire, electrifying the air. Despite the sharp sting of what I've done, or perhaps because of it, our dance of power and defiance seems to have only just begun.

"Well, in that case, may the best player win." I say.

And with that, I turn on my heels swaying my hips as I walk away, knowing I had won this particular battle, leaving Asmodeus standing in the hallway—brooding, dumbfounded, and quite obviously...pissed.

Chapter Twelve

Kali

I stare dully at the cup of coffee in front of me, feeling the weight of exhaustion seeping into my bones.

The seconds crawl by, each one feeling like an eternity in itself.

I stifle a yawn, scrunching my face into a frown. I still find the every-thing about tonight to be nonsense, a demented trick or something that's being played on me; one where my sisters will bust in any moment with the strippers and, hopefully, more booze.

"How are you feeling, sweetie? Are you doing, okay?" Melonie's soft voice quips, breaking the silence that has crept its way in the room.

Okay would be an understatement.

I manage a weak smile, not wanting to burden her with the truth—that I feel as though I'm crumbling inside.

"Yeah, just tired," I mutter, tracing the rim of the coffee cup with my finger.

Melonie doesn't look convinced, her brows knitting together as she studies me, "You know, you're not fooling anyone. It's okay to not be okay."

Her voice is gentle, coaxing, but it feels like a wall I'm not quite ready to scale. It's the acknowledgment I didn't realize I was craving, yet now that it's here, it feels overwhelming. The façade of normalcy I've been clinging to starts to crack, and the dam holding back my emotions shows signs of strain.

"I—I know," I sigh, pulling the cup closer and cradling it with both hands, seeking warmth from its contents. "It's just..."

"A lot to process?" Phil offers.

I nod, looking down at the floor as I try to hold back tears that threaten to spill over, "Exactly," I whisper.

Phil leans forward, resting his elbows on his knees, his expression painted with concern, "I hope one day, we will be able to move past this. I'm not expecting your forgiveness, as we do not deserve it for our deception, but I hope that we can find a new way forward, a path of understanding, maybe. We never wanted to hurt you, but we thought keeping the truth from you was for the best—we were obviously wrong."

I look up at him, the hurt mingling with a flicker of confusion. "I want to understand, I really do. But how could you think keeping something like this from me was ever a good idea? How did you think I'd react to all of this, honestly?"

"I—I guess we didn't." Melonie admits. "The only thoughts I believed we had were: Keep you safe, and then one day reunite you with your mother and your father."

As much as I resent the lies, betrayal, and endless gaslighting, a part of me understands the warped logic in their decision.

Still, it doesn't make it right.

It doesn't erase the sting of deception, the years of feeling like I was losing my mind.

"I still can't believe that she's alive," I whisper, my head shaking slightly from side to side as I try to process the overwhelming mix of emotions going through me. "After all these years, thinking she was gone forever..."

Melonie rushes to my side, arms encircling me in a tight hug. "We never meant for this to cause you so much pain, dear," she says, her voice full of remorse. "In the beginning, we thought she was gone too."

Phil's eyes darken with a sadness that seems to envelop the room. "Yes, it was a shock for us all," He adds. "When we found out she was alive, it changed everything. But circumstances were...complicated. We had to make tough decisions quickly."

I pull away slightly from Melonie's embrace, needing space to think, to breathe.

I let out a forced laugh.

"Complicated." I echo, the word sounding hollow on my breath.

As much as I shouldn't, I want to know to know more—*need* to know more.

I'm already tumbling down the rabbit hole, so at this point I might as well see how deep it goes.

"So, how did you guys even meet my mom?" I finally build the courage to ask.

Melonie's laugh is hearty and deep, the mischievous gleam twinkling in her eyes piercing straight through my heart, like an unintended, yet, well shot arrow.

I'm suddenly envious of all the memories they must have shared with my mother, when I have had so few of my own with her.

"It's hard to believe it's been so long ago now." She says with a slight shake of her head.

"It was actually your father and I who met first." Phil recalls, his voice soft and reminiscent. "It was during the old wars when the mortals and gods of the six realms were entwined in battle against the Titans, and each other. Your parents, my brothers and I, and then, eventually Melonie, formed an unbreakable bond amidst the chaos of war."

My father.

A man I long thought to be gone. My mother said he died shortly after my birth—murdered, ironically enough.

"Your father, Baldur," Phil continues, "Is known as the God of peace and light and man how he could brighten any room or realm he stepped foot in. A skilled warrior for sure, but he was also one of very few that can bring together unity between the gods, mortals, and the other races residing in our realms."

"Wait, so you're saying my parents are gods?" I ask, vaguely recalling a mention of it before.

Melonie nods, a wistful smile playing at her lips, "Some of the best." She replies.

"Indeed." Phil agrees." "And as I recall, Zeus was quite jealous of your father at first." He laughs.

Did he just say what I think he said?

"Wait a minute, Zeus as in *the* Zeus? Like, Olympus is real kind of Zeus?" I ask in astonishment.

The lightest of smiles shades the creases in Melonie's face, "Yes, the very one."

My eyes become slits in my head, "Okay, say this is...*true*...how do you guys know him?"

"He's my brother." Phil answers.

My mouth drops, and I stare at him as I try to connect the family tree.

"So, that would make you a god too?"

He nods, "I am who the mortals refer to as Poseidon."

I blink a few times, trying to process the absurdity of the statement. *Poseidon?*

The man who raised me—the god of the sea, storms, and horses—is sitting across from me in our kitchen, looking as ordinary as any man could.

"But, why—why would you...why live here, like this?"

Phil's gaze softens, and he leans forward, resting his elbows on the worn kitchen table. It creaks slightly under his weight, a mundane sound that contrasts sharply with the gravity of our conversation.

His voice is low, filled with an uncharacteristic solemnity when he speaks, "There are times, even for gods, when they seek solitude from the eternal responsibilities and conflicts of their realms. After thousands of years, the luster of Olympus, the roar of the seas, it became overwhelming, almost stifling. I sought simplicity, anonymity amongst mortals." He goes on. "It has this grounding effect, helps one remember what it's like to live, rather than simply exist. And in some cases," His gaze trails over to Melonie. "It can also teach you how to love."

Melonie matches his affection, her eyes reflecting a deep, quiet love that transcends ordinary human emotion.

"Are you from Olympus too?" I ask her.

"I'm afraid not." She shrugs. "I am but a mere forest nymph. A guardian of nature's grace, tasked with the care of its ancient woods and their creatures. But when I met him," She nods at Phil, "I found a different kind of sanctuary."

An ordinary exterior, it seems, can mask the most extraordinary secrets.

"So, all these years—you both have been...what? Hiding? Living as humans?" I ask.

"Not hiding, per se," Phil interjects, his voice tinged with a hint of amusement. "More like living alongside. Participating, if you will. It's one thing to observe humanity from the heights of Olympus or the depths of the ocean, quite another to walk among them, to share in their joys and sorrows, their triumphs and tragedies. It gives perspective, enriches understanding. And sometimes," He adds, a twinkle igniting in his sea-blue eyes, "It's simply about enjoying a quieter life."

"Exactly." Melonie agrees. "Raising the three of you girls has been the best part of our existence. Watching you grow, learning from you as much as guiding you, has been our greatest adventure and privilege." She concludes with a smile.

"How did you guys meet?"

"It's quite a long story." Phil says.

I raise my brow, "I got nothing but time."

"Okay, okay." Phil chuckles. "Point taken."

Melonie's voice softens as she delves into the memory. "The world was so much younger at the time—as were we."

Bearing witness to centuries passed, along with the rise and fall of many civilizations must be a beautiful, yet tragic thing all at the same time.

Something they've both seemed to have experienced.

Is that what I too will experience once I get my power—to go through endless loss and grief as I watch the people I love and care about age, and die while time stands still for me?

The thought is daunting.

Asmodeus must have gotten over his state of shock because he comes sulking back into the dining room.

"Also...How does *he* fit into all of this?" I ask, pointing to Asmodeus.

A smirk tugs at the corner of Asmodeus's mouth, giving him a devilish lopsided grin. "Go ahead, tell her about me...Uncle," He says with a taunting tone.

Fuck what?

I whip my head towards him, locking him in place with a frosty glare.

"Please tell me he's joking!" I groan, sliding my palms down the sides of my face.

"I don't believe this the time for jokes." Asmodeus snaps at me as he sits down.

Melonie slams her cup down on the table, her eyes burning with fury, "And I don't believe this to be the time for you to try my patience with your rudeness." She warns him, her voice sharp enough to slice through the thick tension in the room like blades.

Asmodeus holds her gaze for a moment longer before looking away, the smirk vanishing from his face as if it were never there.

Phil clears his throat, drawing all eyes back to him. "Let's start from the beginning," He proposes.

"Yes, let's." Crossing my arms over my chest, I slink back into my chair, sending a hateful glare in Asmodeus's direction as I do.

Strong fingers work their way through a thick beard as Phil speaks, "Alas, a time of past life where magic and the gods were as common as the air we breathe today. We were young gods at the time, roughened by the chaos of war and the overwhelming burden of our duties. The Eternals had long left us, and though war had become a commonplace occurrence among the realms and the remaining celestial beings, this particular war, was a war that could end us all."

"The one from the prophecy?" I ask.

"Yes," Phil nods gravely. "However, upon the king's death when Lucius obtained his power, and his throne, he also inherited something he wasn't expecting—a curse. One that would inevitably trap him withing the realm of Tartarus. That is...unless he is to marry someone capable of wielding the powers of creation and destruction—a rare feat for anyone, let alone someone who is fated for an eternity of solitude—or so he believed. Upon learning of his predicament, Lucius became enraged, creating these monstrosities he called *Titans*—colossal and wrathful, they were forged from the darkest depths of Tartarus itself, and they stormed through the realms, driven by Lucius's fury and despair. The lands of the gods and mortals alike trembled under their footsteps, and it seemed as if no force in existence could quell their rampage."

Phil pauses for a breath, taking a sip from the small porcelain cup in his hands as he recalls the horror, "It was during this time that your father and Thor, as young and boisterous as they were, stumbled into our realm of Olympus. They were seeking the legendary Sand Clock of Aetherius, said to control the very essence of time itself. The Sand Clock of Aetherius, as legend had it, was crafted by the Eternal god Chronos himself, hidden deep within the labyrinthine caves that scarred the underbelly of Olympus. A dangerous tool as such wasn't going to be easy to find. Chronos knew that while the Sand Clock had its limitations on how far back in time the user can travel, and how long time can be altered, it was not meant to be wielded by all, especially mere mortals and fledgling gods. This is why it lay hidden within such treacherous terrain, but that made no never mind to your father and Thor. They were willing to die to retrieve it, if it meant they had the chance to change the tide of the war and bring balance back to the realms." A pause lingers for a brief moment, and it gives me just enough time to absorb the information dump. "Granted," Phil's voice picks back up,

"The arrival of your father and Thor was initially seen as an intrusion, a potential threat to the already fragile alliances among the gods, their valor and charm quickly won over many, including myself. Following a lengthy council meeting, it was unanimously decided that we had no other options. However, we knew that any mistakes or rash alterations to the timeline could have disastrous ramifications not only for our realms but for the very fabric of time itself. Your father and Thor, along with the guidance of Hermes, ventured out to find the Sand Clock. Meanwhile, in Helheim and the Underworld, your mother and Hades worked together to combine their forces in hopes of keeping the Titans from reaching Midgard or as we call it—earth. Unfortunately, their efforts were only enough to slow the inevitable. The Titans, relentless in their destruction, breached the borders of Midgard and began their merciless assault on its people."

"I lost almost my entire family when they made their attack." Melonie whispers through her struggle to hold back tears.

A soft kiss from Phil is placed on top of Melonie's head as he pulls her closer, offering a silent reassurance in the wake of her grief.

"I'm so sorry, Mel." I whisper, feeling the weight of her sorrow as if it were my own.

"It was a lifetime ago." She replies wiping a stray tear trailing down the side of her cheek. "We cannot change what has already been lost. But we can still fight for what remains."

I suddenly feel selfish.

All of us have lost something or someone in this detrimental befalling, yet here I am, dwelling on my own pain, when every soul here bears their own scars of battles fought and lives destroyed.

Phil patiently waits out our emotional exchange before he draws a breath and proceeds, "Your mother, as fierce and radiant as the dawn, was not easily swayed by mere bravado or charm. She demanded respect and wisdom that matched her own. It was during a second council meeting when your father first truly caught her eye. He proposed a bold plan to imprison the titans and trap them with Lucious in Tartarus where they could no longer threaten the realms or our people."

I'm on the edge of my seat now, my heart thundering in my chest as I picture the incredible showdown that must have ensued. Phil's voice grows more animated as he delves deeper into the past, his hands gesturing vividly as if painting the scene right before our eyes.

"The plan was audacious and fraught with danger, requiring the co-operation of all who were present." He resumes, "It demanded not only physical strength but strategic cunning and an unwavering resolve. Every deity, from every pantheon, was united in this moment. The human mortals had even put aside their battles with the gods to join forces for a common purpose. Our strategy was simple: we would use the Sand Clock to halt time temporarily, giving us the opportunity to surround the Titans without fear of retaliation. The timing had to be exact, as the Sand Clock's energy could only sustain for a limited time. The battle raged on for what felt like an eternity until we finally found the perfect moment to strike. It was a brutal and exhausting fight."

As Phil stretches and inhales another long-winded inhale, nostalgia heavy in his eyes, I can see the reflection of flames and chaos in their depths, as though the battle still burns within him.

His voice rises, almost thundering against the smooth walls of the kitchen, "Seas churned, heavens split, and the earth beneath our feet quaked as if it too feared the outcome of this great clash. Thunder roared as Thor wielded his mighty hammer, Mjölnir, each strike echoing the determination of our united front. Zeus, commanding the sky, conjured a storm so fierce it seemed like the world's end, and Hades, Asmodeus's father, unleashed the darkest forces of the Underworld, sending spectral warriors and fearsome beasts to join the fray while your mother guided the souls of the fallen, channeling their energy into a spectral veil that obscured our movements from the Titans. She was a force to be reckoned with, raining hellfire down on Lucius's hordes, blazing through their ranks with a fury that could only be matched by the sun itself."

My mouth gapes, and a knowing and prideful smirk grazes the curve of Asmodeus's mouth.

Hades is his father.

What are the fucking odds?

But also, damn…my mom was a total baddie.

Phil's gaze drifts towards the clock, his forehead furrowing as the seconds pass. I notice the concerned glance he shares with Melonie, but I keep my mouth shut.

My attention snaps back to the words still falling from Phils mouth, "Together, we were able to trap the Titans in Tartarus with Lucius. The Sand Clock worked just as planned, if not better. Time stood still long enough for our plan to conclude, and with chains forged from the unbreakable heart of a fallen star, the titans were bound to their molten prison. Persephone's magic ensured that the chains would not only bind them, but also drain their power, preventing them from regaining their strength or breaking free. The only thing that can free them is the death of their creator, and since he was now an immortal king, that wouldn't be an easy task, as there are very few things that can kill a god."

"But it's not impossible?" I ask, plucking a handful of berries off the snack tray Melonie put together.

Asmodeus's smirk transforms into a somber frown as he picks up a grape from the same tray, rolling it between his fingers thoughtfully. "Not impossible, but exceedingly difficult. The gods have their vulnerabilities, but discovering and exploiting them requires more than just power—it requires cunning and often, sacrifice."

He pops the fruit between his full lips, chewing slowly as if savoring the weight of his words. "We all have our weaknesses, but any sane god keeps their vulnerabilities hidden. There are ancient artifacts, much like the Sand Clock, that possess the ability to kill any deity. Finding them, however, is a different story. Many have lost their lives trying to uncover such relics, only to have their efforts die right along beside them."

My interest is piqued.

"Maybe one of these artifacts can help us." I ponder, leaning forward, my hands clasping the edge of the table.

Phil nods slowly, his eyes narrowing in thought. "It's possible," He concedes, "But it's dangerous."

"A lot of times if those who go searching don't die during the search, the guardians protecting the relics will kill them their selves," Melonie interjects, her voice tinged with a cautious tone. "They are the entities who ensure that these powerful objects don't fall into the wrong hands. Each artifact is typically shielded by tests—puzzles and challenges that mirror the inner darkness or desires of those who seek them. It's as if the artifacts themselves can sense the heart of the seeker and adjust their defenses accordingly."

"Wow." I breathe. "That sounds intense."

"Precisely." Phil nods.

I tuck my feet beneath me in the chair, "Okay, okay. What happened next?" I ask, eager for the story to continue.

"Right." Phil says, scratching the top of his head. "Where was I? Oh, yes—together, we were able to imprison the Titans deep in the heart of Tartarus to spend an eternity, but not before they had destroyed most of Midgard. It was during our search for the remaining survivors that I met the most beautiful woman I've ever had the privilege to lay eyes on."

Without a doubt, I automatically know he's referring to Melonie.

Melonie blushes at the mention, her eyes darting away momentarily before settling back on Phil with a mixture of fondness and embarrassment.

"Phil, you always exaggerate," She sighs, shaking her head, but smiling nonetheless as she bashfully tucks her hair behind her ear. "But yes, we did meet during those dark times. It was amidst ruins, yet somehow, amidst that havoc, like a lost seedling finding sunlight through cracks of devastation, our paths crossed and something beautiful emerged from it."

Phil chuckles softly, reaching across the small distance to squeeze Melonie's hand gently.

"As I mentioned earlier," Melonie trudges on, "I lost almost my entire family when the Titans attacked our home. I was bringing as much life as I could back to the trees, the grass, the land...but it felt like trying to breathe life into stones—like painting color onto a canvas that only wanted to remain gray. With every bit of life that sprang up, another piece seemed to wither away. It was during one of my most desperate moments that Phil found me. He was like a force of nature himself, a counterbalance to the destruction that surrounded us."

Phil nods, his eyes reflecting a somber remembrance. "Even surrounded by charred earth and wilted plants, there she was, trying to coax life back into the soil. Never had I seen someone so fiercely determined, so full of hope in such despairing circumstances. It was impossible not to be drawn to her spirit."

I listen contently, captivated by their memories as they weave through the room like tendrils of smoke.

"We spent days together after that, along with your parents, combing through the wreckage, helping whoever we could find. The land was scarred and so were the people, but we rebuilt together, brick by brick, soul by soul. It wasn't just the physical rebuilding that bonded us; it was the shared vision of a restored world, one where beauty and life could sprout anew from the ashes of old wounds. After a bit of time, your mother and father fell in love with one another, and he followed her back to Helheim. My brothers eventually went back to their places among the clouds of Olympus, and the depths of the Underworld, whereas Melonie and I decided to stay here in Midgard."

"Don't get us wrong though," Melonie chimes in. "We all remained good friends and visited one another quite often...at least we did until your mother fell pregnant with you and Loki came back out from beneath whatever rock he was hiding under and chaos pursued once more. Upon your birth Loki tried stealing you, but your mother and father devised a plan to hide you away from him. Loki had promised him you as his bride, ultimately a promise of breaking the curse that keeps him from leaving Tartarus. We thought that if we could hide you until your twenty first birthday, the prophecy would be broken, and you would be safe. Helena asked Persephone to suppress your power at birth to prevent Loki from sensing your presence once you reached the mortal realm. We knew the risk of binding your powers. It was a gamble, sacrificing the essence of who you were for safety, but your mother and father believed it was the only way to keep you out of Loki's grasp."

Trembling lips overcome Melonie's delicate features as she sucks in a shaky breath, her fingers tracing patterns on the wooden table, as if drawing strength from its ancient grains before speaking again, "The night that your mother and father were to flee to Midgard through one of the portals, Loki set his trap. Your mother's guard had betrayed her and gave Loki all the information he would need to put a stop to your parents' plan. He obtained the Basilard of the Damned—a dagger that traps the soul of the victim inside its blade, and he ambushed them just as they were about to step through the portal. A fierce battle ensued, between Loki and Baldur, but in the end, Loki was cunning and swift.

He plunged the dagger into your father's heart as your mother watched in horror. With his last breath, your father pushed her through the portal to Midgard with you in her arms."

The air in the room feels suffocating, like a snake tightening around my lungs, squeezing until breath becomes a luxury.

The weight of the truth is heavy—a brutal realization of my stolen past and the looming threat that grows with each tick of the clock. My eyes dart between Phil and Melonie, seeking an anchor in the storm that now rages inside me.

All the late-night moves, the homeschooling, the isolation and constant vigilance over who knew my whereabouts—it all makes sense now.

The puzzle pieces of my life are slowly clicking into place, yet each revelation feels like a fresh wound. And now, knowing that both my parents have been captured by this monster...my heart beats with a fury that I've never known before. Anger, fear, and a desperate longing to reclaim what was stolen from me burn within my chest.

"We need to save them," I whisper, the words barely escaping my lips as if saying them louder might make them less true.

Asmodeus rises from the table, his towering frame casting long shadows across the room, "We will." He promises. "But first, we need to make sure you're safe. If Loki finds you and makes you betroth that—that—Lucius." His fists curl tightly at his sides, the veins in his hands standing out stark and angry. "Then all will be lost. Not just for you, but for all realms. Marrying you will set him free from the very curse that enchains him to Tartarus. With the influence he already possesses while imprisoned, if unleashed, he would become unstoppable."

Before he can finish his thought, a bloodcurdling scream pierces the air, followed by a wet thud against the French glass doors leading to the back deck. We all jump up from our seats, Melonie letting out a guttural cry as we witness the scene before us.

Rhode stands on the other side of the glass, completely covered in blood with deep gashes marking her bronzed skin from her hairline down past her right eye. It looks as if she were attacked by a wild animal on her way here, and in her arms...she cradles the limp body of a small blonde girl.

Chapter Thirteen

Kali

Phil rushes to the door, fumbling with the locks in haste as Melonie follows closely behind, her hands covering her mouth in horror.

The moment Phil swings the doors open, Rhode stumbles into the room, her knees buckling under the weight of both her injuries and the girl she carries.

A chill courses through my body, leaving me feeling numb and frozen as if I had just jumped into the frigid Arctic waters.

What the fuck is going on?

"Oh my god...oh my god...oh my god." My brain repeats over and over again, my chest heaving with each frantic breath I consume.

I can't panic now—my sisters need me.

Phil catches Rhode lowering both her and the girl gently to the ground. Steadying myself against the wall, I force myself to push past the paralysis of shock gripping me.

Rhode's eyes meet mine, filled with a silent plea for help. Her voice is ragged, each word punctuated by pain.

"It's—it's Liv..." She mumbles through the pain. "She's badly hurt."

Phil's strong arms lift Rhode off the ground effortlessly, but Rhode pushes him away, "No." She shakes her head, point to Liv. "Her. Help her first."

Phil's resistance crumbles. He nods, his jaw set tight as he turns his attention to Liv, who lies pale and still on the floor.

Melonie is already by Liv's side, her usual calm demeanor shattered as she assesses my friend's injuries. I make my way over, my legs feeling like they might give out at any moment but somehow holding me up.

As I kneel beside Melonie, I see the extent of Olivia's injuries—deep gashes across her arms and a worrying amount of blood soaking through her clothes around her stomach. Her breathing is shallow, each inhale a struggle that causes her face to contort in pain.

"Stay with me, Liv," Melonie whispers urgently, pressing her hand against the worst of the bleeding in a futile attempt to stem the flow. "You're going to be okay, just hold on."

I reach out, my hands quivering, and take one of Liv's bloodied hands in mine. Her skin is cold and clammy, and for a moment, she squeezes my hand back, her eyes fluttering open to meet mine.

"Call 911!" I scream, though, no one reaches for their phones.

"No," Melonie shakes her head as Phil rips off his shirt and hands it to her for her to put more pressure on the wound. "There's not enough time for that. Her pulse it too weak, Kali. She's hanging on by a thread. I'm not sure she's going to make it. She needs—" Her head turns to Phil who seems to understand her needs without any spoken words.

"She needs Selene." He finishes for her, speed dialing the shrink's number, and pressing the phone to his ear.

Selene?

"What's Selene going to do? She's a shrink!" I sob, as I watch Phil make the desperate call.

Phil's eyes meet mine, a mixture of desperation and determination shining in them.

"I need you to trust me, Kali."

I nod, my face hot with tears.

After a few grueling moments, she picks up.

"Selene, I need you here, now." Phil's voice is frantic. "It's Olivia. She's badly hurt. I'm afraid she's—"

"Say no more." Selene's voice cuts through the static of the phone, sharp and clear. "Keep pressure on the wounds and make sure her heart still beats. I'm on my way." The line goes dead.

Minutes stretch like hours as we wait. Melonie continues to apply pressure, but the blood seems relentless. I watch Liv's face, her skin growing paler with each fleeting second.

Her eyes flutter closed again, and her breathing becomes even more labored, her mouth opening and closing as she struggles for air.

Suddenly, to my surprise, a shimmering mauve fog illuminates the room and once it clears, Selene appears there in its place. However, her hair is no longer grey, but rather a beautiful long silvery, white braid hangs down her back. Her once leather-like skin now looks smooth and youthful, and her eyes are the most mesmerizing shade of amethyst.

She presses her lips in a thin line as she glances around the space. "What the hell happened here?" She demands.

"That can wait." Phil whispers, noticing the anger flashing through my eyes as my head snaps in their direction.

"Very well." Selene says, kneeling down on the floor next to Melonie who is still knuckles deep in Liv's abdomen as she fights to keep her alive.

"I need space," She commands, not looking up.

Rhode looks just as ghastly, her face pouring a crimson river beneath our feet. She teeters on the brink of collapse, but her gaze remains locked on Liv.

Moving swiftly, Asmodeus crosses the room and steadies my sister, his arms wrapping around her as if she were a fragile piece of glass. Rhode, although weak, nods gratefully at him, her eyes not leaving Liv's still form.

I purse my lips together and mouth a silent thank you to him. His head bobs in understanding, and a small smile tugs at the corners of his mouth in response.

Selene's hands glow with a soft, violet light as she hovers them just above Liv, "I'm afraid her injuries are far too great for me to be able to mend. She's going to need a healer. Death is trying to claim her, but I think can buy her some time. There's this spell—I've only used it once before, and it's risky. It will keep her in a coma like state until we can find a healer who can restore her to full health. Your wounds will be an easy fix." She says to Rhode. "But with how deep the cuts on your face are, it may leave some scarring."

"I don't care about that. Just do whatever you have to do to make sure Liv doesn't die." Rhode replies, her voice harsher than she likely intended for it to be, so she adds a soft please at the end.

Selene acknowledges Rhodes' request with a solemn nod, her hands steadily glowing brighter as she begins chanting in an ancient tongue, the air around her shimmering with arcane energy. The light envelops Liv, spreading over her like a protective cocoon. As Selene weaves the spell, the glow from her hands intensifies, casting long shadows that dance like specters across the room.

I don't think my mouth has closed this entire time as I watch the scene unfold with a mixture of fear and awe.

While watching helplessly, not knowing what else to do, I feel a hand gently squeeze my shoulder. I turn to see Phil standing there, a grim but supportive expression painted across his face.

"She'll make it through," He whispers, trying to assure me, though the uncertainty in his eyes mirrors my own fears.

I nod, trying to muster a smile for Phil's sake, but it feels hollow on my lips.

The violet light begins to fade and the slight rise and fall of my best friend's torso that has assured me that she's still alive—still breathing—ceases to exist.

Selene's face tightens, her eyes narrowing as she presses her palms downward, urging the mystical energies to obey. The silence in the room grows heavy, suffocating almost, as if the very air waits for Liv's next breath.

A knot the size of a boulder forms in my stomach.

Selene steps back, wiping sweat from her brow, her expression unreadable, "It is done." She finally whispers.

"Is—is she dead?" I ask?

"No." Selene says assuring me. "The spell has taken hold, but it is delicate. She is suspended between life and death, in a deep rest that will preserve her until we can find the right healer. Do not fear; her spirit remains strong."

I exhale, reassurance washing over me, though the fear of losing Liv lingers like a shadow in my mind.

Selene makes her way over to Rhode, who also dons a look of relief now.

"You're lucky you didn't lose that eye." Selene tells her.

"Not lucky enough." Rhode grinds out, her voice adorned with a mix of pain and frustration. "If I had been quicker, maybe we wouldn't be in this mess."

Melonie grasps Rhode's hand, "Whatever happened, it wasn't your fault."

Rhodes mouth presses into a thin line as she violently shakes her head side to side, "I should have seen it coming."

Selene places her hands on Rhode's face, the purple mist swirling around her fingertips before seeping into the wounds on her face, her skin faintly glowing as the healing energies do their work.

Rhode's features relax slightly under Selene's touch, the lines of pain softening as the magic commences to mend the deep cuts. The wounds slowly heal, stitching her skin together until the gashes are nothing more than raised white lines.

"Thank you." Rhode murmurs, her voice steadier than before.

Rhode walks over to where Liv is lying on the cold tile and kneels down next to her. She takes Liv's hand in her own, looking at her with sorrowful eyes. "I'm so sorry Liv. I promise I will find a way to fix this, if it's the last thing I do." She places a gentle kiss on the back of Liv's hand before carefully laying it across her chest.

"She deserves to be comfortable."

"Of course." Phil replies, scooping Liv up into his arms. "I'll put her in the guest room."

He strides across the room; his steps echoing softly against the floor and then disappears into the hallway.

Upon his return he can no longer hide the rage in his eyes as he clenches his fists, the muscles in his jaw working. "What happened?" He growls, his question directed at my sister.

Rhode shakes her head, exhaustion etched into every line of her face. "The club is crawling with succubus and incubus demons. It's their fucking feeding ground." She replies, rubbing her temples with her hands. "When we went out for some fresh air, Liv and I were ambushed and taken captive. They held us in the lower level of the club, a section reserved only for members. It was like a torture chamber; men and women were chained up, their souls continuously drained until they were nothing but lifeless husks. It's as if they have no life left in them at all. That's where Eirene found us and helped us escape. But as we made it outside, we were attacked once again. Eirene—Eirene sacrificed herself so I could get Liv out of there and get help." She sobs, her face twisting with anger. "I swear this bitch is going to pay for what she has done! All this time she's been working for him—parading around here like some innocent mortal fool! At this point, I'm not sure how she fits into all of this, but her deceit will now also bring her, her death" My sister snarls, spittle spraying out of her mouth along with her vengeful words.

"Who?" Phil demands, though his features grow dark, like he already knows the answer to his own question.

Rhode's eyes blaze with a fury that could set the very air aflame as she confirms our suspicions with the next word that drips like a poison off her tongue, "Dafina."

Chapter Fourteen

Kali

Hold the front door.

Dafina is involved in this?

After the barrage of events tonight, I think I might have whiplash from all the things being thrown my way.

"This means they already know about Kali." Asmodeus says. "We underestimated him again, damn it!" His fist slams against the wall, leaving a dent in the plaster.

I can't even begin to wrap my head around everything.

It's almost unfathomable that the woman I had entrusted with all my vulnerabilities, who I had confided in and shared my deepest fears and aspirations with, could have been plotting against us this whole time.

What could she possibly gain from harming my sisters and nearly taking the life of my friend?

She's played the part of loving us so well.

But the reality it seems is that she's nothing more than a puppet on a string, and this guy Lucius is her puppet master.

Standing there, arms crossed, I watch Asmodeus pace back and forth like a caged animal.

"We have to move quick. I can take Kali back to the Underworld and—"

"I will go nowhere until I know my sister is safe!" I shout.

Asmodeus halts, his eyes narrowing as he turns to face me. "You don't realize everything at stake here, do you? This isn't some childish rendezvous we're involved in. This is fucking war! And every second you stay in Midgard puts us all in more danger."

I grit my teeth, feeling the burden of his words but also unwilling to leave my sister vulnerable and alone. "Then we fight," I say firmly, meeting his fiery gaze without flinching. "We fight, and we get my sister back. I will not leave until she is safe—I can't."

Asmodeus exhales sharply, his jaw tightening.

He regards me for a long moment, his gaze locking with Phil's before he finally concedes, "Fine." He growls. "But we do this my way, and you are to be with one of us at all times."

I start to argue that I am perfectly capable of taking care of myself but Phil cuts me off.

"I'm sorry, Kali, but I have to agree with Asmodeus on this one."

The feeling of being coddled ignites a simmering anger within me, but I swallow it down. Now is not the time to argue over pride or independence—it's about survival and protecting what I cherish most.

"We need to plan, and we need to plan now," Phil says, his voice all business as he pulls his phone from his pocket. "I'll check the club's property records and see if I can pull up the buildings blueprints."

I watch as Phil starts tapping away on his phone, his brow furrowed in concentration.

Asmodeus starts pacing the floor once again, "The succubae are vile, selfish creatures. They won't hesitate to use any means necessary to get what they want. We need to be careful, more importantly, we need to be clever. They'll try to seduce you—feed on your soul and twist your desires to their advantage. We can't afford to have any weak links."

Dick.

I know that was a jab at me. Yeah...well, fuck you too buddy.

Anxiety rears its ugly head, taking control of my own as I wrestle internally with my rising panic, and the sting from Asmodeus's barbed words.

But what if I am a weak link, and I just wind up being a liability that gets us all killed?

My brain feels like it's going to explode. This day has ripped the sanity from my mind, and extinguished the light from my soul, leaving behind only pure hatred for the monsters that stole everything from me—my childhood, my parents...myself.

And now I want revenge. I crave it—taste it even.

The room seems to close in around me, the walls pressing in with a suffocating embrace. I clench my fists, my nails digging into my palms, trying to anchor myself to something tangible amidst the turmoil swirling inside me. Asmodeus stops pacing and turns to look at me, his eyes narrowing as if he can read my mind and he knows exactly what I'm thinking.

Phil suddenly looks up from his phone, his expression serious. "I've got the blueprints," He announces, breaking the tense atmosphere.

But I'm not listening.

The ground feels like it's shaking beneath me, but I can't tell if it's real or just my body trembling. Nothing seems right, and I'm struggling to keep my limbs from turning into gelatin. Sweat forms on my forehead, my pale skin slick with perspiration as my body fights to regulate its temperature. Suddenly, darkness closes in around me, and a strange electric sensation pulses through every inch of my being.

Panic sets in as I frantically claw at my throat. The air around me feels empty, and my lungs are starting to ache from the lack of oxygen. This is by far the most intense panic attack I've ever had.

"I think it has begun." I hear Melonie whisper.

My eyes dart to the clock.

It's midnight.

All eyes are fixated on me, jaws dropped and gazes wide. Then suddenly, Asmodeus lifts me up into his arms, his strong and defined chest providing a sense of stability and grounding.

"Get her outside," Selene demands. "She needs space. Things could get...messy."

Asmodeus carries me with ease, navigating through the narrow hallway, and living room area, before bursting out of the front door, sprinting down the stone path leading to the beach shore.

A radiant moon looms above us, beckoning me with its tranquil glow to escape this world and bask in its ethereal splendor.

The cool night air hits me like a shockwave as soon as we reach the open beach, and for a moment, it helps. My chest loosens slightly, allowing me to draw a shallow breath. Asmodeus sets me down gently on the soft sand, and I can feel the fine grains slipping through my fingers as I try to ground myself further, pushing my hands deep into the cool, damp earth.

The scent of the ocean fills my nostrils, a mixture of salt and freedom that usually soothes me, but tonight it's barely enough to make a dent in my panic.

The energy swirling within me is cold and dark. It feels like it's clawing its way through my veins, seeking an escape but finding none.

Like an icy wind twisting around my spine, it sends shivers cascading down my body. My teeth chatter uncontrollably, and my breath comes in ragged gasps.

Asmodeus kneels beside me, his eyes piercing through the darkness, reflecting the moonlight like mirrors, "Breath with me. In and out. In and out."

I try to mimic his breathing, focusing on the rise and fall of his chest, but the effort feels monumental. Each breath is a battle, and the darkness within me thrashes wildly, as if angered by my attempts to control it.

Selene arrives next to us, I can hear her voice, "You must let it flow through you, not fight it," She says, her tone gentle yet urgent. "This is no ordinary panic attack, Kali, it's the awakening of your power. You must embrace it, or it will consume you."

I glance up at her, my eyes wide with fear and confusion. How could this terrifying force be anything beneficial? Yet, in the depths of my chaotic thoughts, I sense a glimmer of truth in her words.

"The power was always there," She continues, "It's part of who you are, part of your heritage."

Her words sink in, stirring something primal within me. The darkness, instead of recoiling, begins to pulse rhythmically, almost in time with the lapping waves. With each breath, I feel slightly less like a vessel being battered by an internal storm and more like a conductor of immense, raw energy—I am the storm—pure mayhem and creation intertwined, a force of nature as wild and untamed as the sea before me.

And fuck...it feels so good.

I visualize the darkness within not as my enemy, but as a part of my very essence that I need to understand and harmonize with. My heart starts to beat in sync with the pulsating energy, and I let go of the fear that has been suffocating me.

The realization hits me with the force of a tidal wave, and slowly, I start to harness the energy rather than trying to subdue it. I open myself up to it, allowing it to flow through me like a torrential river breaking through a dam.

I feel hot.

Sickly hot.

Sweat beads on my forehead, trickling down in streams. I can feel every pore on my skin flare open, a network of doors swinging wide to the power thrumming through me.

"She's burning up. Quickly, get her into the water! She needs to cool down before she blows this place apart!" Melonie calls out from somewhere behind us.

What?

Why would she even say that?

I can't focus, everything is a hazy blur.

Hands grab me, firm yet gentle, and in a moment, I'm being dragged toward the sea. The cold touch of the ocean waves shocks my system, sending a ripple of conflicting sensations through my body—chilling cold fighting against the scorching heat within.

The ocean's refreshing chill quickly turns into a scalding heat, surrounding us with bubbling and boiling water. The once small, peaceful marine life now float lifelessly on the surface.

Why is this happening?

Amid my own torment, I catch a glimpse of Asmodeus's contorted features as he gazes down at me, a forced smile etched onto his lips.

"Wha—what is…" I can't finish, the words stumble and die on my lips.

"Breath, little flame. I've got you." He whispers against my neck as he tucks a loose strand of my hair back behind my ear.

Gently, his fingers caress my cheek, his intense gaze seeming to see straight into my soul. His presence is both terrifying and exhilarating, a paradox that I struggle to understand as my body fights against the overwhelming sensations.

He is truly extraordinary, something beyond this world.

Asmodeus lifts me higher, cradling my body against his as we drift deeper into the ocean's embrace. The water around us steams with an intensity that should be unbearable, yet strangely, I find solace in the inferno that we create together.

My body is burning up, as if my skin is melting and my blood is boiling inside of me. The heat seems to radiate from within, torturing every inch of my being, and like a bird that's never seen flight trying its escape its prison, my heart beats frantically behind my ribcage.

Suddenly, my head jerks back, my body convulsing so hard my teeth rattle inside my head.

"It's no use. We're too late." Phil's defeated voice echos against the shadows of night.

"The hell we are!" Asmodeus roars in return. "What happened to you, uncle? You were once a mighty God. Now—now you are a disgrace. The world of mortals has made you feeble and spineless. But I won't succumb to the same fate. I know my purpose here, and I will not falter in fulfilling it."

His grip on me tightens slightly as he carries me to shore, kneeing down beside me, and placing one of his palms against my chest, "Let it out." He demands. "Your power has laid dormant for years, straining to get out. If you don't let go of some of that power, you'll kill us all. Now, let some of it out. Imagine it flowing out of you and into me."

I try to speak—to nod—to do anything at all, but the pain is too insufferable.

I feel like I am going to split apart. A wave of new suffering erupts from within my chest, causing a startled cry to lodge in my throat.

I experience a sensation of weightlessness, as if I am floating on a soft cloud. But the pain that accompanies it is unrelenting and constant. Suddenly, there is a collective gasp from those around me as bright, white flames shoot out of my body and into Asmodeus. His once animate body becomes tense and lifeless, his eyes rolling back into his head.

Oh fuck.

I—I think I'm killing him!

As I attempt to regain control of the power surging within me, the flames grow stronger and higher, engulfing my skin in a mesmerizing display of swirling white and vibrant hues. The intensity only increases as I try to contain it, creating a dazzling kaleidoscope of colors along its base.

My eyes widen in terror as Asmodeus's face is engulfed in flames, leaving nothing but scorched bone behind.

The raw, brutality of all my power, I fear, will soon be the death of us both.

Finally regaining control over my limbs, I shove him aside and he collapses to the ground. With a scissor kick, I thrust my right leg forward to gain enough momentum to stand up again. Tucking my knee beneath me, I use all my strength to push myself back onto my feet.

Enveloped in white flames, I am lifted into the air, weightless and free. I surrender myself to the flames, allowing them to carry me higher and higher until I am suspended above the beach, resembling a fiery angel ready to unleash retribution on those who have crossed her—ready for the sweet taste of revenge.

I tilt my head up, spreading my arms wide as I release a primal scream into the dark expanse above me. All the hurt, deception, and pain that has plagued me in life washes away with each bellowing cry. In its place, a fiery rage takes over, fueling my actions.

The sky responds to my cries with a low rumble, as if the heavens themselves are commiserating with my anguish. Thunder claps sharply in the distance, and the winds whip up around me, fueling the fiery aura that encircles my being.

As the intense flames gradually subside and fade away, I collapse onto the ground.

The moment my feet touch the earth once more, I sprint towards the burnt figure lying motionless on the beach.

Asmodeus's body lies twisted and grotesque, reduced to a charred husk. I reach out a trembling hand, hesitant to touch him, fearing I would only cause him more pain. The sand beneath my feet is warm, almost hot, remnants of the inferno that raged moments before as I drop to my knees beside him.

"Phil, Melonie! Help me, please!" I cry out over the crashing waves.

They quickly come to my aid, and together we carefully roll him onto his back.

He's still breathing.

Despite the grim circumstances, a faint wave of relief washes over me.

"I'm so sorry" I hiccup, cupping his charred face in my hands. "I—I didn't mean to hurt you. I didn't mean to—"

Out of seemingly thin air, Selene pops up next to me, shaking her head, and oddly enough...laughing.

"Oh, love. It takes way more than that to kill one of divine blood." She says, waving a dismissive hand, and jabs her toe in Asmodeus's ribs.

"Come now. Stop being such a drama queen." She scolds him, rolling her eyes in exasperation. "Can't you see you're about to give this poor girl a heart attack? She's been through enough, and here you are acting like a child. It's quite embarrassing and should I also mention that you're wasting valuable time? We still need to find Eirene."

"What?" I question, my bloodshot eyes pinching together.

Asmodeus's body trembles against mine.

The bastard is laughing!

Asmodeus's laughter, hoarse and raspy, cuts through the salty air, a sound so incongruous with his scorched appearance that for a moment, it steals my breath away.

He props himself up with his elbows, flashing a lopsided smile on his incredibly attractive face. I resist the urge to smack it away as he starts dusting off the sand and ash covering his burnt skin. To my amazement, the debris begins to peel off, exposing unmarred flesh underneath.

"Guilty as charged." He says, feigning innocence.

Ugh, he makes me so damn mad!

But at least I didn't actually kill him. As much as I hate to admit it, he's starting to grow on me, despite his asshole-ish tendencies.

"How dare you—you jerk!" My fists pound against his chest in a furious rage as I hurl every profanity and insult, I can think of at him.

I've lost count of how many times I've hit him, five or twenty, it doesn't matter.

Serves him right.

After my relentless attack, I take a step back and meet his intense gaze. His smoldering brown eyes lock onto mine, then hungrily scan down to my mouth as he licks his lips with hooded eyes.

He raises his eyebrow, a sly smirk on his lips, "Have you forgotten my warning so soon, little flame?" He asks.

I fold my arms across my chest and give him a disdainful look, "Did you conveniently forget about mine?" I retaliate, barely containing the smile that quivers upon my lips. "Don't test me, dude. I'll kick your ass"

He chuckles, the sound rich and warm, completely at odds with the dangerous glint in his eyes. "I'd absolutely love to see you try."

The tension between us crackles like a live wire, and for a moment, I can't decide if I want to strangle him or...No, definitely strangle him.

Rolling my eyes, I turn away.

As I take a few steps away from Asmodeus, my heart pounding out an erratic rhythm, the coolness of the evening air finally manages to soothe the heat in my cheeks. I inhale deeply, trying to regain some semblance of control over my flaring emotions and scattered thoughts.

Time to focus.

My sister needs our help.

CHAPTER FIFTEEN

Kali

The blueprints Phil found of the club's building are printed and laid out across the dining table as we stand huddled around it.

His finger traces lines and circles various rooms, his brow furrowed in concentration. "Look at this spot here," He points to what looks like a tunnel behind the wall of the main bar area. "I'm willing to bet this is their escape route for disposing of their victims once they no longer have any life essence for them to feed on."

"Are you thinking that could be our entry point?" Asmodeus asks.

"Possibly," Phil says. "But if I'm right, they'll expect us to come in that way. We'd be better off just going through the front door."

"You've got a point." Asmodeus rubs his jaw. "If we're heading into a trap, we might as well do it on our own terms."

Phil nods in agreement. "We'll need to make sure we're ready for anything. Once we walk through those doors, there's no telling what can happen." He turns to Rhode, "Can you show me where they were holding you and Olivia?"

She leans forward, her eyes scanning the detailed blueprint until she finds the area she recognizes. "Here," She says, pointing to the bottom left corner of the club's lower level. "This is where they kept us."

"Looks like there's only one way in. One way out," Phil mutters, tracing the path with his fingertip. "It's a bottleneck; could work to our advantage if we need to control their numbers."

"And what about surveillance? Any chance they've got eyes on that area?" Asmodeus inquires, his gaze flicking to Rhode.

My sister nods, "When I was there, I noticed several cameras in all the main areas and one right above the entry to the members only section. Once you get down to where they were holding us however, there are none."

"This isn't going to be easy." Phil murmurs.

"You're gods. How hard can it be?" I ask.

Phil chuckles dryly, the sound tinged with a grim shade of humor. "Even gods have their limits. We can still be injured, and we can still die. I can burn but not drown, where Asmodeus here as you could tell from earlier, can burn, but if he were to take my place in the ocean, he would surely drown. Life must always maintain balance, Kali. Without roots, a tree cannot stand, nor can it drink from the land—a god without weaknesses is no god at all, but a force unchecked, and that in itself is chaos."

"And remember," Asmodeus turns to me, "These creatures we're dealing with, they feed on life essence. While they might not be gods or have powers like our own, they literally sustain themselves by draining the vitality of others, making them particularly dangerous adversaries. Their strength increases as they feed, so the longer we're in combat, the stronger they'll become. If they manage to get ahold of any of us, it could be catastrophic for all of Midgard."

"Makes sense." I say, though the reality of their vulnerabilities makes the stakes all the more real and terrifying.

After much planning, the final plan decided upon is, there is no real plan.

No matter how we try to go about things, the only way we're going to get Eirene back is if we take them on headfirst. They're already expecting us, and I'm sure they have their own plot devised.

Rhode excused herself a little while back, and she and Selene went upstairs to tend to Liv. Once Phil and Asmodeus finish arguing about what the best line of defense would be, Melonie and I go to check on them before we head out.

With the assistance of Selene's magic, Liv is now free of any traces of blood and dirt. Her wounds have been carefully stitched up, and she's dressed in a clean set of clothes. However, it looks as though death has already claimed her. Her skin is nearly translucent, drained of all color from the excessive blood loss.

Sighing deeply, Rhode places her forehead against the large wooden bedpost staring down at Liv. She seems so lost, defeated in a war that has only just begun.

The future is still uncertain, and we have yet to uncover the truth about Dafina's involvement.

I can't help but to wonder if she has betrayed us on her own free will, or if someone is forcing her deception.

"Do you want to talk about what happened?" I ask my sister.

She trails her finger along the grooves of the post, a vacuous look upon her face as her fingers dip and slide from each design in the wood.

Rhode slowly lifts her head, her eyes glazed with a mixture of grief and exhaustion. "There's nothing much to discuss," She murmurs, her voice barely above a whisper. "We were outmaneuvered, outmatched. I underestimated them, and now Liv is paying the price."

I put a hand on her shoulder, feeling the tension coiled like steel beneath her skin, "We'll make this right, Rhode. We'll get Eirene back and make them pay for what they've done. We're going to get through this, okay? We have to believe that."

Rhode nods slightly, but her gaze remains distant as she whispers. "I just hope we're not too late." She whispers.

"We're not." Melonie assures her. "Eirene is stubborn and strong. She won't give up easily, and neither will we."

Melonie's words seem to inject a faint spark of hope into Rhode, who manages a weak smile. "You're right." She agrees, though her voice still falters with uncertainty.

My older sister has never been one for physical affection, but she leans into me, and I wrap my arm around her, sharing some of her weight.

I can feel the heavy burden of guilt weighing on her and I wish nothing more than to be able to lift it from her shoulders. But some burdens must be carried alone, and the only assistance one can offer is to walk beside the bearer, so they know they not are not journeying through the darkness by themselves.

"I'm ok." She says through a sniffle.

An obvious lie, but I understand her need to put on a brave face.

"This isn't your fault, sis." I whisper in her hair, hoping to reinforce her with my words. "We were all deceived. It's Dafina who should bear the blame, not you."

"We were all deceived. It's Dafina who should bear the blame, not you."

Rhode tightens her grip on me for a moment, as if the pressure could squeeze out the pain nestled deep within her. "But I should have seen it," She counters with a tremor in her voice. "I should have known better. I was supposed to protect her, and I—I just left her."

She leans back to meet my gaze, her eyes glistening with tears and her hands shaking as she rubs at them, "Eirene sacrificed herself for me and Liv to escape. If I had been more vigilant, she might not have had to make that choice." Her voice breaks, a thin wisp of despair threading through her words.

"You can't think like that." Melonie attests. "You did everything you could under the circumstances. No one blames you, but right now, what Eirene needs from us isn't guilt or regret. She needs us to be strong, to keep fighting, to find her and bring her back home."

Rhode wipes her eyes, takes a deep breath, and nods slowly.

"You're right." She says, "We need to focus on what we can do now, not what could have been done differently." Her resolve hardens, a visible shift in her demeanor that brings back the leader in her I know and admire.

She breaks away from my hug and sits down on the queen-sized bed next to Liv, her expression unreadable and cold.

I walk over next to her and take one of Liv's hands in my own, "They will pay for what they've done," I vow. "Even if I have to burn the entire world down with them."

Selene appears at the door, her silver hair glowing eerily in the light of the pale moon peeping in through the windows. "I'm sorry to interrupt, but ummm...time is of the essence." She reminds us, pointing to her wrist as if she's wearing a watch, which she's in fact not.

"Right. Let's get going then." Rhode replies, standing up from the bed.

"Rhode, sweetheart, "Melonie says calmly, reaching out to touch her arm. "I think—I think you should stay here with Selene. Just in case Lucius has sent more of his cronies. I want you two to make sure Liv and the property stay safe."

Rhode hesitates, her eyes darting from Melonie to Liv and then back again, "Please, be careful. I can't lose you guys too." She chokes out. "Just...please bring her back."

Her face looks worn and aged from the night's stressful events.

"We'll be back before you know it." I smile, pretending that my own anxiety isn't trying to rip the breath right from my lungs.

Selene leads the way, exiting through the bedroom door and descending the staircase with Rhode, Melonie, and I trailing close behind.

We say our farewells and then I quickly retrieve my brass knuckles from a drawer in the cupboard before we leave. I doubt they would do much damage against a demon, if any at all, but it gives me some sense of security having them at hand should I need to use them.

Outside, the world is cloaked in a deep, velvety darkness. The moon, nearly full, casts ghostly shadows across the land as we crunch across the gravel driveway towards my jeep.

It looks like a toy next to the massiveness of Phil. The sound it makes as he slides into the driver's seat is almost comical, as it creaks and groans under his weight, sinking a few inches in the process.

Good thing I have decent shocks.

Melonie hops into the front seat, and I squeeze myself into the back with Asmodeus, our shoulders crammed together in the small space.

As Phil turns the ignition, the jeep sputters to life, and we're off, tires crunching loudly against the loose gravel as we make our way down the narrow tree-lined road.

On all the gods, I hope this fucking works.

Chapter Sixteen

Kali

Upon our arrival at the club, it is unrecognizable from earlier in the night. It resembles a scene straight out of Sleeping Beauty, but with a haunting twist.

Deadly vines the size of tree trunks twist and turn around the area in a dome-like fashion. The thorns protruding from them are razor-sharp and could easily tear us to pieces if we get too close.

It's difficult to imagine Eirene is responsible for creating all of this, but I am beginning to understand why she says we all should fear her.

"How has the town not noticed any of this?" I whisper, astonished by the enormous transformation that had overtaken what was once a bustling hotspot.

"The townspeople won't notice," Phil explains as we exit the vehicle. "Dark magic has been cast over this place, making them oblivious to what truly stands before them. All they see is the same club they've seen every other day. It's an illusion that shields their mortal minds from reality."

We inch closer to what used to be the entrance, cautiously navigating around the gnarled vines. Every step we take seems to echo through the silent night, magnified by the eerie stillness that hangs heavy in the air.

The once-smooth pavement is now a jumbled mess, destroyed by the massive vines that burst through the earth's surface. Their remnants are scattered throughout the parking lot and stretch all the way to the back of the building.

"So," I say, looking around at my fellow comrades. "Any ideas on how to get through all of this?" I gesture, pointing my thumb at the thorny prison.

"I think I have a few tricks up my sleeve," Melonie says, giving me a playful wink.

She pulls her hair back into a ponytail and plants her feet firmly on the ground. Her brow furrows in concentration as she extends her hands in front of her, almost like she's feeling for something. Her fingers twitch and the vines around us start to tremble, slowly unraveling. With a push and pull motion, she guides them until they create an opening large enough for us to pass through without getting sliced in half.

Tilting her head to the side, she grins at Phil, "It's been a long time since we've hunted together, hasn't it my darling?"

"Indeed, it has." He agrees.

"Are you ready to go take down some demon scum like old times, and get our baby back?"

"I was born ready, my love." He responds with a wicked grin spreading across his face.

He playfully slaps Asmodeus on the back as he walks past him, "Don't fall behind now, nephew. Can't have a washed-up God showing you up in front of everyone, can we?"

A mischievous glint shines in Asmodeus's eyes as he stands taller, ready to accept the challenge. "Bring it on, old man."

My veins pulse with adrenaline, and I can feel the fear of what's to come creeping through my body. My knees tremble uncontrollably as I trail behind them, knowing that I am both the last in line and the weakest link.

It's as if Phil can read my thoughts; he abruptly holds his arm out, halting Asmodeus in his tracks. "Keep an eye on Kali for me," He instructs him.

Asmodeus's eyes roll back, and he scoffs. "She's not my concern. In fact, she shouldn't even be here. She's weak and clueless about her powers because you foolishly decided to keep her in the dark about her true identity."

"I did what was best for her and kept her safe." Phil affirms, his body tense with impatience.

Asmodeus huffs, his gaze shifting to me, heavy with a mixture of annoyance and resignation. "Fine. But if she dies, it's on your head." He steps closer, his voice lowering to a rough whisper. "And you better pray she doesn't, because losing her might be the end of us all."

Phil's jaw tightens, his eyes flaring with a protective anger. "She won't," He says decisively, turning back to face the path ahead. "Let's move."

With that, Asmodeus turns sharply on his feet and takes his place at the rear, eyeing me like a hawk watches a particularly vulnerable mouse.

"Hey, I'm standing right here," I interject, feeling frustrated with their condescending tones. "You don't have to talk about me like I'm a helpless child. I can handle things on my own, thank you very much." I snap at them, growing more irritated by the second.

Reaching into the pocket of my dress, I pull out my brass knuckles, sliding them onto my hands. I brought my favorite ones, embellished with large spikes right on the knuckles.

These bad boys can do some damage.

"Try not to get yourself killed and stay out of my way." Asmodeus growls from behind me.

Ignoring his curt remark, I tighten the brass knuckles around my fingers, feeling the cool metal embolden me, "Maybe I don't know everything about my powers, but that doesn't make me useless."

Asmodeus snorts but doesn't reply, his attention already drifting back to the murky shadows that surround us like a thick blanket.

"What the hell did I ever do to you to deserve your hatred?" I clench my fists, the spikes of the brass knuckles catching a faint glint from the weak moonlight that seeps through the dense canopy overhead.

I inhale deeply, trying to steady my nerves as I forge ahead, determined not to show Asmodeus how much his words sting.

"Wha—listen woman...now is not the time for stupid questions." He groans. "We have bigger problems to worry about other than your bruised ego."

"You think I don't understand that? We're here to save my sister, for crying out loud!" I snap back, whipping my head around to face him, looking like a startled owl in the woods.

He quickly averts his eyes to the ground and pauses for a brief moment before resuming his shuffle forward.

"Look, I don't *hate* you, just to be clear, but..." He draws an exasperated breath, "I also shouldn't have to be here babysitting you, when I could be searching for my mother and sister."

His words hang in the air, thick and heavy, and for a moment I'm caught off guard by the raw edge of pain in his voice. It reminds me that beneath the gruff exterior, Asmodeus is fighting his own battles, carrying his own weights that are just as burdensome as mine.

"They disappeared before I arrived. I'm almost positive Lucius or one of his men has taken them prisoner, but I can't be sure, as my family has constructed numerous enemies over the centuries." My heart drops at this information, and we share a moment of mutual understanding.

"I'm sorr—." I try to say.

"You didn't know." He responds, cutting me off mid-sentence. "Let's just focus on getting through the night and finding your sister. We can worry about my family later."

His words, though blunt, bring a shared sense of purpose back into our step, and I come to the realization that he is just as damaged as I am.

Losing your family is a wound that never fully heals; it festers beneath the surface and occasionally breaks open with the slightest provocation. And unfortunately, we both know the sting of that pain all too well, the gnawing emptiness that comes with not knowing the fate of loved ones.

Family is everything to me.

If there is one thing I have learned growing up as a simple mortal it's that, we are much like the wolves that reside in our forest.

We thrive in a pack.

While there are a few loners and outcasts, having a strong bond with someone can bring purpose to life, even for those who have felt hopeless and lost, like I once did.

I have vivid memories of moments when I wanted to give up on everything, but my sisters were always there to reach out and pull me back into the light, despite the darkness that still lives within me to this day.

Rent free, of course.

Speaking quietly, I turn to Asmodeus and whisper, "I can help you find them. After we get Eirene and get her back home safely, I'll go with you, and we can find your mother and sister together. It's the least I can do."

"We will do no such thing." He replies sharply.

I am taken aback by his sudden change in tone. "Why is that exactly?" I ask, trying to understand his refusal to take advantage of the opportunity presented.

"First and foremost, my father would be furious if anything happened to you. It's my responsibility to keep you safe and return you to the Underworld unscathed. Our troops will have to handle the search for my mother and sister." His voice rumbles low, his teeth clenched together as he speaks.

Without explicitly stating it, the weight of my existence and his father's demands weigh heavily on the growing silence between us. I push my way through the prickly barrier, feeling my determination falter with each passing moment of quiet.

No, I can't fall apart right now. I'll have plenty of time to process everything once this is over.

I straighten my shoulders, meeting Asmodeus's gaze with a newfound resolve. "I understand your duty," I say quietly, "But you can't let it chain you."

His eyes flicker with a tumultuous storm of emotions, the depths of which I can barely begin to comprehend. There's a long pause, a silence that stretches out between us like a chasm threatening to swallow any remaining understanding.

Finally, he exhales slowly, the sound almost painful. "Coming from the girl who wore chains most of her life. Ironic, isn't it?" He mocks. "Perhaps you should keep your mouth shut and focus on your own burdens before you try to lift mine."

"I may have worn chains, Asmodeus, but at least mine weren't of my own doing unlike your own." My words cut through the tension like a sword, and I see them strike home.

His face tightens, the angular jaw set in defiance, yet the vulnerability in his eyes betrays his impassive facade.

"You think I choose these chains?" He asks, his voice less harsh, more weary than angry now. "You think I revel in the duties that bind me to an endless cycle of obligations and expectations?"

He laughs.

"Wow. This realm really does produce quite dense individuals, doesn't it?"

This motherfucker right here.

I bristle at his words but hold my ground, "You know what? Fuck you." I flip him the bird and turn on my heel, storming away.

As I stomp away, the ground beneath my boots sends up small clouds of dust, each step punctuating my frustration and anger. I don't care how powerful he is, or what burdens he carries—he's a fucking jackass.

And furthermore, if he thinks for one damn second that I'll be leaving my family behind to go with *him* to the Underworld, my guy is sadly mistaken.

Because as far as I'm concerned right now, he can choke on a fucking Twinkie.

Chapter Seventeen

Kali

As we enter the club, we are greeted by an unusual silence that seems to fill the entire space, making it feel oddly empty. It's a stark contrast to the usual lively atmosphere, there is no music or pulsing lights, just a strange stillness.

The main lights have been switched off, leaving only a faint illumination from the few scattered bar lights. Every step we take echoes through the deserted dance floor, creating a heavy and eerie feeling in the quiet emptiness of the room.

The slick, polished hardwood floor is marred by dark red stains, a clear sign of a struggle. Lifeless figures are strewn about the room, some with missing limbs.

I hope we're not too late.

A nauseating feeling churns in my stomach at the thought, causing the tightness in my throat to constrict even more.

"Oh, my goodness!" Melonie's hand flies to her mouth and I can tell she's thinking the same thing.

Phil pauses for a moment and reaches out to grasp Melonie's hand. "Our daughter is a fighter, my love. She has toughness like no other, not to mention she's stubborn...just like her mother."

His attempt at humor falls flat in the grim shadow of the room, but it brings a small, strained smile to Melonie's lips nonetheless. "I guess I can't argue with that." She replies, as he places a kiss on her forehead.

Carefully, we navigate deeper into the club, stepping gingerly around the bodies and debris.

The air is thick with a metallic scent that mixes with the stale odors of spilled alcohol and sweat. As we move forward, the scene becomes more gruesome and the bodies more numerous.

Shattered glass crunches beneath our shoes, adding an unsettling soundtrack to our bleak exploration. Our eyes scan desperately for any sign of life or movement, each corner we turn offering only more despair.

The office door Rhode told us about earlier, is right where she said it would be—directly past the bar, to the right, and in the very back of the building—the entrance to the members only section, or rather, their feeding dungeon of horrors.

My bones feel tight with anxiety, and a shiver runs down my back, causing me to regret not changing out of the dress I wore earlier. I take a deep breath, trying to calm the overwhelming feeling of dread in my gut.

Goosebumps appear all over my skin, starting on my arms and creeping down to my legs.

Taking notice, Asmodeus peels off his suit jacket draping it across my shoulders. "You should dress more appropriately for battle in the future, little flame."

My cheeks flush hot, my heart beating erratically along with my stuttering words. "Th-thank you," I manage to stammer out.

Our gazes briefly meet, and there's a strange sensation that I can't quite put into words—a pull, so to speak, that I've only ever felt in his presence.

Eh…maybe it's just gas.

The door is locked when Melonie tries to turn it.

Phil steps forward, "Watch yourselves. This isn't going to be pretty." Against Phil's brute force and giant boot, the door is no match, snapping like a number two pencil.

Unfortunately for us, we also probably alerted every malicious sex demon in the vicinity as well.

But they knew we were coming anyway.

As we make our way down to the basement, we encounter another locked door. We'll need a key card to get through, but before I can even relay the message, a blue ball of fire zips past my head and obliterates the door in front of us.

"What in the fuck nuts was that?" I yelp.

Asmo—the name I just decided I will start calling him—waggles his brows as he pushes past me, and through the door he just incinerated.

Okay.

That was kind of cool—I'll give him that.

We step over the charred remnants of what used to be a door, entering a dark staircase that reeks of decay and sulfur.

It's a pit of pure despair.

The air grows colder as we descend, and the faint sound of moaning, and chains clinking echoes up the stairwell, blending with my own shaky breaths. The darkness is thick, palpable almost, sticking to my skin like a second layer, and each step I take feels heavier than the last.

When we reach the bottom and I take in my surroundings, I realize the members only area is set up like it's made for dungeon porn.

Which, I guess in a way, it is.

Rows of beds and moon-shaped couches fill the space, but they aren't being used for rest or relaxation. Instead, men and women are chained to them, their wrists and necks bound by cuffs attached to chains hanging from the ceiling above. They look like hunted animals, captured and unable to escape. But now, they are just empty shells of their former selves.

My stomach churns at the sight before me - it is truly sickening.

The screeching of the demons we disturbed echoes through the moans of the lost souls. They advance on us, hunting us like vulnerable prey.

Their appearance is predominantly human, with the exception of their sharp and pointed teeth and claw-like nails. They are enticing, stunning, and radiate a captivating sexual energy. It would be all too easy to fall under their spell.

My nipples harden under the smooth material of my dress and I feel a wetness between my thighs. I meet the gaze of the Incubus responsible for this effect; his tongue glides over his sharp teeth, and he seems to be getting intoxicated by my arousal.

Gross.

I feel violated and repulsed, yet there's a part of me that's dangerously curious about the forbidden allure they evoke. Asmo senses my conflict and grabs my arm, pulling me closer to him.

"Don't look them in the eyes," He whispers harshly into my ear. "They'll try to ensnare you with just a glance and drag you down into their abyss before you can even scream for help."

He positions himself between me and the rest of the room, my back to the wall so I am protected from any potential threats.

"Stay behind me," He orders, briefly glancing back at me.

I nod, unable to find my voice as fear tightens its grip on my throat.

One of the male demons makes a move towards Melonie, but with a quick flick of her wrist, a vine with sharp thorns erupts from the ground and coils around him. The demon lets out a blood-curdling scream as the thorns tear through his skin and muscle, wrapping tightly around his neck. A sickening popping noise echoes from his throat as thick red liquid oozes from his nose and mouth. He struggles desperately to break free, but there is no mercy to be found here tonight.

With another turn of her hand, the plant tightens its hold, digging its thorns deeper into the incu flesh. The sound of cracking bones grows louder and louder until, with a final pop, the incubus's head detaches from his body and drops to the floor at her feet.

Despite the frenzied look on her face, a small smile of satisfaction spreads across her lips as she revels in the satisfaction of killing one of her daughter's captors.

A curvy woman with red head flashes her pearly white fangs, approaching Asmo with her sultry appeal. He allows his gaze to travel to her plump breast, and she squeals with delight, sure he will be her next feast.

I observe him furtively adjusting the back of his pants, then deftly extracting a gleaming black blade that's as long as his hand.

The succubus bitch wraps her sleazy arm around his waist, teasingly flicking his ear with the tip of her tongue. With bitter eyes, I watch her touch him, her fingertips ghosting down his shirt, to the front of his pants. She cups his groin in her hand, gently stroking at first before increasing her pace and placing delicate kisses on his neck.

A noise escapes my throat, a mix of a moan and a gasp as I watch them. It's hard to tell if it's from jealousy or excitement. He raises the knife in his hand, and it bursts into stunning blue flames. The woman doesn't even seem to notice until it's too late. He plunges the fiery blade into her chest, reducing her to a smoldering pile of ash at my feet.

Like a switch going off in my head, I come crashing back down to my senses just as the demon who moments before had me under his grasp, comes barreling towards me.

My muscles move on their own as I swing with all my might, the spikes on my brass knuckles digging into the creature's face. But it doesn't seem to faze him; he's far stronger and bigger than me. As he pushes me onto my back, fear floods through me and I struggle to break free.

Panic courses through my veins as the weight of his massive form pins me to the ground, his spittle flecking my face, a grotesque grin splitting his features. His hands encircle my throat, squeezing tightly, stealing the breath from my lungs.

My heart is thudding loudly in my ears, and my blood turns to ice, but I focus on keeping my breath steady and my thoughts clear as I strategize a way to escape from his grasp.

With a burst of strength, I manage to break one of my arms free, and I frantically strike him in the eyes over and over again. I may not be able to overpower him, but perhaps I can blind him and create an opportunity for escape.

His hold loosens, and I take advantage by delivering a swift knee to his groin. Using his own momentum against him, I quickly turn and push, rolling him onto his back in one fluid motion. He's caught completely off-guard by my counterattack.

I climb on top of him and start punching rapidly with my fists, my eyes squeezed shut. I keep going until I hear the sound of bone crunching beneath my spiked knuckles. I force myself to open one eye and look at the creature under me, feeling a surge of disgust at the sight before me.

His face looks like it has been through a meat grinder, and he no longer struggles beneath me. The world spins around me like I'm on a never-ending carousel, and it's becoming harder to breathe with each passing second.

I've never taken a life before.

I roll off of him, but my body trembles as I attempt to get back on my feet.

Asmo, who is now standing beside me, extends his hand and I gratefully accept it, allowing him to help me up from the blood-stained ground.

"Impressive." He grins as I lean heavily against him, my legs still shaky from the adrenaline and exertion.

I can only manage a nod in response, too stunned to form a coherent sentence.

The remaining demons shift their focus from feeding on us and instead attack with the sole intent of killing. The desire for nourishment has been replaced by a thirst for blood.

The room becomes a blur as we are bombarded from all directions. Water, fire, and sharp claws clash against each other in a frenzy of attacks. My fists lash out wildly, striking anything within reach.

Asmo pulls me into him, "Stay close to me!" He shouts as he weaves a protective circle of fire around us, the flames licking the air with intense heat. I watch in awe as the demons recoil from the barrier, their snarls filled with frustration and rage.

With a flick of her wrist, Melonie sprouts a massive carnivorous plant, that begins devouring any demons that manage to slip past us.

In just a matter of minutes, the group of fifteen has been reduced to zero thanks to her quick thinking and magical abilities.

As the last demon is ensnared in the gnashing jaws of Melonie's plant, the chaos begins to fade. The creature is eventually reduced to nothing more than a stain on the teeth of the monstrous plant.

"Mom? Dad?" A frail feminine voice calls out from somewhere within the shadows.

We sprint towards the source of the voice, but our efforts are thwarted in the pitch-black back corner of the building.

"Eirene? Sweetie, is that you?" Melonie calls out into the darkness.

We pass countless victims dangling from chains, their limbs stretched like marionette dolls, the expressions on their faces twisted in agony.

The overwhelming odor of death and decomposition hangs in the air, making it almost impossible to swallow or inhale without feeling nauseous. The majority of them are already deceased, adding to the foul smell that lingers throughout the space.

"Give me a moment, I might be able to create light," I suggest confidently, relying on my earlier demonstration of powers.

But in reality, I have no idea what I'm doing. Focusing all of my energy and willpower, I try to manifest a small sphere of flames in my hand.

Nothing happens, of course.

Asmo chuckles and shakes his head before creating a ball of blue fire in his palm. "Is this what you were going for?" He asks with a smirk.

What a showoff.

I nod sheepishly and mumble a thanks, grateful for the light but irritated by my own ineptitude.

We press on through the inky blackness, following the dancing blue flame until we reach a turn towards the back wall. Finally, we come to a halt at a doorway that leads into a small, hidden area.

"You guys came back for me!" Eirene's sweet laughter fills the air, and my heart swells with joy.

"Eirene!" Melonie and I shout simultaneously, and excitement floods my body as I realize we have finally found her.

But then, confusion sets in.

If that was her voice we heard, how is it that she is lying lifeless at the bottom of a cage, covered in her own bodily fluids, and badly bruised with deep cuts on her skin?

I am filled with terror as I take in the gruesome scene before me. My heart sinks when I see that her right arm is twisted at an unnatural angle.

But again, her voice echoes in the room once more, followed by a sinister cackle.

Emerging from the shadows of the room, a figure in a hood comes forward. Bony hands emerge from within the cloak and push back the hood, revealing none other than Dafina. Her eyes are crazed, and she wears a wild expression on her face.

She grins maniacally, stretching her smile all the way to her ears as she speaks in a twisted imitation of my sister's voice. "Aww, what's the matter, dearies? Did you not miss me?"

CHAPTER EIGHTEEN

Kali

Dafina bears no resemblance to the compassionate and affectionate woman I knew growing up. She appears almost alien, similar to the tormented individuals locked away in the nearby corridor, devoid of any rationality or vitality.

I can understand the demons we just fought being evil, but Dafina? It just doesn't make any sense.

But then again, nothing makes sense anymore.

"Why?" Melonie screams at the old woman. "Why do this? We gave you everything, asking for nothing in return! We were family!"

"Family!" Dafina scoffs, a wicked laugh blooms behind her thin lips. "You were a means to an end. Nothing more."

Melonie's eyes blaze with a mix of betrayal and sorrow as she takes a step closer to the old woman, her fists clenched at her sides. "You used us," She hisses.

Dafina's gaze is as cold and sharp as the dagger she casually flips in her hand. "Oh, child, in this world, it's use or be used. I did what I had to in order to survive," She replies, her voice dripping with disdain.

"I'll make you pay for this!" Phil's voice booms with rage as his towering figure looms over Melonie, trembling with the fury pulsing through him.

He is a destructive force fueled by pain and rage, while Melonie is the calculating gusts of wind that feed its power.

Together, they rush simultaneously, their movements in sync with one another as though they have practiced for this moment their entire existences.

Dafina steps back, her eyes widening slightly as she watches them advance. But the expression is fleeting, buried under a mask of impassivity as she braces herself for their attack.

"Fools!" She spits out, just as Melonie and Phil close in on her.

Phil lunges, but she sidesteps with the nimbleness of someone half her age, sending him stumbling past her. Melonie, anticipating this, aims a kick at Dafina's knee, attempting to bring her down to the ground.

However, Dafina's agility prevails as she catches Melonie's foot mid-air, twisting it violently. Melonie yelps in pain but manages to wrench her leg free, rolling away from the old woman's grasp.

"Pathetic," Dafina sneers, looking down at Melonie who is now struggling to get back on her feet on the cold, hard ground. "You think you can defeat me with such a childish trick?"

Melonie grits her teeth against the pain, determination setting her jaw as she pushes herself up. "I don't need tricks to defeat you," she retorts.

With a swift motion, she pulls a small, concealed blade from her boot, the light glinting off the metal. Dafina's eyes narrow at the sight, recognizing the threat now presented.

Phil, recovering from his misstep, charges again with a roar, his large hands stretched out to grab Dafina.

This time, Dafina isn't quick enough. Phil's massive arms envelop her, pinning her arms to her sides in a bear hug that radiates with his pent-up fury. Dafina struggles, her frame squirming as she tries to find leverage, but Phil's grip is unyielding.

With Dafina temporarily incapacitated in Phil's grasp, Melonie seizes the opportunity and limps toward them, "I am going to kill you slowly." She tells Dafina.

Dafina laughs, a harsh, grating sound that belies the precariousness of her situation. "You can try, child," She taunts, "But that's not how this is going to play out."

Suddenly, a vortex of swirling energy forms around Dafina's entwined form, and Melonie pauses mid-stride, the blade in her hand wavering as she senses the shift in power. Phil's grip tightens, his knuckles whitening with exertion, but the air around them crackles with increasing intensity.

Melonie's hair stands on end, and a deep, resonant hum fills the air, growing louder and louder until an earth-shattering pop resounds through the cramped room.

A shockwave blasts outward, throwing Melonie back against a cabinet with bone jarring force. Phil is hurled to the found, his hold broken.

Both knocked completely unconscious.

Once the dust of the blast settles, Dafina still stands there, next to my cage she has my sister in, completely unscathed.

Okay...how the hell?

My jaw drops as I stare in disbelief, and I can tell Asmo is just as surprised when he lets out a shocked gasp, his eyes fixed on Dafina.

That seemed way too effortless.

Phil is supposed to be an all-powerful deity, so how is it possible that a mere shock could incapacitate him?

Where did the bad-assery we had going on thirty minutes ago go?

Something isn't right here.

I turn to face Asmo, trying to conceal the overwhelming emotions that wash over me from witnessing Phil and Melonie's downfall.

Asmo meets my gaze, his eyes equally wide with shock and confusion. For a moment, we're both silent, processing the chaotic turn of events, trying to find our footing in the suddenly altered landscape of our struggle.

Then, he brings his hands up as if he is trying to use his powers to conjure another fire ball like he did earlier to blast Dafina with. But nothing happens, and his face instantly freezes in a silent state of shock.

His hands tremble, and I watch helplessly while his frustration mounts as he tries again, the desperation clear in his strained expression. "It's not working," He whispers hoarsely, the fear evident in his voice.

Dafina watches him struggle for a moment, a cruel smile playing on her lips, and she laughs, shaking her head. "I'm no fool. I know everything there is to know about all of you. Did you really think I wouldn't be prepared?"

She questions. "That I wouldn't anticipate your actions? Your powers are useless in this room; the spell used here is too strong." Her sneer grows as she clicks her tongue and points a bony finger at him. "Especially since I used your own mother's blood to bind it."

A growl emits from his chest, and he lunges towards her but then a plume of bright blue smoke rises from the ground, blocking his path. As the smoke begins to dissipate, it leaves a small girl in its place.

Asmo falls to his knees, his hands shaking as he grabs onto his dark hair and lets out a roar of pure agony. "You did this?" He asks the girl, gritting his teeth so hard they might shatter. "How...no, why would you betray your own family like this?" He chokes out.

The girl crosses her arms across her chest, her eyes gleaming maliciously as she steps closer to Asmo, her smile wide and chilling.

"Oh, Azzy," She clucks sympathetically. "You are so naive and trusting. How could the future ruler of the Underworld miss such an obvious betrayal? You were always the favored one—the heir to the throne—the chosen mentor of the Chosen One...it has always been all about you!" Her voice escalates into a shrill cackle, the sound echoing off the stone walls of the room. "And while you were preoccupied with your destiny, I was overlooked, forgotten, the shadow to your light. But no more."

She glares at me with utter disdain, as if I am a repulsive creature whose presence she can barely stand.

Who is this girl?

Her attention shifts back to Asmo, and she moves closer to him in a seemingly vulnerable manner, almost like she's teasing him. "How could they choose you for the throne when I am more powerful than you could ever dream about being? It's not fair! It should be me!"

Her justifications are as simplistic and childlike as she appears to be in age.

Asmo's anguish transforms into a smoldering rage as he stares at the girl. "Kora, she is our mother! And you let your petty jealousy put her in harm's way? Do you even have any remorse for what you have done, sister?" Asmo snaps back, rising to his feet and closing the remaining space between him and Kora.

Oh, duh.

How did I not realize it sooner?

This girl is his sister. No wonder she looks so familiar.

Out of nowhere, her hair transforms into a vibrant blue hue, similar to the smoke she materialized in. The once wavy strands now resemble dancing flames, gracefully swaying along her shoulders like cobras entranced by a mesmerizing melody.

"Do you truly have such little faith in me, brother?" She questions. "That I would harm our own mother? Yes, I did assist in her abduction—if that's what you want to call it—but it was necessary to expose your incompetence. When father and the council see that you couldn't even do your job bringing back the Chosen One safely, they will have no choice but to reconsider who truly deserves the throne."

Asmo's fury crackles in the air, his eyes burning with a fire that could rival the newly blue flames of Kora's hair.

"You endanger our mother's life just to prove a point? To show that you should be on the throne instead of me?" Asmo's voice booms, filling the chamber with its thunderous wrath. "You risk everything, everything our family has built, on a gamble for power?!"

Kora's lips curl into a spiteful smile, her eyes practically glowing with malice. "Oh, dear brother, you misunderstand me so profoundly. It's almost pitiable. Power is not given, it is taken. And I will take what should have been mine from the very beginning." Her voice holds a cold, calculating edge as she steps closer to Asmo, her fiery hair casting eerie shadows across her face.

Asmo clenches his fists, his knuckles whitening with the intensity of his grip. "And what of the chaos you leave in your wake, Kora? What of the lives that hang in the balance while you play your twisted games?" His voice, though laced with anger, betrays a hint of desperation

Kora laughs, a sound as chilling as the winds of the northern wastes. "Chaos? Dear brother, chaos is but a ladder for the worthy to climb and the weak to fall. Where you may see it as destruction, I see it as opportunity." She steps around him, her smoke magic, or whatever it is, seeps from her fingertips, crawling across the floor and slowly wrapping itself around Asmo. Slowly, it creeps its way up his frame, filling his nostrils, sinking into his lungs. His eyes widen as she pushes the oxygen from his body, slowly cutting off his air with the putrid vapor-like substance.

Asmo struggles to break free, his hands grasping at the ethereal chains that tighten around him with each breath he attempts to draw. Kora watches with a predatory gaze, her satisfaction evident as she witnesses her brother's plight.

I'm aware of the resilience of those with Divine blood, but her immense power and the binding spell in place make me uncertain of how this will turn out. A feeling of helplessness washes over me, settling heavily in my stomach, and my chest constricts with an intense fear that threatens to overwhelm me.

But I know I can't let my fear control me, because if I don't think of some kind of plan, he could die.

Fuck. I'm pretty sure she's just a teenager, and I can't punch a teenager...can I?

No, Kali, No.

Assaulting a minor is against the law no matter what realm we're in.

As she takes another step towards Asmo, I scramble to think of what to do.

Then, in a split-second decision, I lunge forward and extend my left leg, sliding across the ground like a baseball player aiming directly at her. My shin makes solid contact with her feet, causing her to stumble and fall hard onto the concrete.

I'm sure we'll all laugh about this later, yeah?

Asmo finally breaks free from her magical hold, gasping for air. He grabs her and lifts her off the ground, carrying her over his shoulder like a disobedient child. "Father should keep you locked away in the dungeons for a whole month for your reckless actions!" He scolds her.

Kora screams, her legs flailing and fists swinging wildly as she tries to break free from his grip. "Put me down!" She shouts, each word steeped in a toxic blend of rage and humiliation. "I swear Asmodeus, I'll—I'll kill you for this!"

In a flash, she disappears into a cloud of smoke, gone in an instant. But just as quickly, she reappears behind me, draping one arm around my waist and covering my nose and mouth with the other.

A mixture of citrus and acetone fills my nostril and then my head begins to feel fuzzy.

Oh shit, I've been drugged!

I can't believe that bitch just drugged me!

This right fucking here man—this is exactly why teenagers scare people.

I struggle against her grasp, but I feel too weak to fight her and my vision is fading fast. I can vaguely hear Asmo call out my name.

Kora's grasp is tight, her hands almost bruising as she struggles to support both of our weight while I fight against the effects of the chloroform.

Damn. She's really strong for a kid.

I become lost in the cloud of smoke that begins to swirl around me, shielding me and Kora from Asmo's line of sight. I hear him call again, and I try to tell him that I'm here—I'm right here—but the magic cloaking me, Kora, and now Dafina, has some kind of barrier that's hiding us out of sight and somehow keeping the sound of my voice from reaching him.

Without warning, it feels as if I am being pulled into a vacuum. My stomach lurches and drops to my knees as my surroundings begin to dissolve. Asmo and my family disappear along with the room, leaving me alone in this strange void. I can still see them, but they can't see or hear me. All I can do is helplessly watch as they disappear before my eyes.

The disorienting sensation of being transported causes me to nearly lose my lunch, but the abrupt stop of reappearing in another location forces it back down at lightning speed.

Just before I succumb to the overwhelming defeat, my feet touch solid ground and I collapse onto the burnt orange surface.

Through my fading consciousness, I see a striking woman with piercing brown eyes and platinum hair highlighted with shades of blue. It is unmistakably Persephone, mother of Asmo and his annoying twerp sister. She sits beside me, her hands and feet bound in shimmering ropes that seem to emit a soft, ethereal glow. Despite her bonds, Persephone's aura is unyieldingly majestic, her expression stoic yet tinged with a trace of concern.

"Oh, no." She whispers, her voice barely audible over the eerie silence that envelops us. "You weren't supposed to be here. All—all will be lost." I hear the words escape her lips right before the darkness claims me entirely, pulling me into a deep, unnerving sleep.

Unfortunately for me, this wasn't exactly my best first impression.

Chapter Nineteen

Kali

As I regain consciousness, my body aches and my head throbs from the effects of being drugged. The scent of mildew hangs in the musty air, most likely caused by the constant dripping of a broken pipe that I can hear somewhere nearby.

Straining my eyes in the dim light, I try to make out my surroundings.

In one corner of the room, there's an old recliner with a floral print, worn at the edges, the fabric faded and threadbare in spots from age and use. Directly across from me is a small, barred window that lets in only the faintest trickle of light, but it's just enough to reveal the tinged yellow, plastered walls around me that are peeling like aged skin, revealing layers of forgotten paint underneath.

We appear to be imprisoned within a dilapidated motel room somewhere.

But where?

I attempt to move, only to find my wrists bound tightly behind me with coarse rope, the fibers cutting into my skin with each small shift.

Taking a glance around the room, I notice it's just the me and my prison roomie—*aka*—the mother of the man I am weirdly attracted to, in here at the moment.

Escaping should be a breeze.

I clear my throat and turn towards her slowly. "Well..." I say with a hint of humor, trying to ease the tension in the room. "Do you come here often?"

Her laughter fills the air, and she turns to me with a look of pure love, her face lit up with a radiant smile. Despite our current situation—being chained up in a dark, musty room—she remains relaxed and at ease, as if we are simply old friends catching up after years apart.

"I knew my son would find you," She exclaims, her blonde hair swaying as she scoots closer to me. "You are Kali?" She queries, her voice tinged with an accent I can't quite place.

"Yep, in the flesh." I reply.

"You're even more beautiful than I imagined."

I can't quite decipher if her comment is meant to be a compliment or an insult. However, given the fact that my entire world has been turned upside down and there's a chance I could end up dead at the hands of her deranged daughter and my elderly housekeeper, I'm not particularly concerned about it either way.

My thoughts are racing faster than a school of fish trying to escape the jagged edge of a hungry shark's mouth.

What will happen to Asmo—to my family? Will they be, okay? And most importantly, are any of them even still alive?

The haunting images of my sister trapped in a cage and the lifeless expressions on Phil and Melonie's faces flood my mind, and I am overcome with grief.

Why the hell is this happening?

Tears prick at my eyes, blurring the already dim view of the tattered room. I blink them away fiercely, not wanting to show weakness in front of a goddess such as Persephone.

How am I supposed to save the world from destruction when I can't even protect myself from being kidnapped?

By a freaking teenager none-the-less!

This is reality, not some fantastical fruity little fairytale where I'll magically become the stronger than everyone else—or is it?

Honestly, I have no idea anymore.

It's all just a blur.

Just a few days ago, I was completely ignorant of all of this. So, I suppose anything is possible in this bizarre ass world.

Ugh, I could almost laugh at the irony of it all, but the humor of the situation is too dark, even for my taste.

"Kali?" Persephone's soft voice pulls me back from the precipice of my spiraling thoughts.

Choking back the lump beginning to grow in my throat, I scoot my feet and bottom on the floor gently rotating so I can face the woman speaking to me.

"Ye—yes your Goddess-ness.?" I manage through my sniffles.

"I want you to listen to me," She begins, her tone soft yet assertive. "I know this is overwhelming, and I know you're scared. But you are stronger than you think. The power you are said to possess—it's not just a myth. It is real, and it flows through your veins as surely as your blood does. You have a strength that can not only change the course of battles, but also the fate of worlds."

I have the strength?

That's laughable.

More like I have the anxiety. Loads of anxiety and a mounting sense of dread.

But I nod, trying my best to absorb her words. "How can you be so sure?" I ask, the doubt clear in my voice.

Persephone's smile is gentle, "I have seen much in my time, Kali. I have watched heroes rise from less than nothing and demi-gods falter despite their might. The essence of true power lies not in brute strength but in the resilience of the spirit, and the courage to continue even when it feels like you can't. Your spirit," Persephone continues, her eyes locking onto mine with an intensity that pins me to the spot, "Is unyielding. You've faced adversities already, and yet here you are, willing to face even greater threats. That is your biggest power. The ability to persevere, to stand in the face of overwhelming circumstances and still push forward. That is what will carve your path, not just in battles, but in the very fabric of this world. You *are* meant for great things, Kali."

Great things?

I can't even decide what to have for breakfast without second-guessing myself.

But Persephone's words, they kindle something within me—a small flicker of hope perhaps, or maybe the ember of a forgotten courage that had lain dormant under layers of self-doubt and fear. It feels fragile, like a bubble that could pop at any moment, yet it's there, undeniable and growing stronger with each breath I take.

Maybe this is where new beginnings are forged—in the fire of another's faith in us.

"Thank you, your Goddess-ness." I manage a shaky smile.

The sound of her airy laugh gives me goosebumps. "Please, call me Persephone." She encourages. "Ummm, Kali. I—I'd like to apologize for all the *tension* in my family that you've become accompanied to. I'm afraid things have gotten a bit hasty as of late."

"That's one way to say it." I say, bitterly.

She nods in understanding, "Kora's actions have been quite surprising. And I'm sorry that you've gotten tangled up in all of our family drama, along with everything you already have going on." Persephone continues, her expression turning somber. "You were meant to discover your strengths at your own pace, not be thrust into them by necessity. But destiny often has its own timeline, doesn't it?"

I nod, understanding more than I probably should.

The politics of gods and immortals are vast and intricate, far beyond what one might expect. Yet, here I am, right in the thick of it, chosen or cursed—depending on how you look at it.

"My daughter has allowed herself to be corrupted by my mother's influence, and the deceitful promises of power." Persephone says with a sigh. "It pains me to see her so lost, following in my mother's footsteps, and I fear for what my daughter is becoming." Her voice breaks for a split second, "But I still hold hope that the goodness within her will prevail."

"One can hope." I give a nervous laugh. "Also, what exactly do you mean by your *mother*?" I ask, a feeling of leeriness rising in my gut.

Her expression falters briefly. "You know, it's funny in a way—" She begins, "Actually, there's no point trying to make it sound better—she's the mastermind that is behind our kidnappings. And as it turns out, she's been hiding right under all of our noses without any of us suspecting a thing. I must admit, it is quite the scheme she put together, and the patience it took to execute it is horrifyingly commendable."

I swallow hard. "So, your mother is...?" I trail off, not sure if I really want to hear the answer.

"My mother is the woman who you have known as Dafina." Persephone admits, shame coloring her tone. "Though, her true name is Demeter."

My mouth drops.

"Demeter?" I echo. "But Dafin—I mean Demeter was already working for Phil when my mother and I arrived. That would mean..."

My thoughts race back through every interaction with Dafina, struggling to comprehend how a deity such as herself could have remained unnoticed in our own home all these years. "They've always known." I whisper to myself, replaying old childhood memories in my head.

"I fear so, yes." Persephone confirms. "And I think her alliance with Lucius, may even be my fault."

CHAPTER TWENTY

Kali

This woman right here.

My eyes become slits in my face, "Okay, I'm gonna need some additional context on that one."

Persephone presses her lips together tightly, a clear indication that the story she is about to tell is neither simple nor pleasant.

"You see, long ago, when my husband and I first began to fall in love, she forbade me from going back to the Underworld to see him. My mother absolutely loathed him, but the love that burned within me for him could not be quenched by her disdain. It was a tumultuous time, and in her desperation to keep us apart, she went to extreme measures. It started quite mundane at first, little things here and there to try to prevent me from seeing him, weaving small spells or putting up barriers to trap me in the realm of the living. Then, it began to escalate. She summoned storms every time I planned to leave, the sky blackening as though night had fallen in the middle of the day. Lightning struck the earth with vengeance, and thunder roared like a beast unleashed, all meant to frighten me into submission. But my determination was as fierce as her storms, which made her fight against me even more." A tear escapes her eye, trickling down her cheek like a lonely stream seeking the sea.

She pinches her eyes shut and shakes it away as if denying its existence could change the past.

Continuing on, her voice is tinged with the sorrow of old scars. "My heart ached not just for the love I could not see but for the rift that grew between my mother and me. Every attempt I made to explain my feelings, to make her understand, seemed only to deepen her resolve. One day, in her ultimate act of defiance against what she couldn't understand or accept, she went too far. After plunging the living realm into a darkness so profound that it felt as if the sun itself had been swallowed, she unleashed the hounds of winter upon the earth. Frost and ice encased everything, turning the world into a frigid wasteland. She hoped that by making the earth barren, she would force me to abandon my love and stay by her side. When that didn't work, she hired a demigod assassin to kidnap me and bring me back to her. She confined me in a hidden castle along the shores of the North Sea, the structure spelled such that no one could enter or leave without her permission. The walls were thick with enchantments, entwined with the strongest magics she could muster, designed not only to keep me prisoner but to dampen my own powers." Her body trembles at the memory. "Days turned into weeks, and weeks into months. I was isolated, surrounded by nothing but the ceaseless roar of the waves and the howling winds that battered the castle walls. The loneliness was suffocating, an invisible hand tightening around my heart with each passing day. Yet, within the depths of despair, a flame of defiance continued to burn. I knew I had to escape, to find him again and bridge the chasm that my mother's fear had created between us. I spent hours every day by the window, watching the ocean's fury crash against the rocks, letting it fuel my resolve rather than drown it. My powers, though dampened, were not dead; merely suppressed. Slowly, I began to whisper to the elements, to coax and nurture the small spark of magic that still flickered within me. I whispered to the wind, urging it to carry my voice beyond the castle walls, hoping it would find him. Night after night, I sang softly into the darkness, songs of longing and freedom, melodies that wept with my sorrow but soared with hope. Then, one night, under the cloak of a new moon, something shifted. The wind changed its tune, whispering back secrets it had carried over the miles. In its cryptic murmurs, I sensed a presence, a familiar essence brushing against the outer barriers of my prison. It was him; I could feel it as surely as the tides pulled by the moon. Hades had come for me, and he brought your mother with him. They had found a way through the spells and enchantments, a loophole that even my mother hadn't foreseen. But that didn't even matter. When they finally caught up to me, it was too late. My mother had arrived first, sick and consumed with her jealousy. She was convinced that I had chosen Hades over her, and in her twisted mind, if she couldn't have me, then no one could. And she tried to make sure of it by slitting my throat right in front of him."

My eyes fill with tears as I listen, my own heart crumbling at her words "That's so wild. So, how were you able to survive then?" I ask.

"Helena," she responds. "She aided us in using my death as a sacrifice for a soul splitting spell on my mother. We banished her soul to Tartarus, the deepest pit of punishment, reserved for only the most wretched. And then we hid her body here, in the mortal realm, hoping she would never be able to reunite her soul and body. Fortunately, Helena had your father there as a backup. He is a divine healer and was able to revive me before my soul was judged by Charon during that brief brush with death."

"Wow." I mutter, shaking my head in disbelief. "That's so messed up. But the real question lays with, how did she wind up here in the first place posing as our family housekeeper?"

Persephonie sighs, rolling the stiffness out of her neck. "I'm still in pursuit of those answers myself." She confesses. "If I had to make an educated guess, she's likely partnered up to Lucius—or worse—Loki. It makes sense; one of them must have sent her here. Without a physical form, her soul would have turned, and she would have become a Ruhan—a demon capable of possessing non-divine beings. That's likely how she's been able to possess Dafina's body!" She exclaims in frustration.

Cool. Now we're fucking with demons.

"So, what exactly is a Ruhan?"

Persephonie frowns, causing ripples in her perfect, smooth skin. "A Ruhan is a tormented soul that refuses to pass on, clinging to the mortal realm through sheer malevolence. Once they possess a body, they can be extremely difficult to exorcise because they intertwine their essence with their host's, corrupting them from the inside out. They feed off the negative emotions—fear, anger, despair. The more turmoil they cause, the stronger they become. Based on how long I suspect my mother has been inhabiting the body of the woman you call Dafina, it may be impossible to free her from my mother's tormented spirit."

"That still doesn't clarify the current connection. She's been working as a Housekeeper for the Adira family since before my sisters were even born," I point out.

Persephone lifts her head from the dingy wall, "Oh, I think I know exactly how it all connects.

As a young girl, Dafina stumbled upon Poseidon's beach, homeless and alone. He took pity on her and offered her shelter and work. She quickly captivated all of us with her charm and gentleness, becoming someone we all confided in without hesitation. We trusted her blindly, gifting her with our truth of who we were and what gifts we each held. At the time, we were naive and didn't fully believe in the prophecy, so none of us really knew or worried about who she was..." Her voice trails off. "But hey, now we know the truth, yeah?"

Well, she's not wrong there. Now we most definitely know the truth.

"Yep." I state, making an emphasized pop at the end. "So, is it safe to assume you can't get us out of here?"

She raises an eyebrow. "Don't you sense the magic around us?"

I shake my head, responding with a negative, "No, I don't think so."

"Interesting." She mumbles. "The spell that is suppressing our power is bound by three generations of divine blood. It would require someone as formidable as an Eternal to break such a powerful spell."

"An Eternal?" I repeat, though it's more of a question.

Persephone's hair falls gracefully over her shoulders as she tilts her head in a slow, solemn nod. "Yes, an Eternal—one of the ancient beings that existed before the gods themselves. They're said to be the architects of the fundamental laws that govern our universe. Their power is immense, almost without limit. They were the first of us, the originals from which all mortals and magical beings descend."

"I still have so much to understand about this whole magic and divine blood stuff." I groan. "Any chance we might find one of these *Eternals* nearby?"

Persephone laughs.

I'll take that as a no, then.

"They abandoned us a long time ago. Finding an Eternal isn't like picking a flower from a garden. Nor will they bother themselves for the mundane problems of the universe. They are elusive, hidden by the veils of time itself."

I stretch my legs out in front on me, arching my back, trying to relieve some of the throbbing in my rigid muscles. "Right then." I mumble.

I hear the distinct click of a doorknob turning, and my heart pounds against my chest. I tense up, preparing for the worst as I hold my breath.

Dafina and her toadies are surely on the other side of the door, and they'll be coming in any second now to torture us or worse—kill us.

Whatever Dafina's plans are, I know they're not going to be good.

I mean after killing her own daughter over jealousy—there's no telling the lengths this woman will go to get what she desires.

I hear the distinct sound of a feral creature's snarl, followed by a loud, resounding bang on the door. My body freezes as if submerged in ice water. It's the same terrifying sound that has haunted my nightmares since I was a child. The growls reverberate through my eardrums, bringing back vivid memories of my mother's tragic non death.

The door creaks on its old, rusted hinges, abruptly swinging open. A wave of putrid air hits me like a physical force, and my eyes water from the stench of rotting flesh. My heart races and I can feel sweat forming on my palms, and fear takes hold of my body.

I squint as the smoky blue tendrils of Kora's magic seep in through the cracked door, snaking along the grimy floorboards until they coalesce into a shimmering cloud above the lumpy, worn mattress in front of us. As the smoke dissipates, Kora appears, her petite form materializing from thin air.

For a moment, she catches Persephone's gaze, before looking away hastily. Running her fingers through her hair, she smiles, crossing her legs, as she rests her chin in the palm of her hand.

"Well, isn't this a delightful mess you've found yourselves in," She says, her tone both mocking and amused.

Persephone, her eyes wide and her breath caught in her throat, tries to find her voice as Kora's presence fills the small, dank room. "Kora, stop this nonsense now."

"Stop?" Kora tilts her head, examining her finely manicured nails as if the fate hanging in the balance were no more significant than a speck of dust. "Oh, mother, I'm just getting started."

Her eyes flick back and forth between us, and she pops the gum she's been chewing on relentlessly ever since she fucking poofed up in this bitch.

She lets out a high-pitched, delighted squeal and claps her hands together like a giddy child in a candy store. "Oh, come now! Isn't this just the best?" She exclaims, "Just us girls, swapping tales with one another." But then, her expression turns sinister as she addresses me. "Though unfortunately for you, dear Kali, our time together will be cut short. You see, our plan has worked perfectly and now I can finally help Yiayia reunite with her true form. And of course, take my rightful place as heir to the Underworld."

"What kind of curse have you brought onto our family? What did you agree to do Kora?" Persephone demands, her eyebrows knitting together as she glares at her daughter.

"I'm doing what I must to secure my future because you and father have failed in doing so. Yiayia has ensured me a rightful place. I am to break the curse that was put upon her soul so she may breathe life once more and blah, blah, blah." She waves her hand in mockery.

"She intends to kill us all tonight. You know that, right?" Persephone asks her.

Kora's dismissive gesture sends a chill down my spine. The casualness with which she speaks of such dark dealings is unsettling, to say the least.

"Ugh." The girl flips her hair across her shoulder, rolling her eyes. "You didn't get blessed with much of a brain, did you mother? What are you rambling about? She just needs me to do the spell. That's all. She promised me she wouldn't hurt you."

Persephone's eyes flicker with sadness as she averts her gaze to the ground. Her voice quivering as she goes on to explained, "I sacrificed my own life to perform that soul splitting spell, Kora. The Eternals granted me a second chance at life when Kali's father healed me—which Charon is still sour about. But what you don't understand my dear child, is that once Demeter's soul and body are reunited, my physical body will perish, leaving my soul trapped in Tartarus where Lucius holds all the power over my fate."

Shock registers on Koras' face. "No." She whispers, her head swinging back and forth in denial.

It's becoming clear that she too is only a mindless participant in this sick, demented game Dafin—Demeter—whoever the fuck she is, is playing.

Kora's face crumples, the reality of her actions crashing upon her like the harsh waves of a tempest. "But...but Yiayia promised..." Her voice trails off into a whimper.

The hell hound standing on the other side of Kora, massive and menacing, growls softly, its eyes reflecting a fiery glow as Dafina walks in, flanked by two more monstrous creatures with glowing eyes.

Draugrs, I think Phil called them.

Dafina's presence fills the room with a palpable tension, her eyes scanning the scene before her like a chess master contemplating a checkmate. "Promises are such fragile things, aren't they, Kora?" Her voice is smooth, almost soothing, yet it carries an undercurrent of undeniable menace.

"Yiayia?" Kora's voice cracks as she utters the word, the vulnerability of a child seeking comfort where none can be found. "Tell me she's wrong."

In a swift motion, she crosses the cramped room and grabs Kora's arm with a tight grip. She yanks her off the bed and pulls her close, their faces almost touching. "I wish I could say she's wrong," Dafina whispers, her voice low and menacing. "But I won't lie to you, my dear child." She reaches up to brush away a tear from Kora's cheek, still holding onto her arm. "After you perform the spell, I will have no more use for you." She pauses, a smug smile spreading across her face. "So, as your mother predicted, you will indeed be dying tonight."

Chapter Twenty-One

Kali

"You would kill a child? Your own granddaughter?" Persephone wails, tears streaking through the dirt on her cheeks as she struggles against her confines. "Why would you do this? Please, Mother, I beg of you, stop this madness! I can leave Hades if that's what you want. I will swear my loyalty to you once more, just please spare Kora," Persephone pleads, prostrating herself on the ground in front of Dafina.

The old hag kicks her leg forward with a force I hadn't quite expected from someone of her tenor, the heel of her boot meeting her daughter's face with a sharp crack, causing my stomach to tighten in disgust as Persephone's jaw hangs limply to the side.

"No! Stop!" Kora screams at old woman, releasing her magic and letting it swirl delicately in the air around her. "You lied to me! By undoing this curse, my mother will die at my own hands. I won't do it! I won't let her die for my mistakes!"

Demeter lets out a laugh, filled with bitterness and scorn. "You truly are a naive child," She taunts. "Always seeking attention and validation. Of course, I lied to you; it was effortless! You have inherited my best quality, my dear. Always thinking of yourself and disregarding the consequences—it *almost* makes me proud."

"I'm nothing like you." Kora spits, the venom in her eyes starts flashing as bright as the magic swirling around her. "To hell with you and your spell!" She begins chanting in a language unknown to me, her hands shaping the air in front of her as if molding an invisible sculpture.

Demeter only laughs, and Kora's eyes widen in shock, her voice catching in her throat, causing her to stop her chant abruptly. She lets out a sharp cry as she collapses to the ground, her arms contorting inwards towards her body.

Confusion and fear engrave hard lines on her face. "What did you do to me?" She whimpers, finally catching her breath.

Of course.

Leave it to this bitch to be one step ahead.

"Think of it as a precaution. The spell I shared with you earlier was actually a protective one. From now on, any attempt to harm me will only backfire and cause you harm instead," Dafina explains with a smirk. "You were so eager to learn about dark magic and carry out my every request, but in the end, your actions led to your own downfall and that of your mother's."

Kora's breath comes in ragged gasps, her fingers clawing the earth as she tries to stand. Her gaze turns to Persephone, who despite her dislocated jaw, pushes herself up on trembling arms to reach out to her daughter.

"Mother," Kora whispers, tears streaming down her cheeks. "I'm—I'm sorry."

Demeter focuses solely on Persephone once more, crouching down to meet her face-to-face. She grips the jaw she had just shattered, causing Persephone to cry out in agony. Despite the intense pain she must be in, she doesn't show any signs of giving up.

"You should have taught your daughter better, Persephone," Demeter hisses, her voice a cold whisper as she tightens her grip.

"I taught her to be strong, not cruel," Persephone manages to gasp out.

Demeter's eyes narrow, the corners of her mouth twitching into a cruel, mocking smile. "Strength?" She scoffs, releasing Persephone's jaw with a shove that sends her sprawling back onto the ground. "Look where your 'strength' has landed you both. Strength without ruthlessness is just weakness waiting to be exploited."

Biting back the pain Persephone stares defiantly into Demeter's ice-cold eyes. "Try as you will, Mother; you won't break us."

"Oh, but I already have. You just don't see it yet," Dafina retorts with a contemptuous smirk as she takes a step back to admire the destruction she has caused, clearly reveling in her success.

"In the meantime," She continues. "I'm pleased to see that your ability to heal quickly still functions, because hurting you the way you did me—well, it's been a pleasant experience, and I quite looking forward to doing it again, and again. That is, until I'm ready to throw you away the way you did me. Maybe, while I'm at it I'll even snap a few of your precious little girl's fingers." Demeter taunts cruelly.

"Please. Don't." Persephone's desperate plea is only a garbled gurgle as she chokes on the blood that fills her mouth.

Demeter turns to look at the two Draugr standing behind her, then gestures towards the one on the left. "You," she commands, "Put your sword through the small one's stomach. Don't kill her—for now, at least. She still has one final task to complete for me."

With a loud crack, the creature's bones shift as it turns to face its target. It strides towards the teenager, sword in hand. A shrill croaking sound escapes from its mouth, seemingly eager to fulfill its master's bidding.

This is utter chaos.

How can someone do this to a kid?

It's unjust, cruel, and I'll be damned if I'm just going to let this happen.

"Wait!" I scream, trying to direct Dafinas' attention to me. "Hear me out."

Demeter pauses, her head tilting slightly, curiosity flickering momentarily across her features marred by rage. The Draugr halts as well, its sword still poised mid-air, a grotesque statue awaiting further instructions.

"What could you possibly say at this point that would interest me?" She snarls, her words oozing with scorn.

Okay, think Kali.

Hoping she will take the bait, I clear my throat, knowing this probably won't work out the way I intend for it to, but here we go anyways.

"I may not know much about all of this magic stuff..." I pause, taking the time to carefully think about what I'm going to say next. "But I feel like you clearly didn't think this through. Wouldn't you need her at full strength seeing how she's the only one here who can use magic?"

Demeter's expression changes subtly, a flicker of doubt crossing her otherwise resolute face. She considers the words, her gaze shifting back to Persephone, who lies crumpled and weakened on the ground. After a tense moment, she nods slightly at the Draugr, signaling it to lower its weapon. "You make a fair point," She concedes through gritted teeth.

"What's wrong, Grams? Is the old age getting to you?" I ask, poking at the shell surrounding her reserve.

She quickly scurries over to me, her clammy palm sharp as she strikes me across the face. The sting from her slap radiates through my cheek, but it feels like a small victory. Demeter's composure is cracked; she's reacting, not just commanding.

"Now listen here, you impertinent brat," Demeter hisses, her face inches from mine. "Don't for one second think that you have any kind of control here. Ignorance will not protect you, nor will insolence save you."

I taste the coppery tang of blood on my tongue, and I force a laugh, "Is that all you got?"

Striking me again, she leans in closer, her eyes blazing with a fury that could almost set the very air around us on fire. "You are playing a dangerous game," She seethes.

"Maybe," I admit, shrugging as nonchalantly as I can manage, given the circumstances. "But isn't life itself a game of risks and chances? Sometimes you have to play the wildcard, even when the deck seems stacked against you." I keep my voice steady, trying to project confidence despite the throbbing pain in my cheek.

"Mmmm. I couldn't agree more." She says, taking a step back. "Which is why since you seem to have plenty of energy to spare, I have decided that you will take her place." She adds smugly, patting the top of my head.

A chill runs down my spine, but I keep my face impassive.

The smell of her honeysuckle perfume overwhelms my personal space, suffocating me with its overpowering sweetness. Where it used to bring me comfort, now it just makes me feel nauseous.

My lip curls upward in disgust. "Phil should have let you die in those woods."

"And had he, Loki may not have found your mother at all, and I would have never been able to trade her soul for my own. How ironic is that?" She laughs. "And the best part of it all, for me, I think—after I told him where she was—has been sitting back watching you suffer as everyone you trusted, breathed endless lies into your mind." Her words feel like a stab in an already open wound.

To think that we've shared so many sweet memories together as she paraded around my childhood home, making it her playground, twisting everything I loved into something unrecognizable. It's a cruel realization that the person who taught me to see beauty in the chaos was the architect of my deepest sorrows.

But none of those memories are real, and none of them matter.

Not anymore.

She is nothing but a facade of lies I have been forced to live, and I refuse to let someone else dictate how my life goes from here on out.

I swallow hard, choking back the bile stinging the back of my throat, letting my gaze shift to Kora examining her mother's jaw, which seems to be almost entirely healed now.

A light bulb grows brightly in the dimness of my mind, and I know exactly what needs to be done. However, putting it into play is going to be tricky.

Part of me just knows this woman. She can't help but to talk, and it's exactly what I want her to do.

I let the shadows of the room envelop me, shifting my stance ever so slightly to appear as if I'm defeated, broken by her revelations. It's a ruse, of course—a ploy to draw her out, to make her feel as though she has the upper hand.

"Oh?" I say softly, my voice barely a whisper. "You think you've won, don't you?" I continue, making sure my eyes glisten slightly, as if on the brink of tears.

Her smile widens, a sadistic glee suffusing her expression. "Oh, I don't think, dear," She says, moving closer, the scent of honeysuckle intensifying as she encroaches on what little personal space I have left. "I know I've won."

My nose wrinkles at her false claim of victory as she leans in, her breath hot against my cheek. "And now, my dear, it's time for you to understand the full extent of your defeat." She signals to the Draugr and with a long, drawn-out croak it raises its blade before plunging it downward, right through my shoulder.

The pain is instant and searing, but my focus remains sharp, my ruse more necessary now than ever. I stifle the scream clawing its way up my throat and let only a shuddering gasp escape.

Blood, warm and slick, coats my arm, pooling on the floor beneath me.

"Let that be a lesson to you," She whispers cruelly, her face so close now that I can see the tiny veins in her eyes. "Compliance is your only salvation." Her laughter rings hollow in the dank room, echoing off the walls and amplifying the agony spreading from my shoulder.

Stupid bitch.

She briefly turns away to grab an old, worn wooden chair from the nearby table. As she drags it towards her, it accidentally bumps into one of the demons, causing a loud screech to echo from its skeletal mouth. My anxiety levels spike at the noise.

However, I do my best to brush away the unease, knowing that this is not the appropriate moment for my anxiety to be popping out to play peek-a-boo.

The bright rays of the setting sun seep through the small gap in the curtains, casting a harsh light in the room. It may not be much, but if I shift slightly to my left, Dafina won't be able to look directly at me without being blinded by the intense glare.

Using this to my advantage, I inch subtly to the left, grimacing as the movement sends a fresh wave of pain through my shoulder. The Draugr, still hovering by my side, doesn't seem to notice my slight repositioning.

The light flares briefly in Demeter's eyes, causing her to squint and momentarily shield her face with a slender hand.

This small window of reprieve gives me the critical second I need.

I subtly extend my leg, reaching as far as I can without drawing attention, and lightly prod Kora's side with my toes.

She snaps her head in my direction, and as she speaks, her words seem to originate from inside my own mind rather than from her mouth. "What do you want?" She hisses.

Whoa.

This is slightly cool yet weird at the same time.

I attempt to communicate through silent movements and eye gestures towards the door, hoping she will comprehend my message.

However, her sharp voice once again intrudes into my thoughts. "Just think what you want to say, and I will hear you. Our minds are connected. Jeez. Can you be any slower?"

Ugh, this girl is a savage!

"Testing. Testing." I whisper back into my own mind.

"Seriously?"

"I was just making sure. That's all. It's...different."

She rolls her eyes, "It seems being in the mortal realm for so long has turned your brain into a barely functioning organ. How adorable."

"You're a pain in my fucking ass!" I retort, gritting my teeth. "Do you know that? Like, you are literally a twat!"

"Is there a purpose behind this immense headache you are giving me?" She asks. "I have bigger things to worry about."

I press my lips together, summoning all the patience I can muster.

"Yes, there is a purpose," I respond coolly. "We need to get out of here. We're sitting ducks if we stay, and you know it. Can you still do your poof into smoke thing?"

Kora's expression shifts, the irritation melting into a calculating look. "Yes, I can still do that. But it requires a lot of energy, and given our current situation, I'm not sure it's wise to deplete my resources unless absolutely necessary. Why? What are you up to?"

I could choose to stop while I'm ahead, to not put myself in harm's way and risk another 'lesson', but then again, that's never been my style. I am determined to see this plan through until the very end.

"Okay." I commence, letting out a deep breath. "It's just a theory, but it seems that your powers are only affected when you try to harm Demeter. So maybe there's a chance that you and Persephone can still make it out of this alive."

Kora arches a brow, her face reflecting a mix of doubt and intrigue.

"We both know once you finish the spell she needs you for, she's going to kill you. I think if I can catch her by surprise, it will give you guys enough time to get out."

After a moment, Kora nods slightly. "It's risky," She murmurs, "Very risky. But I suppose it beats waiting around for Demeter to finish us off." She studies me for a moment longer, as if weighing the sincerity of my words or perhaps the likelihood of success. "Let me make sure I understand correctly; you're willing to put yourself in danger to assist someone who just kidnapped you. Does that actually seem like a logical decision to you?" Her tone is sharp, but I can tell she doesn't mean any harm by it.

I shrug, "Never said it was logical. Either we take a chance, or we sit here waiting for her to turn us into garden fertilizer. Either way, what do I have to lose at this point?"

"Fair enough."

"Alright. I need to know how she plans to kill us. Aren't we Divine blood, or Immortal, or some shit like that?" I ask. "Doesn't she need a special weapon, or magic, or something?" I ask, remembering Asmo's mention of ancient weapons.

The temporary distraction of the sun has disappeared, and Demeter's focus is now solely on me.

I can feel my face giving away my thoughts, as she stares at me with a fierce intensity that could turn stone to liquid. Her eyes narrow, as if trying to decipher a script written on my face.

Kora shifts uncomfortably, "Not necessarily." Kora's whisper fills the void in my mind. "But my grandmother possesses a dagger forged from the cursed mistletoe created by Loki himself. Legend says it has the power to impede our quick healing abilities, and if the injury is severe enough, our soul will start its journey to the afterlife. I'm almost certain it's the same weapon she used on my mother many years ago." Kora's gaze flicks to Persephone, tears instantly begin to well up in her eyes, and I can see the guilt weighing heavily on her. I know this will be an experience that stays with her forever, scarring her in ways that time might never heal.

Sniffling, she continues, "What I don't understand is how she got it back because I was not the one who retrieved it for her. She didn't share much with me about her dealings or the people she interacted with. I'm sure she only fed me just enough information to keep me in the dark while making me feel like I was part of her plans. I—I can't believe I did this to my family. I was being so stupid—no—I was being a selfish attention whore. All because I couldn't stand watching my brother getting everything handed to him—our entire family legacy, the throne—." She pauses. "I had to put in twice the effort as Asmo ever did just to gain my father's attention, but it still feels like I'm constantly overlooked. I hope one day, maybe, just maybe, he'll see that I'm just as worthy as my brother. As stupid as it sounds now, saying it to someone else, I just don't want to be the only one in my family that's forgotten."

I can see the conflict etched deep into her features, the way her eyes plead for understanding, perhaps even forgiveness. "If it helps, you're unquestionably unforgettable in my opinion." I say, shooting her a tiny smile.

Her eyes brighten slightly, a flicker of hope dancing in their depths as if my words had kindled something within her. "So, what do you need me to do?" She asks.

It's in this exact moment I gain hella respect for this girl. Turns out, she's not all that different from me—always trying to live up to everyone else's expectations, yet, never quite feeling good enough for anyone or anything.

It's that itch that always seems to be present under our skin. Because we know we are meant for something more, but we're only known for our broken-ness.

We are the black sheep—the misfits that never quite fit in.

I glance around the room, looking for all possible exits. If this plan succeeds, perhaps I can find a way out as well.

I have to find out if my family survived and if they are safe. However, as much as I want to deny it, deep down, I have a sinking feeling that I'm not making it back to them.

Demeter's attention is on the hellhound trying to gnaw on one of the Draugr's legs across the room, oblivious to our mind whispered strategizing.

I take a deep breath and steel my mind for the inevitable fight that awaits me.

Not that it's helping much.

Persephone catches my gaze, and I can tell that Kora must have already explained the plan to her. She nods in confirmation, silently conveying her thanks to me.

After mine and Persephone's brief moment of understanding, I delve back into Kora's thoughts. "I need you to leave and make sure my family is safe, alright? I'll take care of everything else. If there's one thing I'm good at, it's pissing people off and causing trouble. Demeter won't expect me to retaliate, especially since she knows my tendency to freeze under pressure, so catching her off guard shouldn't be too hard. I just hope that the spell won't stop you guys from leaving here once I have her attention."

"What about you?" Kora's soft childlike voice asks, full of worry.

"I think we both know how this is going to end for me." I reply, not wanting to think too deeply about it right now and fall down the rabbit hole of fear and despair.

Fear holds my stomach tightly in its vice-like grip, squeezing until it aches.

I know this was what I have to do, but that doesn't mean I want to die at the ripe old age of twenty-one.

Demeter rocks back and forth in the old chair, squinting her beady eyes in my direction, and goosebumps make their way up my exposed flesh, thickening the air with anticipation.

Hoping Kora will still be able to hear my thoughts, I reach out to her once more, "Get ready. It's about to become a shit-fest in here."

"We're as ready as we can be." She confirms.

Fuck me.

Well, here goes nothing.

Chapter Twenty-Two

Kali

Three. Two.

The countdown begins in my head and the room appears to spin, swirling all around me.

One.

I let out a long, held breath in a quick whoosh of air as I forcefully kick both of my feet into the leg of the feeble chair that Demeter is sitting on. The chair topples with an unexpected grace, crashing to the floor with a sound that seems far too loud in the silent room.

Demeter lands with a thud, her eyes wide with shock and confusion. For a moment, she can't seem to process what has happened; her mouth opens and closes, fish-like.

The creatures flanking her shuffle about, their heavy armor clanking as they struggle to find their footing, unsure of their next move. Their bones creak and crack under the weight, adding to the chaos of the moment.

Deprived of Demeter's sharpness, guidance, and commands, they are but benighted souls.

Their ear-shattering screams stab into my core like the fiery blades they wield with their bony, skeletal fingers. The Hellhound, on the other hand, moves with swift dexterity, nearly snapping its lethal jaws around Kora's ankle just as she and Persephone disappear in a swirl of pale blue mist.

Yes!

They made it out.

Demeter springs to life rapidly, catching herself like the fucking Black Widow from all those Marvel movies I watch. In an instant, she's on her feet and pressing a cold, sharp metal blade to my jugular.

I want to squeal with joy as my companions successfully depart, but the dagger pressed against my throat stops me in my tracks.

Demeter flashes a saccharine smile, slipping into the same false persona she's worn since I was a child. "This dagger," She says, gesturing to the weapon in her hand, "Is one of your grandfather's greatest regrets. If he hadn't stabbed it through your father's heart, then your father would have never met your mother. And without that chance encounter, a bastard like you wouldn't even exist, let alone become the lowlife scum that stands before me today. All you know how to do is whine. The oh poor me—all the damn time. You disgust me! I've wasted this minuscule mortal life taking care you, pretending to care about you—" She presses the blade harder against my throat. "Ohhh," She sighs dramatically, "I know, Lucius wants you alive. And yes, I'm supposed to deliver you to him, but I think I might have an even better solution." She purrs, flicking a piece of dried blood off my shoulder.

"So, you're one of his minions?" I can't help but ask, disgusted by the idea that someone like Lucius, who has lived for centuries, would want someone as young as me to be his bride.

Gross.

It's something I just don't understand, nor do I want the chance to find out about it.

"Minion? Oh, my dear, you still understand so little. It's not about being a minion; it's about playing the long game—something that is beyond the grasp of your small and narrow-minded thinking. Aligning myself with Lucius is merely a tactic. He has resources and power that most other gods have trouble contending with. He wants you as his bri—"

"I'd rather just die." I interrupt, my words oozing with sarcasm.

"Funny you should mention that." She sneers, twisting the blade slightly, just enough to make me wince. "Because I was just thinking the same thing."

I swallow hard, the edge of the blade biting slightly into my skin.

She moves.

I move with her.

The dance of desperation begins.

Quickly, I try to calculate the distance to the nearest window—about three long strides.

If I can just maneuver around her quickly enough, maybe, just maybe, I can make a leap for it. The idea is ludicrous, but desperation breeds the best kind of madness.

Without waiting for further provocation, I tense my muscles and push off against the ground. Demeter, expecting a struggle or plea, is momentarily taken aback as I bolt towards the window. Her surprise gives me the precious seconds I need to gain momentum.

As I make my dash, she recovers and lunges after me, her blade slicing through the air with lethal precision. But I'm faster, fueled by fear and the adrenaline that screams through my veins. I manage to dodge the tip of her blade and crash shoulder-first into the glass.

The window shatters with a cacophony that pierces the night air, sending shards flying like silver rain. The brisk air hit my face and for a brief moment, I feel free—until gravity asserts itself, pulling me downward. My arms are still bound behind my back, making it impossible to find a handhold or break my fall in any way. The ground rushes up to meet me, and I brace for impact, my body tensed and ready for pain.

But the fall is broken abruptly as I feel the grip on bony skeletal fingers wrap around my ankle, halting my descent with a jolt that rattles through my entire body.

I dangle precariously, suspended in mid-air. My heart hammers in my chest as I twist my neck to look up.

The Draugr's hollow eye sockets are locked on me as it hisses, "Going somewhere?" Its voice is a raspy whisper, like the sound of dry leaves dragged across cobblestones.

It pulls me up with unsettling strength, back towards the gaping window frame now jagged with glass teeth. My breath catches in my throat as I'm hoisted over the sill and dropped unceremoniously onto the hard floor inside the hotel room.

Demeter stands over me, her expression a mix of fury and grudging admiration. She wipes the blade on her coat, eyes never leaving mine. "Impressive," She says, kicking away the chair that lay overturned from our scuffle.

In the corner the hellhound growls viciously, its jaws snapping together in anticipation, its eyes two embers glowing in the dim light.

"But ultimately futile," Demeter continues, her tone dripping with condescension as she circles me, her footsteps silent on the carpet.

She pauses, tilting her head as if pondering her next move. "Did you really think you could escape from me so easily? No matter how fast you run, how desperately you leap, you cannot escape your fate—your death." She grins, stopping in her tracks.

She wouldn't kill me, would she?

I highly doubt Lucius would allow it, especially since he believes I have the power to lift his curse.

"I actually thought I had it there for a second, yes. And had it not been for these." I jerk my wrists toward the ropes binding them, indicating my helplessness. "I might've made it, too."

"Your humor is something I'm not going to miss."

"Awww, and just when I thought we were really starting to bond," I retort with mock sadness. "Too bad your boss has different plans for me, huh?"

Demeter's eyebrow twitches, the only sign that my words might have pricked some semblance of irritation in her otherwise stony demeanor. She leans down, her face inches from mine, the thin edge of her blade now tracing a slow, menacing path along my jawline.

"I think I've had just about enough of you." She snarls, and with a smooth jerk of her hand she carves her blade deep into my neck, slicing straight through my skin and thick muscle fibers behind it. "And it just so happens," She continues. "That I do not in fact, work for that bastard."

Instinctively I raise my hand to my neck, and I can feel the warm blood oozing out, my fingertips becoming coated in the crimson liquid as I try to stop the bleeding.

I did *not* see that one coming.

My throat feels as though it is on fire, and I am struggling to breathe. I feel like I am drowning, sinking deeper and deeper into the cold, black depths of the ocean. I'm completely paralyzed with fear, unable to swallow or even breathe. She can see the terror in my widened eyes, and she seems to relish it.

"Da—Dafina—" I manage to strangle out before my voice cuts off, swallowed by the gurgling blood.

Her face contorts into one of pure evil, and I swear I can see the demon that's possessing her human flesh suit, peeking through with it's dark ugly face—the monster inside of what once was an innocent teenage girl. "Try not to choke, dear." She laughs, wiping the blade of the dagger on her shirt.

Don't get me wrong we all have our own inner demons, but this is taking it to a whole other level.

My legs give out, and I collapse onto the ground. I struggle to cough up the blood filling my lungs, but it's no use; they still starve, deprived, and desperate for oxygen.

I never realized how much I feared dying alone until this moment.

Funny how that works.

I would give anything to see my family one last time—hell—I'd even settle for hearing Kora's bratty little voice inside my head again.

But there's no time for regrets; survival clings to me like a stubborn shadow I can't shake. I hear Demeter pacing around me, her steps deliberate and mocking.

Suddenly, as if she had been eavesdropping inside my cranium, Kora's voice fills my thoughts with a mischievous tone. "So, I'm a brat, am I? Now, that's no way to talk about the person coming to save you."

"Kora?!" I scream silently in my mind.

"Azzy and I will be there soon! We made it back to your family—they're doing ok for the most part."

"Stop!" I scream. "Please don't come after me. It's too late to save me now. I'm beyond help, and I have no idea what she has in store next. She's not working with Lucius as we originally thought, and since he has my father, it's impossible for me to be healed like your mother was."

"Oh, Kali..." Kora whispers. "Sh—she didn't."

As the tears start to roll down my cheeks, I realize I can't hold them back any longer. "Please let my family know that I love them and that I'm sorry," I whisper. "I'm grateful for getting to meet your family as well, even though you technically abducted me" I try to lighten the mood with a joke, hoping she'll understand that I don't blame her for what happened.

"I wish I could fix this." She mutters.

"Don't be too hard on yourself, kid. We're both just caught in the crossfire of this war. And who knows, maybe this prophecy thing won't come true after all with me dead. Maybe that was my purpose all along."

Man.

I've had some real shit luck in my short life. But...I've also had an amazing little life.

Phil, Melonie, my sisters—they made living with shitty luck, worth every moment of it. They were always there to lift me back up, and made me feel loved and cherished, no matter how dark the days got.

Accepting death isn't easy, but knowing that those moments of joy were real? That they'll live on in their hearts, maybe even grow into something more beautiful in their memories—that brings a special kind of peace.

And no one can take that away.

"Kali, listen to me," Kora's voice takes on a firmer tone, snapping me back to the grim reality of my situation. "You're not just going to lie down and let this be the end. We're not giving up on you, okay? I won't let you say goodbye like this. Azzy and I, we're close now. Just hold on a little longer."

A strained male voice cuts through my thoughts, and I feel a surge of warmth in my chest. "What happened to all the fight you had in you?" He taunts. "Just when I thought you were standing up for yourself, now you're giving in?" His voice is filled with raw emotion., "Please, petite flamme, stay with me, okay?"

I've lost a dangerous amount of blood, and it's a miracle that I'm still even somewhat conscious. "Is that French?" I ask, my words coming out slurred.

I can feel myself slipping away, but I fight to stay present as his voice fills my mind once again. "Yes, it is. Maybe I'll teach you someday when we're out of this mess," He responds smoothly.

The unexpected warmth in his voice, despite the dire circumstances, brings a feeble smile to my lips. My vision blurs and the edges of my consciousness begin to fray, but I cling to his words like a lifeline.

I muster what strength I have left to whisper, "I'd like that."

The room becomes enveloped with blue smoke.

Shit.

They're here.

Both excitement and fear flood through me.

They shouldn't have come for me.

What if she kills them too?

The blue smoke thickens, swirling around the room like a living thing, tendrils reaching out as if searching for someone or something. I cough, the acrid taste filling my mouth, and force my eyes to stay open despite the burn.

"Please! You must leave!" I plead to them inside my head.

"No way!" Kora chimes in. "Selene helped us break the spell protecting her. This bitch is going down!"

"Agreed, but we need to be smart about it," Asmo adds.

The wispy remnants of magic dissipate, revealing Asmo and Kora standing back-to-back in the center of the room. "And once we bring you back to your home," Asmo's focus shifts to me, "You will not leave my sight. Is that clear?"

My nod is weak, barely perceptible, but it's all I can manage under the weight of my fading strength. Asmo looks at me with determined eyes, a fierce protector ready to battle the world.

His eyes darken when he drinks in the bloody sight of me on the floor in front of him.

Rage and raw power radiate from him, his muscles quiver with anticipation.

He looks so primal.

So deadly.

Bound and helpless, lying in a swamp of my own life juice—dying, and I am on the brink of death, yet I cannot resist being drawn towards him. Despite still appearing rough and unkempt from the events of the past few days and clearly not having slept, he remains irresistibly attractive in my eyes.

What is wrong with me?

A lot of things. Obviously.

"You have plagued my family for too long, Demeter." He bellows, his beautiful waves of dark hair abruptly igniting with a cascade of sapphire flames above his head.

He's a fucking beast!

"Go ahead and kill this body." Demeter scoffs, challenging him from her position across the room. "You know my essence will simply find another vessel, and the cycle will continue—you don't have the power contain me."

Asmo smiles, his eyes barely slits, "Oh, but don't I? He looks over at her and pulls out an onyx-colored stone from his pocket. "Charon owed me a small favor."

The stone instantly begins to glow, emitting a soft ambiance of light around him, and for the very first time in all of this craziness, Dafina is the one that's frightened.

Demeter's face twists in fear as the glowing stone in Asmo's hand brightens, its light pulsing like a heartbeat.

"If you truly knew so much about us," Asmo continues. "Then you should have already known that I don't take kindly to those taking or hurting what's mine." He takes a step closer to her, keeping his voice low, "And yet, you've managed to make the mistake of doing both. Time to pay the Reaper."

CHAPTER TWENTY-THREE

Kali

"Kill them." Demeter demands to the hellhound and two Draugr that have been patiently waiting for their orders.

The dog-like creature snarls at Kora, remembering she had bested him earlier in her escape. It lunges towards her, but Asmo is quick enough to notice and he blasts the motherfucker in its flank before it reaches her.

The dog lets out a pained yelp as the bright light hits him, throwing him forcefully into the bathroom door of the cramped hotel room. The two Draugr warriors stride towards Asmo, their swords raised high above their skulls and swinging wildly through the air. Asmo effortlessly dodges each attack, showcasing his expertise as a seasoned soldier.

He and Kora dance in small circles, their backs always touching so they can anticipate any enemy attacks. It's clear they've both undergone rigorous training, given the way they move as a cohesive unit.

Dafina, sensing the urgency of the situation, seizes me by the hair and pulls me through the blasts of magic firebombs engulfing the room.

The piercing screeches and shrieks of the emaciated beings echo around us.

Kora extends her hand and summons a dazzling fiery blue sword into existence. Faint strands of light blue electricity trace along the length of the blade and up her arm.

It's a breathtaking display.

She swings the sword with determination, slicing through one of the Draugr's armor like it was nothing and beheading it effortlessly. The lifeless corpse crumbles to dust and is carried away by the chilling winds of the night through the window I had broken through in my dreadful attempt to escape.

Asmo, noticing the remaining Draugr lunging toward him, pivots on his heel and catches the creature by the wrist. With a swift, calculated motion, he twists and uses the Draugr's momentum against it, flinging it across the room. It crashes into the remnants of a shattered dresser; wooden splinters fly into the air like deadly confetti. The Draugr struggles to rise, its limbs awkwardly tangled in its own armor, but Asmo is already upon it, his eyes ablaze with the fire of battle.

He delivers a crushing blow to the Draugr's chest, his strength penetrating straight through the creature's armor, causing a cacophony of cracking bones that reverberates throughout the confined space. The Draugr's cry of agony is sharp and ear-piercing, a sound that could curdle blood.

Then, the chest of the Draugr explodes as Asmo blasts a fireball directly into the hollow of its dark, decaying ribcage. Flames envelop the creature, consuming it in a fiery inferno that lights up the entire room with a harsh, lapis glow. As the light dissipates, the second Draugr's remains scatter across the floor, settling in a heap of ash and broken armor.

My lungs are on the brink of bursting, and my head feels like it's about to follow suit.

I can't hold on much longer; death is whispering in my ear, it's voice like silken smoke promising an end that seems both terrifying and sweet.

The dizziness consumes me, and the chaos becomes a blur of vibrant hues and deafening noises. Demeter pulls me through the doorway, causing my head to bang against the pavement when she loses her grip on my hair.

The impact sends a sharp pain through my skull. Stars explode behind my eyes, each one a tiny pinprick against the vast canvas of darkness that threatens to swallow me whole.

I try to focus, to claw back from the dark edges encroaching on my consciousness, but it's a tremendous effort.

Demeter utters a string of curses under her breath as she frantically reaches for one of my legs. With all her might, she pulls me off the sidewalk and towards the car that Phil gave her as a present, parked in the lot nearby.

The chilly air causes a sharp pain in my freshly cut scalp and adds to the dull ache in the wound on my neck.

Shit.

She's trying to escape and there is nothing I can do to stop her.

I look helplessly back at Asmo, wishing I could scream out, or somehow let him know I needed his help.

Thank the gods for car alarms.

Demeter's struggle with the locked doors causes the alarm to blare, drawing the attention of Asmo. He charges after us at full speed, his hair wild and his face contorted with rage as he gains ground.

Pure hatred fuels his pursuit.

As he moves closer, his once benign features contort and darken, taking on a sinister appearance. Dark blue flames burst from his skull, dripping out of his empty eye sockets. His nails elongate into sharp claws, now a deep shade of black.

Holy. Hades' son.

"Demeter!" His voice booms, across the vacant lot. "It's time we end this charade." He opens his right hand, exposing the glowing black stone once more.

Demeter freezes, her hand still on the car door handle, and turns slowly to face Asmo. Her eyes are wide with fear and recognition of the power Asmo wields in his grasp.

Watching her fear and knowing that she will ultimately fail brings me a sense of satisfaction. Don't get me wrong, I don't know the full capabilities of this stone; all I know is that it can't be positive if it elicits such terror from her.

And that's enough for me.

Asmo inches closer, digging his claws into the car's hood. "Lucius already knows of your treachery, Demeter. I can only imagine what horrors await your soul in Tartarus when it reaches him." A sneer curls his lips, the deep demonic sound resonating from his throat is jarring to my ears, but I can't say I hate it.

Demeter backs away slowly, her eyes darting between the stone in Asmo's hand and the road, seeming to search for any possible escape route. "We can work this is out, hmm?" She pleads to him, her head bowing in submission. "I can help you save the girl."

What a load of shit.

We both know she can't save me.

No one can.

Not now.

I'm caught in the limbo between life and death. One moment, I catch a glimpse of Charon and his ancient vessel, the next I am struggling to keep my eyes open: struggling to survive.

The stone in Asmo's palm glows brighter with each antagonizing step he takes towards her, and he laughs, the sound thunderous in the air around us. His claws scrape metallically against the hood of the car as he paces closer, cornering Demeter against the vehicle.

The tight hold that Demeter has on my hair finally loosens, and I collapse onto the ground. She scrambles over me in a frenzy, her feet treading clumsily as she tries to escape from Asmo and the stone, pure fear etched into every line of her face. "Please, don't send me back! I—I can help you!" She cries out, backing away from him.

But her pleas fall on deaf ears. Asmo's face remains impassive, "Help? You think you can offer help now?" His voice drips with scorn as he grabs her by the wrist, a devilish grin gracing his lips.

He drags her closer, his grip unyielding.

"It's too late, Demeter. You had your opportunity." In an instant, he lets go of her wrist and forcefully thrusts his claws into her chest, piercing deep into her sternum.

His intense glare flickers in the reflection of her eyes. He relishes in her fear, watching as she struggles against his hold. I'm sure he's taking *some* pleasure in the pain he's causing her.

Blood blossoms from the wound as Demeter gasps, her body convulsing with shock. Dark energy pulsates from the stone, wrapping around her like a diabolical embrace.

"Have a nice trip to hell, Demeter. Oh, and do tell Lucius that I'm coming for him next." Asmo's voice echoes hauntingly as he utters the final words.

Her body stiffens and with a twist of his wrist, he heaves back, forcibly tearing her heart from her chest, leaving behind a gaping void that I can see straight through.

Demeter's cries fade into a gurgle, her legs buckle, and she collapses onto the hard asphalt.

However, a demon then rises from her corpse, looking way more terrifying, than the old lady flesh suit it just shed.

The shadow creature hovers menacingly over Dafina's lifeless body. Its form is indistinguishable, with horn-like spikes jutting out from its head. A glowing orange light emanates from the empty sockets where its eyes should be. The creature lets out a loud screech, clearly angered by the effects of the stone. I can only hope that it is experiencing some sort of pain or discomfort—well deserved in my opinion.

Shadowy hands jut out, clutching its head, and it twitches and flails around aimlessly, the agony seemingly too much for it to bare.

Then, in a quick sudden movement, the demonized Demeter rushes toward Asmo, dissolving into his hardened frame, possessing him just as it has Dafina for so many years.

But how did it end up being able to merge with him? I thought only those with mortal blood could be possessed by Ruhans?

No. This isn't right—it can't be.

Asmo's body jerks violently as the demon merges with him, his eyes rolling back to reveal a sickening shade of black. His mouth opens in a silent scream, the veins on his neck bulging grotesquely as he battles internally for control of his own form.

I refuse to let this demon claim another victim.

I can't and I won't.

I am aware of a new kind of energy stirring within me, like small wisps of clouds gently fluttering across my fingertips, just out of reach. I can sense its buzzing presence, so I dig deeper into my mind to try and grasp onto the potential power.

This magic is different from anything I've experienced before. It doesn't carry the weight of anger and hate that has consumed me for so long. Instead, it's fueled by my sheer tenacity to survive, the need to save Asmo from this demon, and the determination I have to get my parents back from the deadly grip of Lucius.

A feeling of warmth washes over me, followed by a sudden surge of energy that radiates through my body. A mysterious mist pours out of my fingertips, swirling through the air and enveloping Asmo in its white embrace, seeping into his tanned skin

The Ruhan leaves his body with a hiss, my magic like acid to its dark murky form. Asmo collapses to the ground, gasping for breath, the color slowly returning to his face.

The stone that Asmo had dropped onto the blacktop rises up and spins wildly, seemingly suspended in mid-air. The clouds in the sky grow darker and start to swirl against the gusty wind, picking up small particles of dust from the ground and forming a mini tornado.

At first, it's just a small gust of wind, but then it starts to gain momentum. The wind swirls around the frenzied demon, picking up speed until a cyclone is swirling directly above us.

Without hesitation, Asmo jumps on top of me, using his body to shield me from the strong winds and debris flying around us. "I've got you," He murmurs into my ear.

The cyclone rages louder, its howl almost deafening. I can feel Asmo's heartbeat against me, rapid and unsteady. Above us, the Ruhan screams in fury, trapped within the swirling vortex of wind and magic. The demon scratches at the air, trying to claw its way out of its invisible cage.

As the gusts grow stronger, they mercilessly pull and tear at our clothes and hair. The demon puts up a valiant fight, but the twister effortlessly swallows it whole, leaving behind nothing but emptiness. When the winds finally calm and the stone comes to a halt, there is a deafening crack as it shatters into countless pieces that scatter across the deserted parking lot.

Asmo gradually removes himself from on top of me, his attention drawn to the blood seeping from my body onto the pavement. His gaze has returned to its usual silky chocolate color, and his sharp claws have withdrawn, revealing his human hands once again.

The arrogant god that would kneel for no one, is on his knees beside me, taking me into his arms, sheathing me in the warmth of his embrace. *How becoming of him.*

His warmth helps ease the gnawing wintry frost of coldness that dulls my meek senses as he touches his forehead to mine. "Little flame?" He whispers, anguish resting in his tone as the pet name slips past his perfect lips.

His voice is the only thing anchoring me to this world, like a thread connecting my soul to the realm of the living. I can't utter any words, so instead, a small smile twitches on my face to show him that I'm still alive and present—at least for now.

Asmo's tears fall onto my cheeks, mingling with the dirt and blood that has smeared my face. He cradles me tighter, as if his arms could somehow heal the wounds that mark my body and spirit.

He leans in and gently kisses my forehead, his breathing ragged as he struggles to hold back his tears. "Stay with me," He pleads softly, the desperation seeping through his voice. "You—you're stronger than this. You're the daughter of the Goddess of Death—a warrior. You *can't* give up this easily."

Okay, dude...*nothing* about any of this has been easy; I for one, would know.

A sharp wheezing sound escapes my lips, despite the pain that lances through my chest with the movement. It's a laugh tinged with bitterness, born from the irony of his words. A goddess's daughter, yes, but even goddesses can bleed; even warriors can feel fear.

And right now, I'm fucking scared. And I don't know if I'm afraid of death or the fact that I will never seeing my family again.

The coolness of the evening air brushes against my skin, a subtle reminder of the world continuing around us, oblivious to the turmoil confined within this crumbling parking lot. Asmo's eyes search mine, looking for a sign, any sign that his plea has reached the depths where my spirit flickers feebly.

"You *can't* leave, do you understand?" He speaks softly, his words more of a mumble. "You have to fight; you have to hold on. The world needs you...I—I need you."

What a weird thing to say.

He doesn't even know me.

His hand quivers as he traces his thumb lightly over my cheek. It feels almost normal—this tender gesture, but the circumstances render it heartbreakingly poignant.

Admittedly, it's quite nice to see this side of him, compared to the asshole of a man I'd first met.

"Kali, I swear on everything I believe in, if you can fight through this, I'll make sure you're never alone again. I'll stay by your side. You won't have to fight any battle alone, ever again," Asmo promises, his voice breaking as he tries to swallow his grief.

The offer is sweet, or maybe it's the delirium talking, but it warms something in me that I thought was long frozen. I manage another wheezy chuckle, feeling the edges of my vision blur, a sign that either I'm fading or maybe just finally letting go of some of the pain that has been my constant companion.

My fingers twitch, grasping weakly at Asmo's hand as I try to thank him.

He attempts to cauterize the gash in my neck with a torch lit fingertip. The scent of singed flesh meets my nose, making my stomach roll with disgust.

However, the pain is surprisingly dull, a distant throb compared to the agony I had braced myself for. Asmo's face is a mask of concentration, his brows knit together in focus. Despite the gruesome nature of the makeshift treatment, his care is precise, almost tender.

Part of me wants to scream at him for making me feel sick, but another part is grateful that he's here, alive and not under the control of a crazed demon lady thing.

There is still a faint flicker of power within me, almost imperceptible. But I believe I can tap into it. With a mental effort, I grasp onto the small glimmer of hope and try to draw it towards me.

Yes!

I think I got it!

The power courses through my veins like liquid fire, the sensation stark against the creeping numbness. I squeeze Asmo's hand tighter, my fingers gaining strength as the energy bolsters my weakening body.

Suddenly, a white glow oozes from the gash on my neck, and I feel a slight stinging sensation as my injury begins to heal itself from within.

Asmo notices the change immediately. His eyes widen in astonishment "You're healing," He whispers, more to himself than to me.

As the power continues to fill me, the blur at the edges of my vision sharpens, and I take a deep breath—the first full breath in what feels like eternity.

I gulp down as much of the fresh night air as I can, my lungs rejoicing in the sudden infusion of oxygen. Exhaustion overtakes me, and I'm still quite hazy from losing pints of my life juice.

I have no explanation for how I managed to survive, but for now, I am grateful to be safe in the embrace of someone familiar.

"Can you take me home now?" I murmur, peeping up at him through my lashes.

Dark eyes glimmer beneath a cascade of tears as he beams down at me, confusion and awe pervade his face.

Clearing his throat, his deep somber laugh vibrates against my ribcage. "Of course."

He scoops me up effortlessly, as if I weigh nothing more than a leaf caught in a breeze. My head rests against his chest, the steady beat of his heart a soothing rhythm amidst the chaos of the night.

A sharp whistle pierces the air, and Kora appears from the old motel room, her body coated in ash and blood. The fiery blue sword is still ablaze on her left arm, and she holds the scruff of a decapitated Hellhound in her right hand as she runs towards me.

When she makes it over to us she gives us an ear-to-ear grin. "Oh my god, you're still kicking! Damn girl, you've got to be one of the baddest bitches I know!" She gushes, allowing her sword-hand to vanish.

"Can you get us out of here?" Asmo asks, his voice tinged with urgency as he shifts me slightly to make sure I'm secure in his arms.

Kora nods, her grin never fading even as she surveys the chaotic scene around us. "Yeah, let's blow this popsicle stand," She says with a wink.

"You guys ready?" Kora asks.

Asmo looks down at me and I nod.

"Let's get you home then." And with a tiny flick of her wrist, she sends my stomach reeling one more time as we're being siphoned through time and space.

My nails dig deeply into Asmo's arm, holding on for dear life as the world blurs into a dizzying mix of colors and sensations as Kora teleports us. The motion ceases as abruptly as it began, leaving me dazed and disoriented, but unmistakably on solid ground.

I don't think I'll ever get use to traveling that way because it makes me want to hurl, but regardless, I'm really grateful to be back home.

I'm not, however, ready to be bombarded by my family's overwhelming love and concern just yet.

Kora, seeming to sense this, kindly offers to inform our families about the success of her and her brother's mission, as well as my survival.

I happily oblige.

In return, I am left alone with Asmo, who is holding me in his arms like a fragile bird with a broken wing. He hasn't let me go or sat me down yet, and from the way he looks at me...it seems like he has no intention of doing so.

Chapter Twenty-Four

Kali

A re—are you okay?" Asmo whispers.

"I am. Are you going to let me down now?" I question back softly.

Asmo hesitates for a moment, his eyes scanning my face as if searching for something unspoken between the lines. A soft chuckle escapes his lips, breaking the intensity of the moment. "Yes, I guess it is time to put you back on solid ground."

My bed is only a few feet away, but the distance feels like miles as he finally sets me down gently. My legs, however, don't seem ready to uphold the sudden burden of my body's weight. They wobble precariously, prompting Asmo to quickly steady me with his hands on my shoulders.

"Easy there," Asmo murmurs, his voice low and surprisingly gentle. "Take your time. You've been through a lot today."

"Sorry," I say, embarrassment heating my cheeks. "Still a bit shaky, it seems."

"No need to apologize. I'd say you're doing pretty good, all things considered. You lost a lot of blood."

I lower myself down on my black satin sheets and let the cool fabric soothe my overheated skin. Asmo remains by my side, seemingly unsure whether to stay or give me space.

After a moment of silent contemplation, he pulls a chair close to the bed and sits down, his posture relaxed yet somehow still on edge. "Do you need anything? Water, food, more blankets, a painkiller?" His eyes dart around the room, trying to anticipate my needs before I even voice them.

"No, I'm fine for now. Thank you," I manage to say, although the dryness in my throat makes me regret not asking for water. "I just need to rest for a bit, I think."

I look down at my mangled clothes.

My party dress, once a vibrant red, now hangs in shreds on my body, marked with splatters of blood and dirt.

"I'm disgusting." I lament, holding my nose between my fingers.

"I agree, you are certainly not the epitome of cleanliness, but it's not entirely your fault," Asmo comments from beside my bed.

Fuck.

I'd almost forgotten he was there.

"You know what? You're not much better," I shoot back, turning over onto my side so that my back is now facing him.

"Of that, I'm sure of as well." He laughs.

I can't help but let a small smile tug at the corners of my mouth despite the soreness that throbs through every inch of my body.

His footsteps are light as he crosses the room, and I hear the faint sound of water running. Moments later, he returns with a damp cloth and a glass of water, setting both on the nightstand next to me. "Here," He says lightly, offering the glass to me.

I take it gratefully, my fingers brushing against his as I do. The water is refreshing, cold and soothing as it slides down my parched throat. I drink greedily, realizing only when I lower the glass how desperately thirsty, I had been.

Asmo watches me with those curious eyes that never seem to miss a detail. "Better?" He asks as he offers me the wet cloth next.

"Much."

I take the cloth from him, grateful for the coolness against my skin as I gently dab at the dried blood on my face and arms. The sensation is soothing, almost cathartic, after everything that's happened the past few days.

Asmo does not move to leave; instead, he lingers, his presence a silent comfort that I didn't realize I needed until now.

"Should I get someone? Melonie or—?

"No." I shake my head. "Not yet. I just need...I don't know. A moment, maybe?" My voice cracks a bit at the end, and I'm suddenly aware of how vulnerable I sound.

It's not something I'm used to—vulnerability.

But here in the dim light of this room, with my guard down and my defenses shattered, it feels almost inevitable.

He nods, understanding—or at least pretending to understand—my need for solitude wrapped in his silent company. He sits back in the chair next to my bed, his fingers tapping a silent beat on his knee.

We don't speak, yet the silence between us is filled with unspoken words, a mutual understanding that sometimes silence is more comforting than any attempt at conversation.

Asmo's tapping ceases, and he leans in, placing his elbows on his knees before picking up the photograph of my mother and me from my nightstand. "It's odd to see her living like a mortal," He remarks.

His words pull me back from the edges of my own scattered thoughts.

I glance at the image he's holding—a photograph taken years ago, one of the few reminders I have of a life before madness took the reins. "It's strange how the only memories I have of her are complete lies." I huff.

The frame makes a clinking noise as he sits it back down, turning his attention back to me. "Lies have a way of shaping our reality more than truths. Do you think knowing the whole truth earlier would have changed anything?"

I ponder his question, tracing the line of blood still faintly visible on my forearm.

"Maybe," I say with a sigh. "Maybe I would have been prepared. Maybe I would be less...broken. Or maybe I would have just broken earlier." I let out a bitter laugh, the sound hollow in the quiet room.

Asmo doesn't smile, but his eyes soften—a slight change that speaks volumes. "You're not broken, you know. Bent, perhaps. But not broken."

Broken, bent—it feels the same in this moment.

I look away from him, focusing on the shadows dancing across the wall on the opposite side of the room as the flicker of the light plays tricks with the darkness.

"I know things are complicated right now," Asmo continues, "But there's strength in you yet, the kind that endures. Maybe it's not about being unbroken or even unbent, but about how you rise despite it all. You have a fearlessness about you, even if it feels buried under the rubble of your struggles and your past. You showed that when you saved my sister and my mother." His words, like a gentle brush of wind, attempt to untangle the knots of doubt within me

"I don't know if I'd call that fearlessness. More like pure luck." I yawn, flipping over and propping my elbow beneath me.

"Luck then, if you insist. But even luck favors the brave, and not everyone would have done what you did." He replies, sweeping his hand through his unkempt hair.

"You give me too much credit," I argue. "It was a split-second decision, nothing more."

His mouth twitches with amusement and I can hear him quietly mutter, *"Stubborn ass woman."*

If this washcloth wasn't covered in my blood and grossness, I would smack him with it.

"Uh, is there anything I can get you before I head downstairs?" He asks. "You should really get some rest."

I wave him off. "I'll be fine. Well, I might need more water soon. And maybe...maybe just don't leave yet."

He pauses at the door, his silhouette framed against the dim hallway light, turning back to look at me. "You want me to stay?" He questions.

I nod, suddenly feeling the weight of the room's silence crushing me. "Yeah, just—just until I fall asleep. Please? I don't want to be alone right now."

Hundreds of thoughts spin thick webs through my head.

Did I really just say that?

What if he thinks I'm a total freak?

What in the hell was I thinking?

The ominous silence bleeds through the air, and I quietly choke on the embarrassment flowing a heated color to both my cheeks.

He doesn't need another word.

Closing the door softly behind him, Asmo returns to the chair beside my bed, easing himself down into it with a quiet sigh. "If that is your aspiration, ma petite flamme." He replies. "I will give you anything you could ever desire—bend at your every command—break your every fall." His voice deepens, sending little tingles down my thighs.

He's going to be the fucking death of me.

"Come on, enough with the formalities. It's easy, right? Just stay until you hear me snoring," I groggily retort, feeling the weight of exhaustion pulling at my eyelids even in the daft light.

He quickly brings his hand up to salute me and responds, "Yes, ma'am!" A smirk flits across his face, and laughter sneaks past him.

Out of all his characteristics, it's his laugh that I adore the most. It's not something you would expect from someone as stoic as he is. It's light and airy, adding a touch of magic to any room he enters.

His eyes grow heavy right along with mine. I'm sure he's exhausted too.

"You can get some rest in here if you want." I offer. "This is a king, so there's plenty of room. But if you try any funny business, I swear I'm punching you in the dick and kicking you out of here so fast you won't even have time to blink."

He raises his eyebrows, amused by the challenge. "I'll behave," He promises. "But do you always offer a threat along with your invitations?"

"Only to those who might need it," I quip, feeling a bit more at ease now that the momentary tension has passed.

"Duly noted."

He walks to the other side of the bed and takes off his black leather dress shoes, sliding them under the far corner of the bed with one foot. His brooding presence brings me a sense of security, calming my anxiety.

It's hard to explain, but I feel an inexplicable comfort when he's close, like a warm cup of milk and honey on a dark, stormy night.

The bed creaks beneath his weight when he slides himself in next to me. "Is this what you had in mind?"

I give him a thumbs up.

"Yep! All good!" My voice cracks, making me sound like a pubescent boy.

"Just make sure you keep to your side, okay?" I try to maintain a stern tone, but the exhaustion makes it waver.

His chuckle rumbles softly in the dark room. "I'll build a wall if I have to," He jokes, and I can hear the rustle of sheets as he settles in, forming a makeshift barrier between us with the extra pillows.

"Good," I mumble, my words slurring slightly as sleep begins to claim me. "No crossing the pillow fort. Or I—Or I'll have to enforce the consequences." Sleep slurs my warning.

"I wouldn't dare."

Unseen, I smile into the pillow. My heart is racing, feeling as if it may burst out of my throat, and I feel a bit woozy.

Being this close to the Prince of the Underworld is unnerving, yet thrilling in a way that I can't fully comprehend. My nerves begin to get the better of me, and I clutch the edge of my blanket a little tighter.

Over the pillow I spy Asmo as he lifts his arms and crosses them under himself, resting his head on his palms with a soft sigh.

I roll over onto my side and curl up in a fetal position, facing him. My eyes flutter shut

and I breathe in deeply, trying to slow the pounding in my chest. The silence in the room is thick, punctuated only by our quiet breaths.

As if he can sense my unease, Asmo's voice breaks through the stillness, low and soothing. "Rest now, little flame." He murmurs softly. "Worry not about the sun that has yet to embrace the sky, or the problems meant for tomorrow."

His words wash over me like a lullaby, easing the tightness in my chest.

"Asmo?" I whisper.

"Hmmm?"

"Thank you."

"For what?" He asks.

"For this. For being here."

His silence holds a moment before he responds, a tenderness threading through his words. "Eh, I suppose being here with you, isn't that big of a burden." He teases lightly, the warmth in his voice belying his words.

I let out a soft laugh, the sound muffled by my pillow. "Goodnight, Asmo."

"Sleep tight, Kali."

CHAPTER TWENTY-FIVE

Kali

W hen I awake again, the room is touched by the gentle light of dawn filtering through the curtains. Asmo's side of the bed is empty, the sheets folded back neatly, a testament to his quiet departure.

My mind flashes back to close brush with death I had last night, the reality of it still raw and vivid.

Even now, I can envision Charon standing sentinel at the river of lost souls in the depths of my thoughts. My own soul was nearly weighed, judged, and pulled by the relentless currents towards an oblivion that I barely managed to escape from.

It haunts me even now, in the serenity of my own home.

I have no desire to relive that experience anytime soon, or ever again for that matter.

I pull the blanket up to my chin and stretch, feeling the aches in my muscles. Luckily, my neck has fully recovered except for a slight scratchy sensation at the back of my throat.

My back sinks into the plush king size bed, a welcome contrast to being tied up with magical ropes on a filthy, moldy floor in a dingy motel room.

The dress I had been wearing, now torn and stained with blood, no longer clings to my body. Although I am still in desperate need of a shower, I've at least been changed into a soft cotton t-shirt, and loose-fitting shorts.

But *who* changed me?

That's the real question here.

Was it Asmo?

Doubtful.

Though, the thought feels so forbidden and sexy.

My nipples become erect under the loose cotton shirt, and my hand starts to wander lower. But a gentle knocking interrupts me, causing me to jump and quickly cover myself with the blankets like a scared child.

"Who is it?" I yelp.

The door creaks open slightly, and a familiar voice calls out softly, "Hey, sis. Can we come in?"

It's Rhode, sounding cautious but concerned.

I nod even though she can't see me, then call out a faint, "Yes, come in."

Eirene is right on her heals, her blue eyes tinged red from crying, her face pale and drawn.

The way they gently sneak past the door, shutting it gently behind them as they enter, it brings back memories from our childhood, when they would come to my room at night if my nightmares got too intense. We would snuggle and chat until we fell asleep, with my trusty stuffed Pegasus tucked tightly against my chest.

Being in their presence always made me feel secure and protected.

I throw off the comforter and jump out of bed, rushing to their side and wrapping them both in a tight hug.

We all start crying uncontrollably.

Knowing what we've each gone through in the past few days is heart-wrenching, and I can feel their pain as if it were my own. And if that wasn't enough, the fact that I was separated from Eirene without knowing if she was still alive only adds to the heavy burden of guilt weighing on my chest.

Rhode tightens her grip around me, her voice muffled against my shoulder. "I'm so glad you're safe, I was so scared we wouldn't get to you in time."

"I am so fucking sorry that I wasn't there for you, Eirene. I wanted to help but I—I couldn't. I wasn't strong enough. Every moment away from you guys felt like torture," I choke out between sobs. "I thought I was never going to see you guys again."

Eirene pulls back slightly, her hands cupping my face as she wipes away my tears with her thumbs. "It's not your fault," She whispers, her voice trembling. "We're together now, that's what matters."

"What happened?" I ask Eirene, needing to know how she made it out, how she survived. "How did you guys get out after Demeter kidnapped me?"

"When a few hours had passed and you guys still hadn't made it back, Selene and I came searching." Rhode says. "Mom, dad, and Eirene were all unconscious when we found them, and the cage Eirene was in had been spelled. Selene healed mom and dad and then broke the spell on the cage. She transported us back here and began working on Eirene."

"I had multiple fractures, lacerations, and I—I was..." Tears form in her eyes again as she struggles to continue.

It doesn't take more than that for me to know someone hurt her terribly.

Rage flares up in me, white-hot and demanding justice. "Who did this to you?" My voice is a low growl, barely contained.

She wraps her arms around herself, taking a shaky breath, "An Incubus, Demeter's minion who was supposed to keep me from escaping. But he had other plans; after draining my soul, he took advantage of me. Eventually, he brought his friends along too—it was torture." She sobs, wiping at her tears with her shirt sleeve. "If it wasn't for Dante...I—I wouldn't have made it out alive." She looks down at the floor, emptily, her hands trembling. "He stopped them before they could kill me, but my injuries were so severe that I wound up blacking out. He hid me in his dad's office and went to get help. Demeter found me and the next thing I know; I'm doped up and trapped in a cage like a fucking dog. Now, I have no idea where Dante is, or if he's still alive, and it's no thanks to that little witch, Kora!" She declares, her face contorting with rage. "And now she gets to prance around downstairs in our home after everything we endured because of her? It's not fair!"

The agony I feel for her, isn't describable by words. It makes me sick to the stomach, twisting and wrenching my gut into tiny little knots. I can't even imagine the terror she must have felt.

The horrors she endured...

I know there is nothing I can do or say to heal her pain, but I grab her hand anyways. "Eirene, we'll find Dante," I promise, "And as for Kora, I know she's helped cause a lot of trouble, but she isn't evil, just misunderstood. I can ask her if she can track Dante down for—"

"No!" My sisters both shout at the same exact time.

Their reaction is visceral, a unified outcry born of raw resentment and distrust.

"Asking Kora for help is like making a deal with the devil." Eirene spits. "You can't trust Kora, not after everything she's done."

I run a hand through my hair, trying to think of another way to help. "Alright, I understand. We won't involve Kora. We'll find another way."

My gaze shifts between my two sisters, their faces etched with grief and anger, a mirror of the turmoil that has engulfed our lives.

It's clear that the scars run deep, not just on their bodies but in their hearts as well.

I reach out, but Eirene pulls away, her eyes averted. "I just can't right now, okay?" Her voice cracks under the strain of her emotions.

Something has changed between the three of us. I can feel it, even if they don't.

Will our relationship ever be the same again?

I watch her, feeling helpless and frustrated as shes paces back and forth. Even in the bright light of the morning sun her silhouette looks broken, haunted by shadows that I can't chase away no matter how hard I try. The light that once filled her eyes seems dimmer now, overshadowed by the traumas she has suffered.

Rhode embraces me tightly. "I understand that you have good intentions, and we all know Kora is just a kid. But let's not forget that she played a part in all of this chaos. Eirene has been through absolute hell—as have we all. Our wounds may heal, eventually, but the scars that remain behind will be different for each of us." She says, unconsciously tracing the raised milky colored lines on her face.

Pulling away, I nod, wiping my eyes with the back of my hand, still sniffling. "Trust me, I get it. She has been a...*handful,* to say the least.

However, she is merely another casualty of the deception orchestrated by Demeter. She *saved* me. She could have just left me there to die, but she didn't. She came back for me. That has to count for something, right?"

Eirene sighs, her eyes softening, but the lines on her face remain taut with unresolved tension. "Yes, it counts for something. It does. But it doesn't erase everything else, it doesn't undo the pain she's been a part of, intentionally or not. It's just really hard right now." She continues, "I do understand she came back, and that she saved you, but it was also her that kidnapped you to begin with. I get it." Eirene says, throwing her hands in the air as she walks a small path in front of me. "She had her reasons for doing what she did. And now I have *my* reasons for doing what I need to do. I'm not ready to forgive her—at least not right now. I need some time, and I hope you can understand that."

"I'm with Eirene on this one." Rhode interjects. "We've all been pushed far beyond what we thought were our limits. If it had just been me Kora hurt, this would have been easier to handle. But it wasn't just me. This hurt my entire family...and it hurt Olivia." She whispers, fresh tears welling in the corner of her hazel eyes as she shares a sorrowful gaze with Eirene.

I nod slowly, understanding the depth of their pain. "You both have every right to feel the way you do." My voice is soft, reflective of the heavy atmosphere that surrounds us. "Maybe there's no perfect answer. No right way to handle this kind of betrayal and hurt, but we can navigate it together, as a family."

Eirene stops pacing and shares a weird look with Rhode.

There's something they aren't telling me.

And I can feel it isn't going to be good, whatever it is.

Rhode clears her throat, shifting uncomfortably from one foot to the other. She avoids my gaze, fixating instead on something over my shoulder.

I decide to confront the issue head-on and address the elephant in the room. "Alright, what's the deal? I know you're hiding something from me. Spill it," I say forcefully.

Rhode exhales sharply, her shoulders sagging as if relieved to be unburdening herself of the secret. "Do you want to sit dow—"

"No, I don't want to sit down!" I snap, rolling my eyes. "Just tell me. My brain is already feeling like it's about to implode, and I'm in no mood for beating around the bush."

They quickly glance at each other once more, Eirene rocking back and forth on her feet. "I'm sorry Kali, but...we're going to be going away for a while."

Eirene's voice wavers as she continues. "We need some space, some time to heal and think things through. It's not just about what Kora did; it's about rebuilding ourselves, and about us fulfilling our destinies in this web of chaos as well."

I feel a sting in my chest, a mix of surprise and betrayal. "Going away? Both of you? For how long? Why didn't you tell me sooner?" The words tumble out, edged with hurt and confusion.

And just like that, the waterworks are on again, assaulting my already swollen eyelids.

Rhode steps forward, her expression tight with regret. "We didn't know how to tell you. Everything has happened so quickly, and you're so new to this godly duty stuff. We weren't entirely sure that we were going to be getting sent off so soon. But with how close Lucius has been to you this whole time, he must already have some kind of plan in motion to get to you. The best thing right now is for you to go with Asmodeus and Persephone to the Underworld. You'll be safe there. Eirene and I begin our training in Olympus. There is a war coming, Kali. A war unlike any we've faced before. We need to be prepared, and so do you."

"I know." The words are heavy in my mouth, tasting of cold reality. "I know there's a war coming. But how can I prepare for something I barely understand? How am I supposed to just accept all of this?"

Rhode grabs my hand, "You don't have to understand everything at once, Kali. That's not how any of this works. What matters now is that you're safe and that you begin to learn. You have powers that you haven't even begun to tap into, and Asmodeus and his family will help you harness them."

Rhode squeezes my hand, her grip strong and reassuring. "Trust us, please. We wouldn't be doing this if we didn't think it was necessary."

I nod, swallowing the lump in my throat, feeling the weight of fate pressing down on me. "Okay." I whisper, feeling the resolve settle within me like sediment in still water.

Rhode gives me a small, sad smile and releases my hand. "We'll be in constant contact, I promise. And before you know it, we'll be back together, fighting side by side."

"Yea." Eirene adds, stepping in close and wrapping an arm around my shoulder. "This isn't goodbye, not forever. Just for now."

"Okay, enough of the sad stuff, come on." Eirene says, guiding me over to my bed. The three of us clamber to the top of the mattress and sit cross-legged, facing one another in the triangle we created.

"So, where will you guys be going, then?" I ask, becoming the first to break the silence.

"Olympus." Eirene says. "From there, we will be able help you by finding out everything we can about these weapons the Eternals created."

"That's right," Rhode confirms. "According to Persephone, Zeus possessed one in the past. He reportedly held onto it as a trophy after slaying its former owner. These weapons have the power to annihilate both the physical body and the essence of the Gods. It's the sole thing from which they cannot recover. If we're to have any chance of overcoming Lucius, we must acquire one of these weapons."

As much as I dislike acknowledging it, they've got a point. To rescue my parents and put an end to this madness, we'll have to acquire one of those weapons.

But still, the pressure in my chest intensifies, weighing me down like a thousand anvils "So, just like that...you twats are going to leave, huh? How long do you have before you guys have to go?" I force the words out, my voice quivering slightly more than I'd like.

Eirene lets out a sigh and reaches into her pocket. She retrieves a slender, elongated object and brings it to her mouth. Taking the red BIC lighter from my bedside table, she ignites the end of the rolled leaf held delicately in her small hand.

A pungent aroma surrounds us as she inhales.

The light curls of smoke, sway along in the air, circling and entwining within themselves. Blowing out a cloud of smoke, she leans over handing me the sweet tempting grass.

I take it hesitantly, feeling the weight of the farewell looming over us. Drawing in the smoke, I let it fill my lungs, holding it there for a moment before exhaling slowly. The room spins gently, and the sharp edges of my anxiety soften just a bit.

"We leave tomorrow morning." She finally says, nibbling on her perfectly manicured nail.

I take another draw, inhaling it deeply, reveling in the slight burn it gives my throat. "Wow. I wasn't expecting it to be that soon." I admit.

The tick of the clock in the corner of my room seems louder now, like it's pounding on the doors of what little time we have left together.

Rhode looks at both of us, her eyes serious as she picks up the conversation. "We didn't expect it either, but the situation with Lucius is escalating faster than we anticipated."

"That's true." I nod, reaching to pass the rolled leaf back to Eirene, but Rhode snatches it from my fingers.

She inhales a small amount and proceeds to erupt into a coughing fit that resembles the sounds of an injured baby seal. I raise my eyebrow, surprised at her sudden strange behavior. She has never even considered smoking anything before this moment.

Once she quits coughing and she can finally gulp down some air without choking, "I figure I have nothing else to lose right now, so why the hell not." She grins proudly.

Rhode's unexpected boldness brings a weak smile to my face. It's strange how tragedy and impending separation can push us to do things out of our norm—acts of rebellion against the uncontrollable forces steering our lives.

Eirene chuckles softly, shaking her head with a mixture of amusement and concern.

She places a comforting hand on Rhode's back. "Lucius won't know what hit him with you being such a badass," She jokes.

Rhode's laughter fills the room, "If only badassery could be inhaled," She quips with a wry smile, passing the good-good back to Eirene who takes it with a solemn nod.

Eirene takes a long drag, her eyes fixed on the smoke as it curls upwards before slowly dissipating into nothingness.

The room falls into a companionable silence, each of us lost in our own thoughts as the smoke swirls lazily above. The weight of what awaits us seems momentarily lifted by the haze, though we know it's just an illusion, a brief respite from our reality.

"So, are you guys just going to *poof* there?" I ask, making a blowing up motion with both my hands. "Because if you are, I'm just going to let you know...it fucking sucks traveling like that."

Eirene giggles, shaking her head, her curls bouncing playfully around her face. "No. We travel through the portal that's outside in the hidden grotto. Most people need to use a portal to travel between realms. Only someone with immense power can jump without one."

"We have a grotto, and I'm *just now* finding out about it?" I huff. "This is bullshit!"

How did I not know about a whole ass grotto?

Eirene exhales a ring of smoke from her lips, which are formed into a small *'o.'* "It's cloaked," She explains. "To uncover it, you need to chant an incantation along with some plant magic. We've only experienced it a few times ourselves."

Rhode reaches over for another drag, her hands slightly trembling now. "You'll see it tomorrow," she says with a half-crocked smile, "When you watch us make the jump." She seems a bit out of it now, swaying slightly while sitting on her backside, her eyes reduced to mere slits on either side of her nose.

She is blitzed!

My heart skips a beat at the casual mention of tomorrow; the day looming like a storm on the horizon. I try to mask my rising anxiety with an attempt at humor, "Great, a magical grotto adventure followed by a heartbreaking farewell. Can my day get any better?"

Eirene chuckles, sending more smoke twirling into the air. "And here I thought I was the drama queen." She teases, nudging my shoulder with her own.

I shoot her a mock glare but can't help the grin that spreads across my face. "Whatever." I retort, rolling my eyes for added effect. "Can I meet you guys downstairs? I'd prefer not to be caked in dry blood and smelling like roadkill when I see you guys off, so I want to take a shower. Plus, it looks like Rhode can use a minute or two to catch her groundings." I let out a small laugh.

Mouth wide open, Rhode flatly gazes up at us, shaking her finger in the 'no-no' form you would use to scold a toddler.

"I'm go-ood." She sounds out.

Eirene and I burst into uncontrollable laughter.

She is most definitely *not* good.

"You go get cleaned up, I'll handle this mess," Eirene says through fits of giggles.

She tries to get Rhode off the bed and onto her feet, eventually succeeding and guiding to the door. I remain seated and watch my sister struggle, as any good sibling would do.

"Meet us in the kitchen when you're done," Eirene calls out before disappearing with Rhode.

I nod in response.

"Oh, and make some coffee while you're at it!" I shout after them as they disappear behind the closing door.

"Hell no!" Eirene yells back.

Ahhh. Sisterly love.

CHAPTER TWENTY-SIX

Kali

The hot liquid in the large tub below me sends steam rising into the air as I add my preferred floral-scented oil. Carefully, I sprinkle in small rosebuds and watch as they gracefully glide across the surface of the water, entranced by their beauty.

As the rosebuds drift, their petals slowly unfurl, tinting the water with hints of pink and the air with a delicate fragrance. My shoulders ache as I raise my arms and remove my shirt, letting it drop to the ground. I reach behind me and unhook my bra, feeling a slight bounce in my breasts as I wiggle my hips while slipping off my panties—which are currently being swallowed by my ass.

I dip my toe into the bath, testing the temperature—it is just right. With a sigh of contentment, I ease myself into the welcoming warmth, feeling the stresses of the day.

A moan breaks free from my pursed lips when the hot water brushes against my sensitive lady bits.

It burns, but in that relieving kind of way.

The water envelops me, and I sink deeper, allowing the heat to penetrate every muscle, every fiber of my being. I close my eyes, exhaling deeply, the world outside this bathroom fading into insignificance. My hands float lazily to the surface, fingers tracing small circles on the water, mingling with the rose petals around them. The floral scent is intoxicating, amplifying the tranquility of the moment. I let go of all my thoughts, my mind emptying into the bathwater, merging with the warmth and the fragrance.

This is exactly what I need right now.

Normalcy.

I am aware that this brief moment of calm will dissipate as soon as I descend those stairs, but I cling to it nonetheless.

They are all counting on me...expecting me to become this great and powerful goddess they believe I am destined to be.

My sisters will be departing, I will be shipped off to the Underworld, and everything that has been my reality since I was six years old will cease to exist.

My family will once again be shattered—just like before.

But for now, floating here, I am just me—no titles, no prophecies, just the warm embrace of the water and the scent of roses. I wish I could stretch this moment into eternity, hold back the future with these soft, wet hands—but reality is relentless, always creeping at the edges of serenity.

I bring my knees to my chest and squeeze them tightly, curling into a small, compact ball of emotions.

The pain of loss resurfaces, knocking on the door of my mind and inviting me to join in its sorrowful dance once again.

I hide my face in my hands and cry, feeling a deep ache in my chest as I let out a mournful wail.

My heart feels like it's going to burst from the anguish.

Tears mix with the bathwater, indistinguishable from one another, as I sob quietly in the hollow sanctuary of the tub. The soothing warmth that once cradled me now seems to mock my fragile state, a reminder that nothing, not even this perfect warmth, can shield me from the inevitabilities of fate.

Suddenly, a loud knock resounds throughout the room, startling me out of my thoughts, and the bathroom door flies open with absolutely no other warning at all.

Asmo's hulking form appears before me and all my naked glory. His eyes are covered with his hand, and he spins on his feet until his back is facing me. "I—I heard you crying." He stammers, the huskiness of his voice coiling my stomach into tightly woven knots.

"And I wanted to make sure you were ok. I also thought you may need a towel, since your sisters were downstairs laughing about how they hid them all, so here..." He keeps his palm across his eyes, and reaches his arm backward, feeling around in the air until he hits the towel rack, then struggling for a moment before finally draping the floof of cotton on the hook.

Of course, those bitches hid the towels.

His gesture, awkward yet heartfelt, pulls a reluctant smile from my tear-streaked face. "Thank you, Asmo," I manage to say between sniffles.

He nods, still not turning to face me.

Shifting on his feet, he clears his throat and asks, "Are you okay? Can I get you anything else?"

I wipe the tears from my cheeks, attempting to compose myself. "I'm okay. I reply. "Just trying to wrap my head around everything and make sense of it all."

There's a hesitation in Asmo's stance, his broad shoulders rising and falling with a deep breath. "Alright," He begins, "But if you want to talk about it—or not talk at all—I'm here."

The offer hangs in the air, sincere and simple.

For a moment, I consider asking him to leave, to let me wallow in my sorrow alone. But that feeling of isolation that had been my comfort only moments ago, now feels more like a shackle.

So instead, I scoot up so I'm sitting cross legged in the tub, the water sloshing wildly from the sudden movement and say, "I still haven't had the chance to give you a proper thank you for coming back to save me."

His breath hitches. "Oh, well...I was just doing my job. I am the protector of The Chosen One. Couldn't just leave you there, could I?"

"I mean, technically you could have."

Asmo chuckles, a deep, resonant sound that vibrates against the bathroom tiles. "Suppose I could have," He admits, finally lowering his hand from his eyes but keeping his gaze fixed on the polished ceramic floor. "But then what kind of protector would I be?"

"You'd be a pretty terrible one," I joke, my voice finally finding a bit of its usual spark.

"Exactly." Asmo says. "And I can't have you thinking I'm terrible at my job. It's all I've got going for me."

I let out a small laugh, the sound surprising even myself. It feels good, almost cleansing. "Well, I guess you're not *terrible* at it. You might even be considered pretty good," I concede.

"Pretty good, huh?" He asks, his eyes finally meeting mine.

My bath bubbles cover all my private parts, but that doesn't stop the heat that crawls up my cheeks as his gaze holds mine with an intensity that feels like it could melt the very walls around us.

The air in the room thickens, and for a moment, everything but Asmo's dark brown eyes fades into obscurity.

He shifts again, this time closer, leaning against the bathroom counter, his expression softening. "You know," He begins, voice lower, "I think I can live with that." His smile is faint, almost shy, which seems ridiculous for someone of his imposing stature.

I observe as his fingers dance along the edge of the countertop, tracing shapes only he can see. As my eyes roam over his bare chest, I can't help but admire his toned muscles and the way they flex with each movement.

My gaze then shifts to the elaborate tattoo that covers his back. It's a masterpiece. Intricate designs and patterns shift with his every breath. It's a symphony of lines and shapes that tells a story—a story that I long to uncover.

It's a work of art that leaves me breathless.

Asmo seems to notice my fascination, and his lips curve into a more pronounced smile. "Like what you see?" He teases, and there's a playful glint in his eyes that wasn't there before.

"In your dreams, loser." I retort, though the flush of heat in my cheeks betrays my attempt at nonchalance.

"Maybe," He concedes with a wink, "But you're the one standing here admiring the view."

I roll my eyes, trying to mask the flutter in my stomach with a scoff. "Admiring is a strong word. Observing, maybe."

"Semantics," He quips, pushing off from the counter to stand a little straighter.

His proximity is disarming, and the faint scent of his cologne mixing with the steamy air, makes my head spin just slightly.

"Well," He continues. "I should really let you finish your bath in peace. Don't want the old folks talking about us. But before I make my grand exit, is there anything else you need?"

His offer hangs in the air, teasing yet serious, adding an extra layer of heat to the already steam-filled room. I hesitate, biting my lip as a million responses flit through my mind.

"Actually, there is one thing," I say, my voice steadier than I feel. The words hang between us, suspended in the steam like droplets of water.

Asmo raises an eyebrow, his interest clearly piqued. "And what might that be?"

I take a deep breath, gathering my courage. "Can you get my back?"

His eyebrow arches higher, the playful glint now mixed with something softer, more tender. For a moment, he just looks at me, as if weighing the seriousness of my request. Then, without a word, he nods.

"Turn around," Asmo instructs, his voice low and surprisingly gentle.

I obey, turning my back to him, feeling the heat of his gaze like a physical touch. My heart beats loudly, resonating within the confines of the humid room. I hear him move closer, the slight rustle of his clothes, the soft pad of his footsteps on the wet floor.

He picks up the loofah from the edge of the tub, and I feel the slightest brush of his fingers against my skin as he does so. Tension coils within me, a mix of anticipation and something else, something deeper.

His touch is tentative at first, as if he's testing the waters. Slowly, he begins to move the loofah in gentle, sweeping motions across my back. The scrub is methodical, almost meditative, and each circle he draws seems to ease the tension knotting my muscles.

Around us, steam rises, cloaking the room in a warm, foggy veil. The sound of water dripping from the faucet plays a soft background melody to the hush of our movements. With each stroke, Asmo's hands become more confident, the pressure firmer, more assured as if he's sketching a map on my back, charting unseen territories.

"You should relax," He murmurs, his voice close to my ear, sending a shiver down my spine despite the warmth of the water. "You're tense."

I nod, attempting to loosen the stiffness that has settled in my shoulders, though his proximity makes it difficult.

Gradually, I find the tension beginning to dissipate under his skilled touch, the steam and the rhythmic strokes coaxing my muscles into relaxation. My breathing deepens, syncing with the slow, deliberate movements running up and down my spine.

I moan when he hits a particularly tight muscle, causing the slightest of delays in his expert movements before he gently digs in a bit deeper, the discomfort melding into relief. His hands adjust, applying more pressure now, his fingers working expertly as though they were meant to find and soothe each of these aching spots within me.

"Better?" Asmo's voice is a low rumble, soothing yet laden with desire.

I nod again, unable to form words, my senses overwhelmed by his touch and the dense, steamy air that envelops us. The intimacy of the moment, confined within these four walls, feels like a world unto itself—exclusive and detached from reality.

As the minutes pass, the boundaries between us seem to blur, melting into the humid air that wraps around us like a cocoon. My breathing quickens as I feel his other hand leave the loofah and gently trace a path along the contours of my arm, raising goosebumps despite the steam. The simple touch is electrifying, sparking currents that race through my body, igniting every nerve with acute awareness of his closeness.

The loofah is abandoned now, his hands taking over completely, molding and kneading the flesh beneath them with a mix of gentle caresses and firm, dedicated strokes. His touch is both healing and provocative, each glide of his fingers a whisper against my overheated skin.

Asmo's movements become less about cleansing and more about exploration. His hands travel from my back, over my shoulders, and down the sides of my arms, tracing patterns that send tingles through every nerve ending. Each touch, each contour followed by his fingers, drawing invisible lines that connect dots of sensation across my skin.

"So," I begin, finally finding my voice. "This is a pretty big tub, isn't it?" I manage a small, breathy laugh.

"Indeed, it is," He replies, his voice a soft echo in the steam-filled room. *Do I even know where I'm going with this?*

A moment of awkwardness floats between us. His response hangs in the air, his hands momentarily stilling on my skin as if he's considering his next words—or actions—carefully.

The silence lasts for a moment longer than I'm comfortable with, so I jump in to break it. "I was just thinking...I mean, if you want, we could...Maybe you can join me?" I manage to say, awkwardly stumbling over my own words.

Asmo's hands pause their ministrations, and for a moment, he seems to consider my invitation.

I hold my breath waiting for his response.

Then, his hands resume their movement, a softness in his touch that wasn't there before. "Are you sure?" His voice is low, almost cautious, as if he's treading on the edge of something significant.

I turn around to face him, meeting his eyes, which hold a mix of hesitation and curiosity.

He slides his hands up to cradle my face, his thumbs gently sweeping across my cheekbones. The intimacy of the gesture catches me off guard; it's tender yet loaded with unspoken questions. His gaze searches mine, looking for a sign, an affirmation.

"Yes," I whisper back, the word feeling like a key turning in a lock, releasing whatever hesitation hovered between us.

Asmo's eyes darken slightly, the corners crinkling in a subtle smile that suggests both relief and excitement. "Then, your wish is my command."

With a fluid motion, he stands and begins to undress, his movements deliberate and unhurried. The air around us seems to ignite with anticipation as each piece of clothing drops to the tiled floor, revealing more of his sculpted form. I watch, entranced by the grace and confidence with which he exposes himself to me.

My mouth waters at the thought of having my lips wrapped around the massive cock that is now bobbing freely above his thighs. His eyes roam over my curves, making my nipples harden under his intense gaze.

This is the last thing that should be on my mind, but here I am, acting like a horny hormonal teenage girl, just trying to get her rocks off.

To be honest though, I absolutely fucking deserve to have this moment.

I shift my weight, creating more space for him to join me. I can sense his firmness pressing into my lower back before he repositions himself and presses me against his body.

"Are you okay like this?" he whispers.

My heart pounds in my chest, but I manage to reply, "Yes."

It's hard to believe that I'm actually doing this, but it just feels so perfect—so natural.

Once again, his hands find their way to my shoulders, and he kneads into the tense muscles with the heels of his palms, working out the knots.

His hands should be a sin.

Closing my eyes, I let my head fall back, resting it on his shoulder.

"Mmm...this feels amazing." I breathe.

Asmo's breath is warm against my neck, his lips grazing the sensitive skin just below my earlobe, sending a shiver down my spine. "I'm glad to hear that," He murmurs, his voice a sultry whisper that seems to resonate within my very core.

"Please don't ever stop."

His hands quit moving.

"The fuck?" I groan. "I'm pretty sure I said *don't stop.*

Asmo chuckles, a low, pleasing sound that vibrates against my skin. "Patience. All good things come to those that wait." He teases, his breath tickling my ear.

His fingers resume their dance across my skin, now lighter, more teasing than before. The touch is electric, sending sparks of desire shooting through my veins. I can feel every detail of his fingertips, every trace as they move slowly down my arms, raising goosebumps in their wake.

There's a sense of cynicism that emanates from him. It's something raw and primal, almost animalistic.

With each casual stroke, he unravels me further, weaving a silent promise of more to come.

A light bite at my neck elicits a gasp from me, and I can't help but press closer into him, seeking more of his touch, more of this exquisite pain mixed with pleasure.

"Asmo," His name is like a prayer on my lips, a whispered plea for more.

His response is immediate, fingers pausing before diving deeper, exploring with more intent as his other hand encircles my waist, pulling me even closer into the heat of his body.

"Tell me what you want," He demands.

"I want..." My voice trails off as his fingers trace a particularly sensitive spot just along the curve of my spine, sending waves of heat cascading through my body. "Everything," I finally breathe out, the word heavy with desire.

Asmo's laughter is rich and knowing, a sound that wraps around me as tightly as his arms. "Greedy," He accuses, but there's no reprimand in his tone, only delight.

His lips find mine in a searing kiss that steals my breath, deep and lingering, tasting of promises and secrets yet to be shared.

His hands glide up my body, gently caressing my skin until they reach my breasts. He cups them in his hands, teasing my nipples with his thumb and index finger. As he places soft kisses down my neck, one of his hands moves lower and his fingers begin to rub slow lazy circles on my sensitive bundle of nerves.

He releases my nipple with a soft *'pop'* and grabs the body wash. With a quick twist, he opens the cap and lets the shimmery pink liquid pour over my chest, down my stomach, and onto the hand that is still teasing my clit.

His touch sends shivers down my spine, each stroke of his fingers igniting a spark that spreads through my entire body. His hand spreads the soap across my skin, covering every inch with its lather.

My eyes close in pleasure as my body responds by arching into him. Delicate moans slip past my parted lips as I clutch onto him, my nails making small crescent imprints on his skin.

He cups his hand and dips it between our legs, using the warm water to rinse away the dirt that has claimed my skin.

I'm incredibly aroused...so wet and eager for him to be inside me. The way this man can pleasure my body until I'm on the brink of losing control is unbelievable.

I'm putty in his hands.

He puts one...two fingers inside of me.

The sensation is electric, a delicious stretch that makes me gasp as he moves slowly, deliberately, feeling every contour. His fingers curl inside me in a beckoning motion, finding that tender, secret spot that makes my entire body jolt.

His other hand continues to tease and stroke, amplifying the waves of pleasure that are crashing over me. The combination of his fingers inside me and on me is overwhelming, pushing me closer and closer to the edge.

Asmo's lips return to mine, swallowing my moans as his kiss deepens, his movements becoming more urgent, more demanding. The heat builds, coiling tighter within me, each of his strokes fanning the flames higher.

I feel the hardness of his cock jabbing me in my lower spine, and the walls of my pussy tighten around his fingers.

He senses my mounting urgency, the tremors that race through my body and tighten around his probing fingers. His own breath grows heavy, his chest heaving against my back.

I'm so close—almost there—almost. "Oh, fuck!" I moan loudly, as my orgasm reaches its trembling crescendo.

The wave crashes, sweeping me along in a rush of intense, all-consuming pleasure. My body clenches and unclenches rhythmically, each throb pushing me further into a state of blissful delirium.

Asmo's fingers continue their expert movements, prolonging the ecstasy washing over me. "That's a good girl. Come for me." His voice is low and strained, as he nibbles the bottom part of my ear.

Black dots line my vision.

Just as I'm on the verge of climax, he abruptly stops rubbing and instead smacks my swollen, abused clit. His other hand continues to caress me, hitting that spot that leaves me breathless and on the brink of exploding all over him.

The sudden sharp sensation sends another shockwave through my already trembling body, pushing me over the edge once more.

My cries fill the air. "Oh fuuuuck! I'm—I'm coming!"

My entire body is in spasms.

He kisses through my tiny whimpers as I ride out the high of the mind-blowing orgasm he just gave me.

When I finally stop jerking, he rubs his thumb along my lower lip, pushing past the barrier until I can taste the sweetness of my own come on my tongue.

Fuck, this is so hot.

I melt against him, forgetting everything else, but us and this moment.

I *almost* feel whole again—like a person and not just a collection of frayed nerves and shattered thoughts.

"Watching you come undone like that," Asmo whispers into the hollow of my neck, his voice both tender and triumphant, "Is the most beautiful thing I've ever seen." He gently pulls his fingers away, and I feel the cool air hit my heated skin, making me shiver in his arms.

"I bet you say that to all the girls." I giggle.

"Only the special ones," He replies, his voice laced with amusement. "And you, little flame, are by far the most exceptional."

"You don't even know me." I brush off his compliment. "I could be some weirdo psycho killer or something and you'd be none the wiser."

Asmo chuckles, "Then I suppose," He mutters, tracing patterns lazily across my skin, "I am exceptionally lucky that my last moments would be so divinely spent."

His words render me speechless, the audacity of his charm leaving me unsettled and unnaturally drawn to him.

Well played, prince.

Well played indeed.

Chapter Twenty-Seven

Kali

As we step into the kitchen, we are met with raised eyebrows and accusatory stares that seem to bore straight through us.

They're onto us.

Phil glares at Asmo as he walks past, but he's unfazed by all the attention.

Persephone playfully smacks his arm when he gets closer, causing his arrogant grin to grow even wider.

"We should've been more discreet," I whisper to Asmo, feeling the weight of everyone's eyes on us.

Asmo, ever the provocateur, just shrugs, "Where's the fun in that?" He replies, his smirk unwavering as he scans the room, relishing the discomfort we've caused.

We head to the coffee machine, an oasis in this desert of scrutiny. Eirene follows, sporting a mischievous smile—she's enjoying this far more than I am.

As I fumble with the cups and try to find the sugar, Eirene leans in close, "You two really stirred the pot, didn't you?" She laughs, reaching around me to grab a spoon from the drawer. "I haven't seen dad that red since the Christmas debacle a few years back."

Asmo chuckles, giving Eirene a wink. "Oh, come on, it's not as if we planned to make a scene."

I can feel my cheeks heat up under their teasing.

"Well maybe someone," She says glancing pointedly at me, "Should be a little quieter next time if they don't want the whole house to hear their moans of ecstasy in the middle of the day." Her laughter rings out, clear and unapologetic.

I blush deeper, wishing I could sink through the floor, groaning as I cover my face with my hands. "Please, let's not make this any worse."

Asmo's laughter joins Eirene's, the sound booming and infectious. "It's a little late for that, don't you think?" He jokes, leaning back against the counter with an ease I envy. "Besides, it's not like we committed a crime."

"More like a misdemeanor," Eirene quips, still giggling as she stirs her coffee.

Rhode finally gets up from the chair she's been plastered to, the effects of our smoking session clearly still lingering as she staggers over to us. "You know, this is far better entertainment than anything on TV." She says, giving a lazy grin.

"Glad to be of service," I mutter, finally managing to get the sugar into my cup without spilling it everywhere.

Rhode reaches out, steadying herself on the edge of the counter as she leans closer into our little group. "Seriously though, did you guys have to go at it like rabbits when you knew everyone was just one wall away?" She stifles a chuckle.

"It wasn't even like that!" I protest, my voice rising a bit too defensively. "It just...happened."

Eirene bursts into another fit of laughter, her voice singing through the kitchen. "Oh, please! You two were louder than the fireworks on New Year's Eve. It definitely 'just happened' loudly."

I throw up my hands in exasperation. "It's not like we planned for it to be that...audible."

Rhode snickers, taking a sip of her now lukewarm coffee. "Would've been less conspicuous if you'd just sent out invitations."

Eirene slaps her knee, her laughter peaking. "Invitations with a schedule, 'Please attend our unintentional live performance at 3 PM sharp!'" Her mimicry of a formal invite sends another round of giggles through the room.

Poor Phil is beet red.

He's trying his damnest to ignore our barrage of jokes, focusing intently on his breakfast and his ongoing conversation with Persephone.

Phil's efforts are futile, however, as even Persephone can't help but let a sly smile slip through her usually composed demeanor. "It seems," She says slowly, "That our children have turned our quiet breakfast into a morning comedy show."

Persephone's comment only amplifies the laughter around the table, her dry wit catching Phil off-guard as he tries to sip his coffee. He chokes a bit, coughing, which elicits a pat on the back from Melonie.

He's still not used to us girls not being little girls anymore.

It's hard for him, I guess, watching us all grown up and getting into antics that are more adult than he'd like to admit we're capable of.

He clears his throat, setting his coffee down with a firm clink. "Alright, alright, enough about last night," He grumbles, trying to steer the conversation towards safer waters.

Eirene, still chuckling under her breath, nods her head and wipes a tear from her eye. "Sure thing, Dad. We'll put a pin in it—for now." Her tone teases that the topic might resurface again at any given moment, but she offers him an affectionate smile that softens her playful jab.

Phil offers a half-smile, the corners of his lips twitching upward as he accepts the momentary ceasefire. His eyes scan around the breakfast table, lingering on each face, perhaps trying to imprint this scene in his memory—the laughter, the familiarity, the unabashed comfort of family.

The rest of breakfast passes with a muted kind of joy, the kind that acknowledges both the preciousness of the present and the impending distance of the future.

I glance over at Rhode who seems to be feeling a bit more sober now, "Feeling better?" I ask, playfully poking her in the ribs.

She takes a sip from her own cup. "Honestly, I kind of liked smoking with you guys. It was...relaxing."

"Ha!" Eirene shouts. "She says, *after* smashing an entire bag of chips, and the last slice of cheesecake I had been saving!"

Rhode rolls her eyes, grinning guiltily. "Desperate times call for desperate measures," She retorts, shrugging her shoulders as she shoves her last forkful of scrambled eggs in her mouth.

Phil shakes his head, the earlier sternness melting into a begrudging amusement. "You girls," He sighs, but there's a trace of pride in his tone. "Always an adventure with you."

Melonie leans over and refills his coffee cup, "That's what helps keep us young, my love." She winks.

"Well, I suppose you're not wrong," He concedes.

My chest tightens, realizing that I am about to leave this behind. Our back-and-forth banter, and everything else that makes us who we are—I'm going to miss it so damn much.

"Will you guys have cell service in Olympus?" I ask my sisters, trying to sound casual but feeling a tinge of anxiety at the thought of being cut off from them.

"Not so much cell service as it is—'magic service'." Eirene grins, her fingers doing little air quotes in front of her.

"Magic service?" I raise an eyebrow, intrigued and bewildered all at once. "I can't wait to see how that works."

I turn to Asmo, "Will I have this magical cell service stuff in the Underworld?" I ask half-joking, half-hopeful.

"You will." He confirms.

Asmo's confirmation sends a small ripple of relief through me, but it's quickly followed by an avalanche of questions. "So, how does it work exactly? Do I just...think really hard?" I try to infuse some humor into my tone, but my curiosity is genuine.

"Not quite." He explains. "It's more structured than mere thought. There's a network, akin to the phones here but powered by enchantments and runic scripts. You'll have a device—small, easy to carry."

I blink at him. "Like a phone?" I ask, though I'm picturing some sort of magical, glowing artifact.

Asmo nods. "Very much like your phones, but it doesn't require charging. It draws energy from the ambient magic around you, and in the Underworld, there's always plenty."

"That sounds...actually pretty cool," I admit, my skepticism melting into a childlike wonder. "And I can communicate with anyone? Even up here?"

"Absolutely," Asmo assures me.

I lean back, trying to take it all in. The idea of blending such ancient magic with modern convenience is fascinating—and comforting. Knowing I won't lose touch with everyone makes the whole daunting prospect of going to the Underworld a bit easier to swallow.

Eirene leans forward, her eyes sparkling with excitement. "It's not just for communication, either. There are functions I haven't fully explored yet—maps that change as the realms shift, news feeds filled with updates from all corners of the mystical realms, and even a marketplace for trading spells and artifacts."

Kora, after sitting in silence all morning, refusing to look at anyone or speak, finally lifts her head cracking a small smile, "The marketplace is probably one of my favorite features."

"The way that doesn't surprise me." Eirene scoffs, sending her a death stare. "Let me guess, you used it every day while you planned the demise of my family."

Kora's smile fades as quickly as it appeared, and she shifts uncomfortably in her seat. "It wasn't like that, Eirene. I never—" She hesitates, clearly searching for the right words.

"Save for someone who cares enough to believe you." My sister snaps.

Phil raises his hand, signaling for silence. "Enough of that now. We're not here to reopen old wounds." His voice, though gentle, carries an authority that quiets the room instantly. "This is no way for a future guardian to behave."

Eirene clenches her jaw but nods, acknowledging Phil's reprimand with a reluctant silence.

Kora's eyes drop to the floor, her hands fidgeting in her lap. The tension in the room is palpable, but Phil's authoritative presence keeps it at bay, like a lid on a simmering pot. I look around, feeling an uncomfortable mix of pity and frustration.

"Well, I think I'll go to our quarters and prepare for our departure." Persephone says, standing up from the table. "Come, Kora."

Kora hesitates for a moment, glancing at Eirene and then back at Persephone.

She gets up slowly, biting the bottom of her lip as she tries to hold back her tears, "I—I'm so sorry for the pain I have caused your family." Her voice breaks on the last word.

Eirene's expression softens marginally, a flicker of conflict crossing her features as Kora's apology hangs in the air. She looks away, conflicted, her hands gripping the edge of the table as if steadying herself. After a moment of uncomfortable silence, she mutters, "Just—just go."

Persephone places a gentle hand on Kora's shoulder and gives her a small smile, "Come, daughter. Wounds are fresh and hearts are tender. You need to give them time. Forgiveness is a journey, not a destination. It cannot be rushed." With a comforting squeeze, she leads Kora away from the table and towards the door.

As the door closes behind them, Phil turns his attention back to Eirene. "Your feelings are valid," he begins, his tone more fatherly now. "But we must strive for unity. Holding on to resentment will only poison your own heart, not hers. It is important to strive for understanding and, if possible, reconciliation. This is part of what it means to be a guardian."

"Yes, daddy." Eirene nods, her gaze still averted.

Phil sighs, sensing the reluctance still simmering beneath his daughter's calm exterior. He moves around the table, pulling up a chair beside her. "Eirene, look at me." His voice is soft but firm.

Reluctantly, she lifts her eyes to meet his.

"I know it hurts." He says, gently taking her hand. "And I would never ask you to pretend it doesn't. But remember, pain can either define you or refine you. Choose wisely. You are stronger than your hurt."

Eirene's eyes fill with tears, the embankment barely holding. "It's just so hard, Daddy. Every time I see her, I remember...everything."

Phil gives her hand a reassuring squeeze, understanding the weight of her past struggling against the present. "I know, my dear. It's never easy, especially with wounds so deep. But we cannot let the past chain us down. We must learn to look forward, to build from our pain rather than dwell within it."

He pulls her close, enveloping her in a warm embrace as her tears finally spill over. Eirene clings to him, her body shaking with the force of her sobs. Melonie, Rhode, and I join in the embrace leaving Asmo sitting awkwardly by himself at the table. He fidgets with the cuff of his sleeve, clearly uncomfortable with the display of emotion across the room.

Asmo's discomfort grows until he can no longer remain silent. Clearing his throat, he stands, his chair scraping slightly against the floor, "I'm gonna—" He points with his thumb and without another word, slips out the French glass doors, and disappears outside, onto the back deck.

This morning has been full of unexpected events, to say the least. It's probably safe to say that this was the biggest dumpster fire of a family breakfast we've ever had. Buuuut, no one died, and no one got kidnapped.

And that my friends, is definitely a win.

Chapter Twenty-Eight

Kali

Morning comes too quickly.

My bags are packed, sitting idly by my bedroom door, yet I can't bring myself to move them any farther. I stand by the window, watching the sun rise over the horizon, casting a warm golden hue over the soft, sandy beach below. This will be the last sunrise in who knows how long that I'll be able to witness from this window. The thought squeezes my heart painfully tight, reminding me of what I'm about to leave behind. My friends, my family, the only life I've ever known.

I hear a soft knock on the door and then it opens gently. "You ready?" Rhode asks, peeking her head in with a small, sympathetic smile.

"No." I chuckle weakly, despite the ache tightening in my chest. "But when are we ever *really* ready for big changes?"

Rhode steps into the room, shutting the door behind her. She walks over and sits beside me on the window seat, reaching out to take my hand in hers. "Big changes," She repeats softly, her gaze following mine out to the sunrise. "They're scary, they're unpredictable, but some-times...they're necessary. You know this is a good thing, even if it hurts."

I nod, the lump in my throat growing.

"You have the chance to see your mom again, and finally get to meet your father too."

"Yea, if I don't die first." I attempt a laugh, but it comes out more as a choked sigh.

"You're not going to die," She assures me. Then, with a playful nudge, she adds, "And if you're worried about that, just remember who taught you how to throw a punch."

I manage a real smile then, grateful for my sister's attempt to lighten the mood. "That's true. You did teach me how to throw a mean right hook." I reply, my spirits lifting slightly, though it's a fleeting feeling.

"And don't forget," She continues earnestly, "Wherever you end up, whatever happens, we're just a call away. You're not going through this alone. We're going to figure out a way to rescue your parents, and Liv, you're going to go learn about your past and get your powers under control, and this nightmare is going to be ended once and for all."

"But what if we fail"

"But what if we don't?" She stands up, pulling me up with her as she does. "Then we succeed, and everything changes. You have to believe that the possibility of success is just as real as the possibility of failure. Otherwise, you've lost before you've even started."

Rhode's words resonate with me, vibrating through the core of my fears and doubts. I take a deep breath, feeling the early morning chill seep in through the open window, carrying with it the scent of dew and the distant sea.

"Alright," I breathe out, gritting my teeth against the nervous flutter in my stomach. "Let's do this."

***

My bags make a loud thud as I drop them to the kitchen floor. Melonie looks up from where she is flipping pancakes on the stove, a worried expression crossing her features momentarily before she masks it with a smile. "You girls all packed then?" She asks, trying to keep her tone light and cheerful.

The air is thick.

We've always been terrible at goodbyes.

I nod, forcing a smile. "Yeah, all set." My voice cracks slightly, betraying the turmoil inside me.

Rhode steps forward, her own bag slung over her shoulder. "We'll be back before you know it," She says confidently, more for my benefit than Melonie's.

Eirene looks up from the pancake she's nibbling on, her red eyes welling up with tears that she quickly wipes away. "Yep!" She nods, "It's really no different than going to college. Except, you know, with potentially world-altering stakes, and the possibility of being un-alived." She adds, her attempt at humor falling flat in the heavy air.

Melonie sets the spatula down and comes over to hug us tightly, one by one.

She inhales a deep breath, trying to hold back tears, "We always knew this day would come, but how does one prepare for the loss of all of her children?" She manages a shaky laugh.

"It's not a loss, Mom," Rhode reassures her, hugging her tightly back. "Think of it as an investment. We go, we grow, and then we come back stronger, ready to protect not just this family but the whole world."

Melonie laughs, "You're too much like your father." She jests, rolling her eyes at Rhode.

Phil, who had been quietly leaning against the doorframe, finally steps forward. His eyes are rimmed with red, but his posture is firm. "Hey now, I would say she's just the right amount of him," He replies, managing a wry smile. He wraps his massive arms around us all, enveloping us in the kind of hug that seems to try and squeeze the fear right out of our bones. "Remember, every challenge, every adversity you face, it's all part of the journey." His voice is gruff with emotion, and he clears his throat before releasing us from his grip. "You girls be smart, be strong, and above all else, trust in your instincts. You are the daughters of gods, after all. Your senses are sharper, your resilience greater than most. Use that. Never underestimate yourselves."

As we pull away from the embrace, the morning light begins to filter through the windows, casting long shadows across the kitchen tiles. The scene feels almost surreal, a moment suspended in time as if the sun itself pauses to watch our departure.

Eirene picks up her bag, adjusting it on her shoulder, "Let's get this show on the road, then," She declares with a shaky smile, trying to muster the courage that her words imply. "Mytikas Guardship Academy awaits, and I don't want to be late for our first day."

Rhode dramatically clutches her chest in mock surprise, "You care about being late for something?" She teases.

"Very funny." Eirene rolls her eyes but the corners of her mouth twitch upward as she gives our sister her famous *Tinkerbell* fist shake.

We share a laugh before Rhode's face turns to stone, and she points upwards toward the guestroom where my best friend is barely clinging to life "What's going to happen with Liv?" She asks.

Her question makes the looming departure an even more difficult pill to swallow.

My best friend of eight years almost died and is under a spell that has completely stopped her heart, frozen her in a comalike state, and preserved her just as she was at the moment of the spell's casting—keeping her just out of Charon's reach.

Her fate, as well as ours, hinges in the balance—a delicate thread in the complex tapestry of destiny we are all entwined in.

"Oh honey!" Melonie exclaims, grasping Rhode's hands. "I am going to keep her as comfortable as I possibly can until we find a healer that can save her. Selene has already contacted a few covens she knows, that still practice old healing magic. We will find someone, I promise."

Rhode nods, biting her lip as she looks toward the ceiling, clearly picturing Liv in her mind's eye. "Okay." She whispers, her voice barely audible, laced with worry and hope tangled together like vines. "Just keep us updated, okay?"

Melonie nods solemnly, her eyes glistening with unshed tears. "Of course, darling. Every step of the way." She pulls Rhode into another tight embrace.

"Okay, okay..." Rhode pulls away, clearing her throat and wiping a stray tear from her cheek. "I guess I shouldn't make this any harder than it has to be. We have a mission, right?"

Eirene grins, "MGA won't even know what hit them when the two of us show up."

"Try not to cause too much trouble." I wink.

"No promises on that front." She quips, the tension in the room seeming to dissipate as her lightheartedness takes the edge off the grim situation for a moment.

Phil stretches his long arms around all of us, engulfing us in a warm bear hug. "This might be the last time I can hold all my girls together." He says with a hint of sadness in his voice.

"Daddy, we'll come back!" Eirene says with a grin, squirming out of the group hug.

"Yeah, you better," He playfully grumbles.

"It's hard to believe this is really goodbye," I announce suddenly, clapping my hands together and startling everyone in the room.

"Yeah," They all echo in unison.

"Are you nervous about going into the Underworld?" Eirene asks, grabbing her coffee, and taking a sip as we head out to the back deck where Asmo, Persephone, and Kora are waiting for us. "You were kind of just smacked with all of this. How are you not going nuts right now?"

I shrug off the goosebumps prickling up on the back on my neck, "I'm absolutely scared shitless! Look!" I hold my trembling hand out in front of me, "I'm fucking shaking!"

Eirene laughs, "At least your honest."

Rhode gives a sheepish smile, the fear temporarily pushed aside by the camaraderie. "Well, honesty seems like the only policy when you're about to dive headfirst into hell, literally."

"Thanks, guys. Your words of wisdom have made me feel so much better about this." I crack, my voice dripping with sarcasm.

"You'll do fine." Persephone assures me. "My husband is far sweeter and more reasonable than the myths suggest."

Asmo kicks off the banister he's leaning against, tossing back his head in a deep rumble of laughter, "Our father...sweet and reasonable? We are talking about the same person, aren't we?"

Persephone shrugs, a playful sparkle lighting her eyes. "Well, maybe I just bring out the best in him."

Kora leans in, her voice a conspiratorial whisper. "Or he's just terrified of you. Which is basically the same thing."

Persephone's laughter peals out, bright and clear, cutting through the morning air. "Either way, it works in our favor."

"But really, there's nothing to worry about." Asmo promises. "I will be with you every step of the way—we all will."

Kora and Persephone nod their agreeance.

"And besides," Asmo continues. "The Underworld isn't all doom and gloom. There are gardens, libraries, even a river that mirrors the stars at night—it's not what you expect."

Maybe this won't be so bad after all. I've only ventured out of California a handful of times after my mother brought me here—a few family vacations, and a couple of school trips—nothing that ever really took me out of my comfort zone.

But this, venturing into the literal Underworld, is beyond anything I could have imagined a month ago. Despite the unnerving destination, a sense of adventure begins to simmer within me. Perhaps, there's a part of me that craves the unknown, a part that's been dormant, waiting for an excuse to wake up and really live.

"A river of stars?" I murmur, the idea captivating my imagination. The fear that clung to my bones begins to thaw, drip by drip, replaced by a tentative curiosity. "It sounds beautiful."

Asmo's grin broadens, catching the shift in my tone. "It is. At night, the surface glitters as if the sky has fallen into its depths."

"However," Persephone interrupts. "The beauty of Lethe also comes with its dangers. The river will tempt you to drink from its waters, but you must resist. One sip and you'll forget every sorrow, but also every joy. You'll lose your past entirely."

"Oh. Well, that's...nice." I reply with a nervous half-smile.

Rhode places her palm on my shoulder, "Don't even think about forgetting any of us, got it? Because if you do wind up forgetting us, I'll have to kick your ass so hard, you'll have no choice but to remember every single moment you spent with us." The threat is delivered with such a dramatic flair that I can't help but laugh.

"There's that warm, caring sister we love so much." Eirene jokes.

Rhode grins before punching her lightly in the tit, causing me to burst out with another fit of giggles.

As the laughter dies down, Phil glances around the group, his clear blue eyes reflecting a serious undertone beneath his usual jovial demeanor. "I hate to say it but, Melonie, my love. Would you lead the way to the grotto? I'm afraid it's time."

Melonie nods. "Of course, dear." She gestures for us all to follow her.

Eirene grabs me by the arm and starts shaking it, "You are going to love this." She squeaks.

We follow the path hidden in the trees along the beachline, each step shifting from soft sand to firmer ground as we approach the cavernous entrance of the grotto. The air grows cooler as we draw nearer, the salty tang of the sea mingling with a sharp, earthy scent.

A small hill rises before us, thick with ferns and wildflowers.

Melonie, leading our group, pauses at the foot of the hill. Then, she begins to twirl and dance around the base of the hill, a melody of words escaping her lips—a song that seems as old as the moon itself, yet utterly fresh and alive, resonating with the magic of the place.

Her voice is soft yet carries through the air, weaving between the whisper of the leaves and the distant crash of waves. The Earth—entranced by her beauty and power too, moves along with her delicate rhythm, as if swaying to the same celestial tune. The ferns flutter gently, and petals from the wildflowers lift into the air, circling around her in a whirlwind of color.

It's breathtaking.

Out of nowhere, the earth starts to shake, causing my legs to tremble and throw me off balance.

Asmo throws his arm around my waist, breaking my fall and jerks me back, pinning me against him. "Already falling for me, I see." He laughs, with a devious smile glued to his face.

"Don't flatter yourself." I scoff, pushing away from his chest with feigned annoyance, though the flush creeping up my cheeks might tell another story.

He clutches his chest as if a bullet has pierced it. "Oh, the pain," He groans. "Just when I thought we were becoming friends, you wound me so deeply."

"Wouldn't it be more like friends with benefits after yesterday's free concert?" Eirene chimes in, her voice lilting with amusement.

Touché.

In the midst of her dance, Melonie's movements come to a sudden halt as the trembling ground beneath us calms.

She stands still, and in front of us, an extraordinary tree sprouts from the earth. Its sheer size able to dwarf even the tallest skyscraper. The roots shoot upwards, expanding across the land and twisting until they form a magnificent basin within the tree's trunk. Water flows along the weathered wood, filling the hollow space with its gentle trickle.

It's the most beautiful thing I've ever experienced.

Melonie approaches the colossal tree with reverence, her earlier dance now a silent march of awe and wonder. Her fingers brush against the rough bark, sending ripples through the pool of water collected in the basin. The petals and ferns that had danced with her now settle around the tree's base, as if paying homage to this new marvel of nature.

Asmo, Eirene, and I watch in silent wonder as the scene unfolds. Melonie's touch seems to bring even more life to the already miraculous tree. A soft glow begins to emanate from the water, its light reflecting off her face and casting ethereal shadows against the thick bark.

Melonie smiles, running her fingertips across the top of the water, creating a series of sparkling waves "Behold, our portal."

I gaze around, captivated by the marvels in front of me. "I still can't believe that I never knew about this place." I pout.

Melonie wipes her brow, her face distraught with guilt. "Kali, I'm so sorry we lied to you all these years. Had we known this was how things would have turned out —" Her voice catches.

"It's...okay." I say, pausing to gather my thoughts.

And for the most part, it is.

I'm slowly beginning to accept my new reality even if it means reevaluating everything I've ever known, and the sting of deception is lessening with each passing moment.

"Besides," I continue. "It builds character."

Melonie's laugh, light and airy, rings through the silence like a silver chime. "Well, if it's character we're building, then you'll be as solid as this tree before long."

Persephone wraps her arm around Melonie's shoulder. "We all make mistakes, my friend. But our flaws don't define us—how we rise from them does." She gestures to the tree, encompassing its grandeur with a simple sweep of her hand. "This tree has weathered many storms, yet here it stands, more majestic than ever. Let it remind us that growth comes from adversity."

"I couldn't have said it better myself." Phil agrees, nodding his head with a soft and reflective smile.

"Okay, so how does this portal thing work exactly?" I ask.

"It's pretty simple." Melonie begins. "You think of the place you want to travel and then step into the water while holding that vision in your mind. The tree or whatever the portal is linked to, acts as a conduit, reaching into different realms, transporting us to wherever we wish to go."

"Fascinating. So, we can literally go anywhere?"

"Well, anywhere that exists in time and space." Rhode corrects.

"Wow. It's like having the universe at our fingertips." I murmur, the possibilities sending a thrill through me.

"Yes, but until you get used to traveling this way, you should have a travel partner. That way you don't wind up somewhere unintended—or worse, minced meat." Eirene adds, her tone half-joking, half-serious.

"Noted." I take a deep breath, glancing at the shimmering pool beneath the ancient tree. The water is calm, reflecting the mottled light filtering through the leaves. "Who wants to be my travel buddy then?" I ask, looking back at Asmo and Persephone.

Asmo steps forward with a mischievous smirk, "That would be me. You know, since it's my duty and all to protect you, oh, Chosen One." He shoots Kora a playful wink, and I can almost see the steam rising from her cheeks.

"Yea, yea, Whatever." She mumbles under her breath, clearly still ashamed of her previous actions stemmed by her jealousy.

"Very well, guardian," I reply, trying to match his teasing tone. "Lead the way."

"Alright," Eirene salutes the group, "Until next time, fam! I'm really going to miss you guys. Oh, Kali, I almost forgot...here's something for you before I go." She reaches in the bag slung over her shoulder, pulling something out of the front zipped pocket.

It's my stuffed Pegasus!

"Just in case." She winks, throwing the winged horse at me.

Rhode gives me a stiff hug, ruffling my hair with her right hand. "Stay out of trouble, will you?"

"Always." I reply.

After another round of goodbye's, they ascend the natural staircase formed by the tangled roots of the tree. The water sparkles, a multitude of hues dancing in a mesmerizing display, combining with the ethereal white light that radiates from below. With excitement, they wave at each other before swinging their legs over the edge and plunging into the depths below.

As soon as their heads are submerged, they disappear from sight, swallowed up by the mystical world beneath the surface.

Holy. Shit. Fuck. Batman.

That was incredible.

It's our turn to go next.

Asmo pulls me close to his chest and grins at me, "Are you ready to have your mind blown?" I shake my head in response, knowing that I am not prepared for what is about to happen.

But whether I'm ready or not, here we go.

Without any warning, Asmo pushes us over the side, but I feel safe and secure in his embrace. The rush of air whips against my cheeks as we are sent on a thrilling adventure ride.

I'm weightless.

If being carried on a cloud, inside the northern lights was ever a thing, this would be it.

Vibrant hues swirl around our entwined bodies, filling me with unadulterated happiness. My veins are flooded with serotonin and I am consumed by the euphoric sensation. As gravity begins to take hold once again, the colorful lights dim and a stone chamber comes into focus. The portal room in this location looks vastly different from the one we just departed from.

As we emerge from the water, blue and white steam envelops us and dances over the glowing surface. Kora and Persephone appear behind us a few moments later.

I glance down at my clothes in surprise; somehow, they're still dry despite being submerged. With a sense of wonder, I take in my surroundings, trying to absorb every detail.

It's even more beautiful than I imagined.

The room has an elegant yet eerie aura, with light reflecting off its stone walls like tiny diamonds embedded within them. A shimmering mist hangs in the air, casting a seductive spell over everything it touches, making the stone chamber feel like a hidden world suspended in time.

A small light zips past my head, catching my attention. I turn my head to follow its path, needing a second look.

Could it be a butterfly?

No.

As I focus on it, I suddenly realize it's not an insect at all.

I am in awe when I notice that it is, in fact, a miniature dragon; its body constructed from delicate flames tinted with the faintest hint of purple.

I'm dying!

My toes do a tip tap dance, and my breath catches in excitement. The cuteness overload is almost too much to handle.

"Do you see this?" I squeal.

Asmo laughs beside me, his amusement evident in the deep chuckle that resonates within his chest as he places a kiss the top of my hand, peering down at me with those soft brown eyes. "Welcome to the Underworld, little flame."

CHAPTER TWENTY-NINE

Kali

As we walk through what seems like a corridor, the sound of our footsteps bounces off the stone floors and walls.

The path is illuminated by flickering silver flames from the torches, creating dancing shadows that seem to sway and move in a haunting performance.

Suddenly, a loud, ominous rumbling noise fills my ears with its intensity. I freeze in place, my heart pounding in my chest as if trying to escape.

A high-pitched shriek echoes through the air, accompanied by the sound of sharp claws scraping against the stone—likely an indication of some kind of dangerous creature lurking nearby.

Its footsteps are deafening—or is that my heart?

I can't even fucking tell anymore.

I swear if I get attacked again so damn soon, I'm going to lose it.

The low growls are getting louder, causing the floor to vibrate with each one that rips from its throat.

No one moves; it's as if the very air has solidified, trapping us in this nightmarish tableau. The growls crescendo into a deafening roar, and the scraping grows louder, more desperate.

It's getting closer.

The look on Kora's face causes me to panic even worse than I already am. I have no fucking clue what to expect in the Underworld.

Demons?

Cursed souls?

Her eyes, wide with terror, dart frantically from shadow to shadow, trying to pinpoint the source of the sounds that encroach upon us. She grabs my arm with a strength born of fear, her grip tightening as the creature's growls reverberate in the confined space.

"Get ready," She whispers.

We take our battle stances. Preparing ourselves for the fight ahead.

Because if it's a fight this fucker is looking for, it's a fight that it's going to get. I slip on my brass knuckles, not that I believe they will make much of a difference, but it gives me some peace of mind.

After what feels like an eternity, the creature turns the corner and comes into view. And when I finally see it, my jaw drops in shock.

It's colossal, easily the size of a small school bus, with three heads filled with sharp pointed teeth. Saliva drips from its jowls, creating puddles on the ground where it stands. It almost resembles rottweilers from the mortal realm, except much larger in size.

I would be nothing more than a Scooby Snack if this thing decides it wants to eat us right now.

Hackles raised, teeth bared, it lunges forward to attack.

Uhmmm...no...not attack.

It pauses, its massive heads swiveling as if assessing us—calculating, deciding. In a move that makes no sense, it suddenly stops its advance and sits back on its haunches and begin licking the faces of my *'oh so terrified'* comrades.

This—This is the big scary monster I was afraid of?

The dog beast bounces up and down on its front paws, its big butt wiggling high up in the air.

Each head seems to express a different personality; one looks eager, the second appears cautious, while the third carries an expression of sheer joy. It's a bizarre sight, one that shatters the terrifying illusion I had built up in my mind.

I jerk my arm from Kora, "Seriously?" I mutter angrily. "I can't believe you just made me think I was about to be eaten alive; you jack ass!"

Kora, unable to stifle her laughter, doubles over, holding her sides. "I'm sorry! I just couldn't resist," She manages to gasp out. "Kali, meet Cerberus. He's not exactly the ferocious guardian of the underworld today, more like a giant, overgrown puppy really keen on making friends."

I reluctantly lower my fists, now feeling foolish with my brass knuckles still firmly in place. I remove them hastily and shove them back into my pocket.

My shoulders slump as the adrenaline fades, replaced by a mix of irritation and relief. I glare at Kora, but the sight of Cerberus, with one head nuzzling into her hand, another head trying to playfully chew on her sleeve, and the third simply watching us with what could only be described as puppy eyes, melts my anger away. It's hard to stay mad when faced with such an un-threatful display of affection.

"Alright, big guy," I say, cautiously approaching Cerberus. "You got me." Extending a hand tentatively, I'm surprised when the eager head gently nudges my palm, its tongue lapping at my fingers in a sloppy welcome. The cautious head remains a bit aloof but watches intently, ears perked and eyes bright with curiosity. The joyful one, on the other hand, leans forward to plant a wet kiss on my cheek, causing me to laugh despite myself.

"See?" Kora grins, wiping a tear of laughter from her eye as she watches the interaction. "He's really just a big softie once you get to know him."

I nod, now fully engaged in petting Cerberus, each head vying for more attention than the last.

Kora steps closer, her laughter subsiding into a warm smile as she watches me, and Cerberus interact. "You know, most people don't get this side of him. You should feel special," She teases lightly.

I shoot her a playful glare, then turn back to Cerberus, who seems to revel in the attention. "Lucky me." I reply, scratching behind the ears of the cautious head, which finally closes its eyes and leans into the touch. "Guess I have a way with mythical beasts."

Cerberus flops lazily onto his back, his butt doing the cha-cha while Asmo proceeds to give him belly rubs. "He's such a ham." Asmo shakes his head.

I don't know how to explain it, but being here just *feels* right. The feeling settles in my chest, warm and unanticipated, like the sun emerging on a cloudy day.

I feel more alive than I've ever felt before.

Here, I can sense my power simmering just beneath the surface of my skin, a latent energy that seems to pulse in synchrony with the heartbeat of this mystical realm. It's an exhilarating sensation, both terrifying and liberating, as if I'm standing on the precipice of understanding something profound.

"Asmodeus? Persephone taps her son's shoulder. "Perhaps you should show Kali to her quarters?"

Asmodeus nods, his gaze shifting from the playful giant at our feet to me. "Of course, Mother. Come on, Kali, let's get you settled." He stands and offers me a hand up, which I accept, slightly reluctant to leave the warmth of Cerberus's affections but curious about what else this enigmatic realm has to offer.

Persephone lets out a sharp whistle, and immediately Cerberus comes running towards her, nearly bowling over anyone in his way. "I'm going to take this nuisance with me and get him fed before he starts thinking he can snack on the lesser demons again." She says with a wink.

Cerberus's three tongues loll out to the side and his stubby tail starts wiggling excitedly at the mention of being fed.

"When you guys are ready, meet us in the throne room. I'll have food delivered there." She continues.

"Thank you so much for your hospitality, your goddess-ness." I say, awkwardly tapping my pointer fingers together.

She wraps her arm around my shoulder and gives it a squeeze. "Kali love, there is no need to thank us. You are like family, ok? And no rush at all, take your time getting settled in and make yourself at home."

I express my gratitude once more before she whirls around, the giant three-headed pup bounding ahead playfully.

"Come along Kora." Persephone calls to her daughter.

"Why do *I* have to go with you?" The sassy teen snaps.

"Because *you* have some reconciling you need to do with father after the stunt you pulled." Persephone responds with an equal amount of sass. "You put this entire kingdom in jeopardy with your little escapade.

It's high time you learn to uphold the responsibilities that come with your lineage."

Kora rolls her eyes, "Seriously mother, I have better things to do than hearing one of father's lectures."

But Persephone's gaze sharpens, and her voice drops to a cold whisper, "I wasn't asking." She says, and with a twitch of her hand, Kora is floating in the air.

"Mother!" Kora shrieks, kicking her feet. "Put. Me. Down!"

"Enough, Kora. You will come now," Persephone commands firmly.

Kora ceases her protests, though her scowl deepens. "Fine. Can I at least walk on my own?" She asks, crossing her arms over her chest.

Persephone pauses, studying her daughter's defiant pose, then with a flick of her wrist, Kora gently floats back down to the ground. "Very well," Persephone says, her voice softening just a touch. "But make no mistake, I will not tolerate any more of your antics. Am I clear?"

Kora nods, albeit reluctantly. "Yes, Mother."

"Good," Persephone replies before turning her attention back to me and Asmo. "And I will see the two of you shortly. Kali, please don't hesitate to ask if you need anything at all."

As Persephone leaves, guiding a still-muttering Kora down the ornate hall, Asmo turns to me with raised eyebrows. "Ready to see your room?"

I nod, still slightly overwhelmed by everything—the grandeur of the palace, the mythical figures trotting casually around, the casual display of magical authority, and not being in the familiarity of my own home. "Yep. Let's do it."

Asmo leads me down a hallway lined with towering marble columns that stretch towards a ceiling painted with scenes of celestial bodies and mythical creatures intertwining. The floor beneath our feet is a polished obsidian, reflecting back the flickering lights from the torches that line the walls. Every few steps reveal another extravagant tapestry or ancient artifact.

The air is thick with the scent of pomegranates and myrrh, creating a heady mixture that seems to wrap itself around us as we walk.

We stop before a massive set of double doors adorned with intricate carvings depicting the four seasons—each season meticulously represented by a series of divine figures and mystical beasts entwined in an eternal dance of growth, harvest, decay, and rebirth.

Asmo pushes open the doors with ease, and I'm immediately taken aback by the opulence of the room beyond.

The chamber is vast, with a high domed ceiling painted like the night sky, twinkling with stars and a crescent moon delicately etched in silver. The walls are draped with velvet curtains the color of deep-sea blue, and the floor is scattered with plush, thick rugs in shades of midnight and indigo.

In the center of the room stands an enormous four-poster bed made of dark wood, its posts carved with intricate designs of climbing ivy and blooming flowers. The bed is dressed in linens of the softest silk, embroidered with threads of silver and gold that catch the light with every subtle movement.

Beside the bed, a large bay window offers a view of the palace gardens below, moonlight streaming in to bathe the room in a ghostly, tranquil light. The gardens themselves are a masterpiece of design, with winding paths, fountains that seem to dance under the moon's gaze, and exotic flowers that glow softly in the darkness, their colors muted but still vivid.

Asmo strides over to a small table near the window, where a crystal decanter and two glasses sit atop a silver tray. He pours a deep, ruby-red liquid into each glass, the scent of spiced wine mingling with the castles already intoxicating fragrance.

Handing me a glass, he gestures towards the plush seating area near the fireplace where large bookshelves are filled to the brim with any book I could ever dream of reading. "I hope it is to your liking."

With a nod, I accept the glass, the rich aroma of the wine drawing a deep breath from me as I take in my surroundings. The room feels like something out of a fairytale, surreal and beautifully overwhelming. The fire crackles softly in the grand fireplace, adding a comforting warmth to the luxurious chill of the chamber.

I sink into one of the plush armchairs, velvet soft against my skin, and take a tentative sip of the wine. "It's absolutely perfect." I breathe.

Asmo smiles, a glint of satisfaction in his eyes as he settles into the chair opposite me. "I'm pleased you approve," He says, his voice as smooth as the wine we're sipping.

"It's all so…beautiful. But why all this for me?" I ask, the question escaping my lips before I can reel it back.

He raises a curious brow, "Why not?"

Asmo's response hangs in the air, a beguiling smile playing at the corners of his mouth as he watches me carefully, gauging my reaction. "Do you not feel deserving?"

I shift uncomfortably in my seat, unsure of how to respond. "It's not that," I begin, searching for the right words. "It's just more than I'm used to."

Asmo's smile deepens, his eyes reflecting the flickering flames from the fireplace. "Well," He murmurs, almost to himself. "Perhaps, it's time for you to get used to more, then."

He takes a slow sip of his wine, watching me over the rim of his glass with an intensity that makes my heart quicken and a heat spread directly to my core.

"The flowers outside," I shift the subject. "They're unlike anything I've ever seen. Are they always in bloom like that?"

Asmo sets down his glass, his gaze shifting toward the towering windows that showcase the expansive gardens under the gentle glow of the Underworld. "They are special," He begins, his voice carrying a hint of pride. "Enchanted to bloom eternally, they reflect the perpetual state of the Underworld itself—timeless, unchanging, yet always alive with beauty. Each one was carefully selected to thrive here, to bring light and color where you might expect none to exist. My father had the gardens designed for my mother after she became bound to his realm for six months of the year. It was his gift to her, a piece of everlasting spring in a land thought barren and cold. Similarly," Asmo continues, leaning slightly forward, the shadows from the fire dancing across his sharp features, "I wanted to offer you something unexpected, something uniquely breathtaking."

I clear my throat and clench my thighs together, feeling strangely aroused by his confession. "You definitely succeeded." I say, with a nervous laugh.

"Listen, Kali...I'm sorry about being such a dick to you. You never deserved that."

I wave my hand in the air dismissively, "I wasn't the peachiest myself." I admit. "So, how about we call a truce?"

His stands up from his seat, walking over to me as he extends his hand. "A truce it is then." He runs his tongue across his bottom lip, and my clit tingles with excitement.

"A truce it is, then." Asmo's hand feels warm and firm in mine, his grip tightening ever so slightly as he helps me to my feet.

The close proximity suddenly makes the room seem smaller, the heat from the fireplace more intense. His perfect lips are so close to mine, begging for me to taste them. My breathing quickens, my heart racing with anticipation.

His gaze lingers on me for a moment, an unreadable expression crossing his face, then slowly, he releases my hand. "Come," He says softly, "Let me show you the gardens up close."

I follow him through endless corridors, down countless stairs, until we emerge through the castle doors and onto a stone pathway that winds through the sprawling garden.

It's even more magnificent up close, the flowers glowing softly under the light of the bioluminescent plants scattered throughout.

Asmo guides me along the path, pointing out some of his favorite blooms. "This one here," He says, stopping before a cluster of luminous violet petals, "Is called the Night Whisper. It blooms only under the light of the stars and is said to bring calm and peaceful dreams to those who inhale the pollen it releases at night."

He plucks one of the delicate flowers, its petals shimmering with an ethereal light, and tucks it carefully behind my ear. His fingers brush against my skin, sending a shiver down my spine. "For sweet dreams," He murmurs, his voice low and enchanting.

The simple gesture feels intimate, and a flush of warmth spreads across my cheeks. "Thank you." I almost whisper, smiling up at him, my heart feeling lighter than it has in ages.

Asmo smiles back, placing his hand on the small of my back, "There's much more to see." He says, leading us further down the path.

The garden reveals itself to be a labyrinth of beauty and mystery, each turn unveiling new wonders that enchant the senses. We pass under archways entwined with jasmine vines, towering hedges sculpted into fantastical shapes, and small pools of shimmering water that reflect the light of tiny glowing orbs in a dance of silver ripples.

Asmo's presence beside me is both comforting and electrifying. Each glance, each touch, although slight, feels laden with a magnetic pull that I find increasingly difficult to resist. As we wander deeper into the garden, our shoulders occasionally brush, sending sparks of warmth through me.

We arrive at a particularly secluded nook surrounded by tall foxgloves and ferns that sway softly in the gentle otherworldly breeze.

Here, hidden from the view of the castle and shrouded by the thick greenery, Asmo stops and turns to face me. His eyes hold a depth that seems to pull at my very soul, and in this secluded enclave, the world outside our little circle fades away.

"This place," He begins, as he gestures for me to sit on a small bench made of twisted vines and blooming cushion. "Is a sanctuary, not just for the flora and fauna, but for souls seeking solace and clarity."

He takes a seat beside me, the bench giving slightly under our combined weight. The air around us is saturated with the fragrance of wet earth and fresh blooms, creating a heady mixture that makes every breath feel like a gulp of pure life.

Asmo's arm brushes against mine as he leans back, looking up at the canopy of leaves above us, dappled with the soft light of the moon filtering through. "I come here often when the world becomes too much, when the noise drowns out the music of my thoughts. It's a place where I can hear myself think," He explains, "And it's where I come to remember what it feels like to feel, unburdened by the expectations of others."

His words sink into me like the roots of the surrounding trees into the fertile earth, nourishing something deep within me that I had not realized was so parched. I feel a kinship in his vulnerability, a mirror reflecting my own hidden pains and pressures.

A sigh presses past his lips and seems to blend seamlessly with the rustling of the leaves. "I brought you here because I hoped it might do the same for you." His gaze meets mine again, piercing yet gentle, as if he's trying to unravel the complexities that I've woven around my own heart.

"I…thank you." I manage to stammer out, my words catching slightly. "It helps—this place. It feels like breathing after being underwater for too long. Here, I don't feel the weight of the prophecy or everything that's expected of me. It's like I can just be."

Asmo smiles, a warm, genuine curve of his lips that makes me feel as if the world has slowed down just for us. "That's exactly it," He murmurs.

His hand brushes against mine, tentative but seeking. I hesitate for a moment, then allow my fingers to intertwine with his, feeling the roughness of his skin against mine.

As our fingers lock, a comforting silence, a silence that feels both comfortable and filled with a thousand unspoken words. The canopy above us seems to embrace the moment, the leaves whispering their ancient lullabies, coaxing the world into a gentle repose.

"Well," Asmo finally breaks the silence. "I guess we should head back." The words hang in the air, a faint echo of reluctance threading through them.

I nod, the movement slow, not quite ready to sever the connection that has formed between us in this secluded haven.

He stands up, brushing the dirt and leaves from his pants with a casual swipe of his hands, then extends one to me.

"I guess it would be pretty bad to keep the God of the Underworld waiting." I joke.

A laugh bubbles from Asmo's chest, "I dare say he'd survive a few more minutes without us." He pulls me to my feet, and for a moment we stand close, closer than before, his hand still clasping mine. There's a hesitancy in his eyes, as if he's contemplating whether to say something more or let the silence speak for us.

His head dips lower, "We can take the long way back, if you prefer." His breath is warm against my cheek, stirring the air between us.

"Yes, let's take the long way," I find myself saying, my voice steady despite the fluttering in my chest and the tingling in my pussy.

There's a part of me that wants to stretch this moment into eternity, to stay lost in this forest where prophecies and destinies don't seem to reach.

"As you wish." He replies, though he doesn't move.

My heart is a drum in my chest, relentless and thrilling. His proximity is intoxicating, and I find myself leaning in, drawn by the seductive pull of his presence. Our eyes lock again, and the world around us blurs into insignificance. Time seems suspended, held captive by the intensity of the moment.

Asmo's gaze is a mix of mystery and warmth, a contrast that sends shivers down my spine. His thumb caresses my cheek softly, tracing the line of my jaw. He lowers his head, his lips only inches from mine.

The anticipation builds, a delicious tension that threatens to overwhelm me. I can feel my arousal, slick between my legs, as every nerve in my body screams for his touch.

When his lips finally meet mine, it's a gentle collision — soft and testing at first, then deepening as if we're both searching for answers in each other's embrace.

Asmo's lips move against mine with a purpose, his hands sliding up my back, pulling me closer until there is no space left between us. I melt into him, lost in the rhythm of his touch, each caress of his fingers igniting sparks that leap through my veins. Our kisses grow more fervent, more urgent, as if driven by some primal hunger that neither of us can deny.

My hands find their way into his hair, tugging him closer, desperate to feel more of him, to lose myself completely in this embrace.

His body responds with a fervor that matches my own, his arms tightening around me, anchoring me to him as if we might otherwise drift away into the wind.

When he finally breaks the kiss, I'm left breathless, my lips burning from the intensity.

Asmo rests his forehead against mine, "Careful, little flame. He warns, his voice husky. "If you keep kissing me like that, you might make me fall in love."

My laugh, breathless and disbelieving, fills the small space between us. "Loving someone you've just met is utter madness."

"Well, if love is madness...may I never be sane again."

Fuck.

I hope to hell he's joking...because that shit's weird.

CHAPTER THIRTY

Kali

The throne room is like stepping into a sparkling, crystalline dream.

The walls are adorned with elaborate silver and blue designs, glinting in the light filtering through grand stained-glass windows. In the center of the room, a raised platform holds two magnificent thrones, crafted from shimmering white gold and studded with sparkling blue gems. The air seems to be charged with magic, giving the room an otherworldly aura. Simply being in this majestic space takes one's breath away.

Hades sits on the larger of the two thrones, Persephone sitting beside him with a beaming smile, her gown a flowing masterpiece of midnight and frosty blue fabric that cascades down the steps of the dais.

Persephone clasps her hands together, standing from her seat, "You two made it just in time! The kitchen staff are getting ready to serve dinner. I do hope you're hungry."

"Starving." Asmo replies.

"You my dear, are always hungry." Persephone laughs. "I was talking to Kali."

Hades laughs at his wife's jab at their son as he stands up and greets Asmo with a slap on the back and a warm, enveloping hug. "It's good to see you, son." His voice rumbles through the vast room.

Asmo grins, returning his father's hug with equal fervor. "It's good to be back, Father. The mortal realm is fascinating, as always, but it lacks the quiet grandeur of home."

Hades roughs up Asmo's hair, "I'm proud you. You did your mission well."

Asmo nods and Hades turns his attention to me, "Kali...you look just like your mother." He pauses, taking one big stride towards me, his gaze softening as he pulls me into a gentle embrace. "It warms my heart to see you," He says before pulling back to look at me. "I owe you my deepest gratitude and admiration for the courage you showed saving my family. You have proven yourself to be more than worthy of the title the prophecy has bestowed upon you." Hades' voice is sincere as he places his large, weathered hand on my shoulder, his piercing chromatic eyes meeting mine with undisguised respect.

I lower myself to my knees, bowing my head in reverence for the God of the Underworld and his Goddess. "Thank you, Lord Hades, for your kind words and for welcoming me into your home." I say, my voice barely above a whisper due to the overwhelming emotion of the moment.

Asmo grabs my elbow and pulls me up, his intense gaze conveying that I have either made a mistake or caused offense with my dramatic entrance. "*You* are a Goddess." He says, his correction more informative than harsh. "You kneel to no one." He lowers his head toward my ear, his lips grazing the delicate flesh as he whispers so no one else will hear, "Unless it's before me in my chambers. Understood?" He winks at me, his audacity eliciting a quick, involuntary smile from my lips despite the seriousness of the gathering.

I nod, standing straight, still fighting off the blush that threatens to color my cheeks, and smooth out the front of my fox ear hoodie.

Persephone, noticing the interaction, steps forward with a graceful swiftness unique to her divine presence. "Indeed, Kali, here in our realm, you are among equals. We welcome you not just as a hero, but as family."

"Speaking of family," Hades interrupts. "Kali, I am so sorry about your parents. I swear to you, I am doing everything I can to rally enough allies and resources to ensure their safe return."

The gravity of his words falls heavily around us, like the thick blanket of darkness that perpetually shrouds his domain. My heart clenches at the mention of my parents, their fate a constant shadow on my soul's landscape.

Persephone nods solemnly, her eyes filled with a maternal kind of concern. "Their fate weighs heavily on us all," She says, reaching out to squeeze my hand reassuringly. "But we shall not lose hope. We have the might of the gods, and now, with you among us, a new strength that cannot be underestimated."

"Thank you, Your God and Goddess-ness," I manage to say through the tightness in my throat. "But I'm afraid that I'm not as powerful as you believe. I have no idea what I'm doing. I can't even tap into my power at will. It just sort of...happens." I add.

"Please, just call me Hades." The Lord of the Underworld says with a dismissive wave of his hand. "And as for your power...that is not unusual for someone newly awakened to their divine essence, Kali. Power as profound as yours often requires time to understand and control. Think of it as a wild river that must be channeled into productivity. In time, and with practice, you will command it as easily as breathing."

"You got this." Asmo chimes in. "And let's not forget, you've got me now—master of charm and wit—at your side." He grins.

Persephone shakes her head, disapproval gently played across her features before she turned her attention back to me. "Asmo does have a point, though in his own...unique manner," She said, a small smile replacing the previous concern. "We all are here to support you, train you, and provide whatever assistance you may need. The path ahead is not an easy one, but it is yours, and we believe in your ability to walk it."

The double doors behind the thrones open, and a figure steps through, casting a long shadow that stretches across the cold marble floor.

"Pardon the interruption." The man bows low, his voice a melodic baritone. "But the dining room has been prepared for your presence, and dinner is served." He straightens up, revealing sharp features softened by the gentle glow of the flickering torches lining the hall.

"Ah, Thanatos," Persephone greets him with a nod. "Thank you for letting us know. We shall join momentarily."

Thanatos nods in acknowledgement and retreats, his cloak whispering against the marble as he moves. The assembled group rises, and Persephone extends a hand to me. "Come," She says softly, "Let us take this opportunity to replenish ourselves before we continue our discussions."

"Wonderful idea, my love." Hades agrees, reaching down to place a gentle kiss on the back of her hand.

She smiles sweetly back at him before turning to lead the way toward the dining room, her robes sweeping gracefully behind her.

The smell of exotic spices and roasted meats ornate the air as we approach the grand dining hall. The long table set in the center of the room is adorned with golden candelabras and crystal goblets, shimmering under the ambient glow of chiseled sconces. The chairs, each carved from dark wood and cushioned in velvet, stand ready to embrace their guests.

Asmo pulls out a chair, offering me a seat next to him with a mischievous wink. "Best seat in the house," He declares, waiting until I'm comfortably settled before sliding into his own chair beside me.

Kora is already seated, a scowl on her face as she glares at her parents.

Persephone catches her daughter's gaze and raises an eyebrow, an unspoken conversation passing between them. Kora averts her eyes, focusing instead on arranging her silverware by her plate, clearly still irritated by her and her mother's earlier interaction.

Servants in muted tones of gray and silver glide silently between us, filling goblets with a richly aromatic wine and setting plates heaped with an array of dishes before us. Each plate is a masterpiece of culinary art: tender slices of spiced venison paired with vibrant, honey-glazed vegetables; a delicate tower of roasted root vegetables encircled by a rich balsamic reduction; and a centerpiece of grilled fish, its scales glistening under a drizzle of lemon herb sauce.

The variety is dizzying, the presentation flawless.

Hades raises his goblet, allowing the clinking echoes to summon attention. "To old friends, new alliances, and ending this war with Lucius once and for all." He declares.

Glasses rise in unison, a chorus of agreement resonating around the table. "To peace," Persephone adds.

I nod, though, worry begins to creep like a shadow at the back of my mind.

Despite the comforting warmth of the gathering, the mention of Lucius brings a chill that wine and laughter cannot dispel.

I clasp my goblet a bit tighter, my fingers tracing the cold rim as I listen to the murmurs of assent around the table. The conversation shifts seamlessly from toasts to tales, stories spun from past adventures and old battles that paint the air with both nostalgia and laughter.

Asmo leans closer, his voice low. "Are you okay?"

"I'm fine," I whisper back, knowing full well that my reassurances are only partially true.

He offers me a half-smile, not entirely convinced, but lets the topic drift away with the rising bustle of conversation.

But the truth is...I'm not okay.

I'm scared, I miss my home, and I feel utterly unprepared for what we're up against with Lucius.

The next step is training; and fuck me with a silly willy—*it* starts tomorrow.

Nope. I'm not ready for any of this. None of it. Nilch. Nada. Zero.

But time isn't going to wait for me to be ready. It marches on, indifferent to fears and hesitations.

So, I raise my goblet slightly higher than before, a silent pledge to myself more than anyone else. To be braver than I feel, and stronger than I seem.

Chapter Thirty-One

Kali

T raining day.

The morning arrives with a heavy fog that seems to mirror the thickness in my chest. As I lace up my boots, the leather stiff and cold against my fingers, I take a deep breath, trying to dispel the icy dread coiling in my stomach.

The courtyard is still as I step outside, the mist curling around my feet like a living thing, whispering secrets I'm not sure I want to hear. The air is sharp, biting at my skin, reminding me that this is no ordinary day.

Asmo is already there, stretching his limbs with the grace of a warrior or perhaps a cat.

Could be either.

He catches my eye and nods, a silent gesture that somehow steadies me. "You ready?" He asks, his voice cutting through the morning stillness like a blade.

I muster what I believe might pass for a confident smile. "As I'll ever be," I reply, though my voice wobbles slightly at the end.

We both know it's a brave front, but it's all I have to offer right now.

Asmo walks over and claps a reassuring hand on my shoulder. "You'll do fine," He assures me.

He believes in me more than I believe in myself at this moment.

I let out a slightly sarcastic laugh, "Oh, yea. Totally."

My attempt at humor does little to ease the tightness in my chest, but Asmo's chuckle is warm and genuine. He guides me toward the center of the courtyard where the fog seems to shy away, revealing a collection of training dummies inside a small training arena.

"You see those?" Asmo gestures towards the dummies arrayed in various poses of attack and defense. "By the end of the day, you should be able to summon your own hellfire and blast these fuckers to smithereens. Or at least singe them a bit."

I eye the demon dummies, their straw-filled heads mocking me with silent, stitched grins.

"We'll start slow," Asmo continues. "First, we focus on breathing and feeling for the magic feeling the energy around you. You need to connect with that power, feel it in your bones. It's not just about throwing fire; it's about being in control."

Breathing deeply, I attempt to calm the riot of nerves inside me and focus on the energy Asmo speaks of. It feels elusive, like trying to grasp at smoke with bare hands.

"Close your eyes," Asmo instructs. "Feel the ground beneath your feet, the air on your skin. Channel every sense into locating that spark within you."

Obediently, I shut my eyes.

The cool air brushes against my cheeks, and beneath my feet, the earth feels solid and real. I try to ignore the mist that continues to swirl around our little arena, coiling like serpents between my ankles.

Slowly, the static of my own thoughts begins to dim. The whispering anxiety recedes into the background, overshadowed by a growing awareness of something deeper—a warm, pulsating energy that begins to flicker within me.

I can feel a warmth in my gut, slowly spreading like a gentle fire. "I—I think feel something." I say, my voice strained with the effort of concentration.

"Good! Keep focusing on that feeling," Asmo encourages, his voice steady and supportive. "Let it grow, but keep it controlled. Imagine it as a flame within a lantern—bright but contained."

I nod, focusing intently on the warmth that seems to swell within me. With every breath, I relax a little bit more until finally it's right there.

I let out the loudest, most raunchiest fart that echoes against the stone walls of the courtyard, frightening off a flock of small flying creatures nearby.

Embarrassment floods through me, but before I can apologize or make a hasty escape, Asmo bursts out laughing.

"Not exactly the kind of fire I was talking about, but you've definitely got some power in there!" He snorts, doubling over with laughter. "Let's try channeling that into something a bit less...explosive."

I feel like I might die from embarrassment. Though, I'm curious to how that would work since I'm already in the Underworld.

Trying to recover my dignity, I take a deep, steadying breath and attempt to refocus.

Asmo's chuckles subside as he stands up straight, wiping a tear from his eye. "Okay, okay. Go ahead and try again."

With a sheepish nod, I close my eyes once more, willing my cheeks to stop burning.

This time, I dig deeper, trying to find the spark Asmo spoke of, not the accidental inferno I'd unleashed before.

My focus sharpens, the earlier embarrassment transforming into a fierce determination. By the afternoon, I still haven't been able to conjure anything more than a headache, growing impatience, and an attitude.

Though, the attitude is mainly because I'm hungry.

"Can we be done already?" I whine as I flop to the ground and sprawl out on my back, my arms stretching out on either side of me.

Asmo sighs, shaking his head but with a smile tugging at the corners of his mouth. "Fine, we can take a break. But don't think you're off the hook. We're just getting started," He says, offering me a hand to pull me up from the ground.

I grudgingly accept his hand, rolling my eyes, "I wouldn't dream of it."

Once I'm upright, he keeps hold of my hand for a moment longer than necessary. "You'll get the hang of it. Stop trying to rush it or force it. Embrace the process."

"I don't have time to embrace the process." I snap, jerking my hand free. "My parents don't have time for me to *embrace the process*. If I'm expected to stay hidden and to learn how to control my powers like a good little chosen one so Lucius can't get to me and commit world domination, or whatever his overambitious plans entail while my parents are going through who knows what kind of torture, then why can't these alliances in which your father spoke of, or all these other gods, demigods, and otherworldly creature things rescue them? Why must we wait for me to master something I can barely grasp?"

Asmo's expression softens, and he releases a long, drawn-out sigh. "Sometimes, waiting is the hardest part of a battle. Not because we aren't eager to fight, but because the timing must be right. Rush in headlong and we risk everything, including the lives of those we aim to save. My father and the others are not sitting idle, believe me. They are strategizing, finding the right moment to strike where it will make the most impact with the least cost. I *know* how hard this is, little flame. I was literally just in your shoes—feeling powerless and torn apart by the burden of not knowing whether my mother and sister were alive, but I still had duties. Our duty, no matter how bitter or twisted it feels at times, is to be ready when that moment comes. To not falter under the weight of our own impatience."

"I'm not you, Asmodeus! I'm not a prince who got to grow up with mommy and daddy while being fed from a golden spoon and had everyone waiting on me hand and foot. You at least grew up with your family. You weren't convinced they were dead and that you were never going to see them again. You didn't have to find out on your birthday that the people that raised you duped you for your entire life about who you really are. You never had to question anything about your parents because you knew they were alive and that they cared for you." Tears well over the brim of my eyes, stubborn and molten, like the fire I was supposed to control but never felt within my grasp.

I turn away from Asmo, feeling the jagged breaths tearing through my chest as each word I had hurled at him carves itself into my heart.

"I never meant to imply our situations were the same, but don't tell me that I don't understand loss, or fear, or sacrifice," Asmo replies, his voice pinched with a sharp edge of pain. "I've seen cities fall, friends turned to dust, and yes, I grew up with a crown waiting for me, but that crown came with its own set of shackles. I get it, I've had privileges, lots of them, but those privileges never shielded me from suffering or from the harsh realities of this universe. You think I haven't felt helpless? You think I haven't been scared out of my mind, not knowing if the next day would be my last or if I'd ever see the people I love again?" His voice breaks a little, and the anger seeping through his words thins into something more vulnerable, more raw. "I've been right where you are—in different circumstances, yes—but the pain? It doesn't discriminate based on your title or lack thereof."

I squeeze my eyes shut, trying to push back the tears, but they don't stop coming—they never do when I need them to.

The silence that stretches between us is suffocating, but then Asmo rests his hand lightly on my shoulder. "I didn't choose this path any more than you did, Kali," He continues softly, his anger dissipated into the frigid air around us. "But we're here now, and we have to face what's in front of us. We can't change our pasts, but we can shape our future. Both of us have lost, both of us have been lied to, and both of us are fighting not just for ourselves but for something greater."

I open my eyes, the tears distilling my vision making the world seem as if underwater. Asmo's face is blurred, softened around the edges by my watery gaze, and for a moment he doesn't look like a prince, or a god, but just a man, burdened by his destiny as much as I am burdened by mine.

Swallowing the lump formed in my throat, I nod slowly, acknowledging his words and the truth they carry. It's easy to see Asmo as otherworldly, to place him on a pedestal that separates him from pain and fear. But here, in this moment, our shared vulnerabilities lay bare the simple fact that beneath the crowns, the titles, and the power, we are both human.

Scarred, perhaps, but still capable of fear and hope alike.

"I'm—I'm sorry." The words struggle out, choked and heavy with unshed sorrow. "I never meant...I didn't mean to dismiss your experiences or to imply that you've been spared from hardship. It's just..." I falter, searching for the right words.

Asmo gives me a light smile, his eyes crinkling at the corners, "Sometimes it's hard to see past our own pain?" He offers.

I nod.

"My mother once told me that, in the heat of our struggles, it's easy to feel alone in our battles, to feel as though no one else could possibly understand the depth of our pain. But that's not true. We all carry burdens, we all have stories of grief and hardship, and in that, we are connected, not separated," He says.

I feel a shift inside me as his words sink in.

He's right.

In our own ways, we each wrestle with our shadows, our own kinds of demons. It doesn't make any one of our struggles less significant than the other's—it only means that we are not as alone as we sometimes believe.

And I presume *that* has been the true lesson of the day.

CHAPTER THIRTY-TWO

Kali

It's been two weeks now since my arrival in the underworld.

It's crazy to think about how much has already changed in such a short time. I sometimes struggle to believe it's all actually real—me, living among gods and monsters, discussing escape routes like it's a normal Tuesday activity.

My powers are getting a little easier to control.

Well, sort of. I blasted my first demon dummy a few days ago, and that felt like a real breakthrough, but that was my first and only time.

Since then, mastering my abilities has been more of a frustrating dance of two steps forward, one step back. Each session at the training grounds leaves me exhausted, both physically and mentally. But Asmo keeps reassuring me that this is all part of the process. That even gods had to learn how to harness their powers once.

Today however, is a rest day and I'm taking full advantage of it in the library.

The library in the castle is unlike any other I've ever seen. Shelves made of dark, gnarled wood stretch endlessly upward, disappearing into the shadowy heights of the ceiling. Rolling ladders stretch along the walls, allowing access to even the highest shelves.

Books of all shapes, sizes, and ages are crammed into every available space, and the air smells of old parchment and mystery, a scent that stirs a thrill of excitement within me every time I step through the giant arched doorway.

Asmo enters the room, and I lift my gaze from the book in my grasp, grinning as he settles into the recliner beside me.

"Hey." I greet him warmly, my mood lifting further at the sight of him.

"Hey yourself." He replies, stretching out his legs in front of him. "Enjoying your day off?"

"Definitely," I reply, flipping the page of my ancient tome. "I've already wandered through three different dynasties just this morning."

Asmo chuckles, and a deep warmth spreads in my chest. "Three adventures already, huh? And it's not even lunchtime yet," He adds, his dimples deepening as his smile widens.

"I know, right?" I laugh. "At this rate, I might just solve the mystery of the Lost Scepter of Nyx by dinner."

Asmo raises an eyebrow, a playful smile tugging at his lips. "Is that a challenge? Because you know I can't resist a good mystery."

I playfully toss my book onto the table beside us, my energy renewed. "It's a race then. First one to figure out the location of the Scepter wins bragging rights."

Asmo nods, his eyes sparkling with competitive fire. "And the loser," He continues, drawing out the suspense with an impish incandesce in his eyes, "Has to add an extra day of training to their schedule."

I groan theatrically, covering my face with my hands. "You drive a hard bargain, sir." I peek through my fingers at him and add, "But you're on."

With that, the quiet of the library transforms into a vibrant battleground of wits and wills. We each race to grab stacks of books from various sections, ancient texts on magical artifacts, dusty chronicles of forgotten kingdoms, and tattered maps that promise secrets hidden in their creased folds.

The afternoon slips away as we immerse ourselves in layers of history and mysticism, piecing together clues from texts that haven't felt the warmth of sunlight in centuries.

I rise to my full height and extend my arms in a long stretch, feeling the satisfying pop of my back after being hunched over books for hours.

As I glance around, I catch Asmo's gaze fixed on me from behind his writing materials. "What?" I raise an eyebrow, self-consciously wondering if I have food stuck in my teeth or something equally embarrassing. "Is there something on my face?"

His response only confirms my fears. "Yes," He says with a smirk, "Only the most breathtaking beauty that has graced the Underworld...and any other realm, for that matter. But also, you have ink just there," He points, his grin roguish, gesturing to a spot on my cheek.

Laughing, I rub at the spot he indicated. "You could have led with that, you know."

"I could have." He shrugs. "But flattery is an art form best savored, don't you think?"

I throw a cushion at him from the settee nearby, but it only makes his laughter ring out louder in the quiet library. "Alright, charmer, let's see if your detective skills are as polished as your flattery. Found anything yet, or are you too busy sculpting more compliments?"

"Can't I do both?"

Yes. Absolutely. I love it.

"No."

"Ah, your loss, truly." Asmo retorts with a light sigh, returning his attention to the sprawling cartography spread out before him. "But I digress."

I shake my head, my shoulders shaking from my fit of giggles. "I can't with you right now." I laugh, my fingers gliding across the page in my book.

Stiffling a yawn, I put down my book and snuggle into the plushness of the recliner, tucking my feet underneath me.

"Ugh, my brain feels like it's turning to mush." I complain.

"Break?" Asmo questions.

"Sounds perfect." I sigh, grateful for the pause.

Slipping off the recliner, I make my way over to the cart of coffee and snacks that had been delivered earlier by Amelia, one of the Imps, that works in the castle. She's like an elemental fairy demon thing—all fluttery movements and bright eyes, she's quite pretty actually, and always seems to be hovering just out of sight, ready to assist or vanish with equal alacrity. I pour myself a steaming cup of dark roast, the rich aroma enlivening my senses, and grab a couple of sugar-dusted pastries from the tray.

Asmo watches me for a moment, his eyes lingering on the way my fingers clumsily wrap around the warm mug, then he stands and joins me.

"Little flame?"

"Yea?" I ask around a mouthful of scone.

"Wanna take this out to the gardens?"

I nod, wiping crumbs from the corner of my mouth, but before I can reply, I'm being sucked into darkness.

Sounds start to filter in around me. I'm no longer in the library, or the castle, for that matter. The scent of the dark roast coffee fades, replaced by the acrid smell of fire and brimstone.

My eyes struggle to adjust to the sudden change in environment, the oppressive heat wrapping around me like a thick blanket.

I'm in a whole new realm, standing on a scorched landscape, surrounded by towering, jagged rocks that pierce the smoky sky.

Fear creeps in, tightening its grip around my heart as I try to comprehend how I ended up here.

But before panic can fully take over, I feel a hand on my shoulder—an unfamiliar touch.

Oh, no...I begin to choke on the lump forming in my throat.

The dark soul demon, like the one that had taken control of Dafina is glaring at me from its position at the end of a fiery leash.

I'm frozen—too afraid to move, so I slowly allow my eyes shift upward and meet the face of the person in control of it.

It's a man that looks to be around my age.

He's stunning.

He looks as though he were carved by the Eternal Gods themselves—a painful beauty, I dare not touch.

Shaggy hair, as white as freshly fallen snow, frames his face, and his eyes seem to be made of the same fiery lava that rushes through the molten river next to our feet.

My eyes widen when the realization of who this man is crashes into me like a wave of ice-cold water. It's Lucius, in the flesh—The Devourer of Souls and ender of all worlds.

You've got to be fucking kidding me!

How—just...how?

Amusement dances behind his pupils, his nostrils flaring slightly as though he is trying to breathe in my scent.

A crooked smile spreads across Lucius' lips, revealing a set of unnervingly perfect teeth. "Alas," He says, "I finally meet my bride."

Epilogue

ASMO

This is the fourth demon I have killed tonight, and it still isn't enough.

It's never enough.

As long as she continues to be gone, I could care less about how many deaths are on my hands, or how many of Lucius's minions I incinerate.

I *want* to piss him off—to challenge him.

Somehow that bastard got to her, and I've been trying get into Tartarus, ever since. But no matter how many doors I open, barriers I break, the gates to that infernal abyss remain firmly closed to me.

My veins are burning with rage as I wipe the black coagulated blood of my latest victim on the front of my suit.

The smell makes me crunch my nose.

Whatever magic that has been used on the entry to Tartarus that's keeping me from saving her, is strong.

I've never experienced anything quite like it before.

Despite my mother and sister's tireless efforts, they have been unable to break through the barrier.

I know it shouldn't but angers me each time they fail.

I know it's not their fault, but still, I can't help the surge of frustration that swells within me each time they report back with nothing new. Every failed attempt feels like a personal defeat, a reminder that Kali is still trapped, suffering somewhere beyond my reach.

These have been the absolute worst weeks of my entire existence.

I feel sick without her—weaker somehow.

The prophecy must be right; she has to be my soulmate. But soulmates are rare. There hasn't been a true soulmate connection in decades.

I approach the diminutive figure huddled in the corner of the cold stone chamber. My claws extend and my eyes glow with fiery intensity. A small scream escapes from his tightly clenched jaw, a clear indication of his terror.

Such a simple, foolish creature he is, cowering before me.

A thrill of excitement snakes its way down my spine as he pisses himself under the scrutiny of my glare.

"You can save yourself, you know, and your family. All you have to do is tell me who this spell belongs to." I press my brows together, straightening my tie.

"I—I don't kno—know." He sputters.

The fear in his eyes intensifies as I lean closer, the heat from my breath brushing against his quivering face. "Think harder," I whisper, a dangerous calm seeping into my words. "Because if you truly don't know, then you are of no use to me anymore, and I have no reason to let you live.

Fuck. It seems like another waste of time.

My frustration boils over, and in a fit of rage I swing my hand, my fist connecting perfectly with his frail chin. There is a loud crack from it breaking that seems to bounce off the lifeless walls of the dungeon, resonating through the cold and darkness.

"Then tell me who the fuck does!" I scream.

The man's body slumps further against the wall, his eyes wide with the fresh shock of pain, tears mingling with the blood that trickles from his split lip. He whimpers, clutching at his jaw.

His feeble attempts at speech are now garbled by the swelling rapidly overtaking his face, but his eyes—those wide, terror-stricken eyes—screamed a silent plea for mercy that I find myself momentarily considering.

Mercy, however, is a luxury I can scarcely afford.

"Your time is running out," I growl.

The man's breaths become rapid and shallow, each inhale a tortured gasp. He nods feverishly, the acknowledgement in his eyes mingling with the pain.

"Look man." He finally croaks. "All I kn—know is Var'Un is the one who put the curse on it."

His words, though fractured and weak, send a ripple of surprise through me. Var'Un—a name reputed in dark circles for his merciless nature, potent magic, and knack for accepting any job that pays well. A formidable enemy, or an invaluable ally, depending on one's perspective and current standing in the dark underworld of sorcery and ancient crafts.

Though, he will regret his decision for crossing me.

I straighten up, smoothing the front of my shirt as I step back from the crumpled man before me. A thin smile curls the edges of my lips—not out of pleasure, but as a precursor to the wrath about to be unleashed. "Var'Un," I murmur under my breath, "Good to know."

I bring my foot down, slamming the heel of my boot into his ribs.

"Please!" He pleads. "Just let me go."

I have no reason to end his life.

He has willingly shared more information than anyone else before him. And I'm sure he's a decent person, with a nice family.

But unfortunately for him, decency and familial bonds hold no currency in the caverns of darkness that I now tread. A tortured soul like mine finds no solace in the pleasantries of the morally upright. My mission is singular and my path, clear.

"You've done well," I acknowledge.

She was still alive, to some degree.

"Th—thank you." His voice trembles, laden with the hope of salvation after revealing his last piece of useful information.

I reach out my hand towards him, offering to help him stand up from the cold floor. Despite his trembling, he takes my hand, and I gently pull him back onto his feet.

He eyes me nervously.

He should be nervous.

As he stands, I keep a firm grip on his hand, "Oh. Just one more thing."

His eyes widen.

"I can't chance you telling Lucius that I know anything. Your family will survive, but they will live on without you I'm afraid."

His face goes pale, the color draining away as if I had already struck him dead. "No." He whispers.

I nod solemnly, the weight of my decision anchoring my resolve. There is no room for hesitation in this game of shadows and secrets.

"It's unfortunate," I continue, my voice as cold and detached as the stones lining the dungeon walls. "But necessary."

In a single, decisive motion, I plunge my razor-sharp claws into his chest and grasp onto his rapidly beating heart. My grip tightens around the pulsing organ as I swiftly remove it from his body, blood spraying onto my face as he crumples to the ground and disintegrates into ash.

Ma petite flamme.

I'm one step closer to getting her back.

Finally.

I wipe my hand, stained with blood, through my hair and smother the flames. I regain some of my composure before taking a bite of the heart in my hand and flinging the rest against the wall.

The metallic taste of his life essence fills my mouth, a harsh reminder of the lengths I must go to regain what has been taken from me. My stomach churns, not out of disgust, but an unsettling blend of satisfaction and necessity.

"Guards!" I yell.

Two figures immediately appear from the shadows, their footsteps quiet but quick.

"Clean this mess up." I point to the blood and ash. "I have a warlock to find."

Amber is an author of Beautifully Broken Romance. She resides in Ohio with her amazing family and dogs. When she's not creating fantasy worlds and sinfully delicious romance, you can find her with her family, gaming, playing board games, or of course, snuggled up with a cozy blanket and a good book. Some of her favorite genres include fantasy, paranormal, mythological, ect. but she's a total sucker for any kind of romance.

Amber has multiple tattoos and piercings but she wants/needs more. She has an unhealthy addiction to coffee and yes...she does believe in magic, and you can't convince her otherwise.

(Her pet dragon wouldn't allow it anyway.)

Also by

Of Gods and Muses:

Bonded by Secrets
Bound by Flames
Tempted by Fate (TBD)

A Twisted Princess Collection

A Pursuit of Madness
A Taste of Revenge
A Spindle of Nightmares (2025)

Secret Projects:

Title TBA (A Dark Mafia Romance)
Marked By Death: Kingdom of Lost Souls

323

Thank you to everyone that made this book happen.
A special thank you to my PA, Haley (She is a goddess in her own right),
for helping to keep me somewhat sane throughout the process.
And of course, thank you to my readers. You all are so amazing, and I
appreciate each and every one of you. Thank you so much for allowing
me to share my stories with you—it's an absolute honor.